I0527014

PRAISE FOR REVENANT

"An eerie gothic mystery with a central character as intriguing as he is unsettling. Jackson's writing is superb—the prose is polished, and as ethereal as the psychic powers at work. I'll never walk by a mirror without a second look again."
— N.J. ALEXANDER, AUTHOR OF **FOG-BOUND**

"Revenant has everything I could want: Gorgeous prose, brilliantly crafted characters, and an undercurrent of terror that wraps itself around the reader and doesn't let go until the final page. I want to both live in this fascinating world Jackson has written, and hide under the covers and hope that nothing from it can find me."
— QUENBY OLSON, AUTHOR OF **MISS PERCY'S POCKET GUIDE TO THE CARE AND FEEDING OF BRITISH DRAGONS**

"Revenant is filled with beautiful prose framing a pervasive yet creeping dread intrinsic to gothic stories that follows the reader from page to page. The mystery unfolds in a languid sort of way that beckons like a

sly wink or a hastily caught glimmer in a window's reflection."
— MEL POLK, AUTHOR OF **ROSEBANE**

"Mirrors don't always reflect the truth. Jackson weaves a delicate tale of intrigue and suspense in Revenant. Her first person prose is as usual, exquisite. And the witty sibling relationship was a nice change from the typical dark romance. Though the mysterious Lucian has his own secrets as he works his way between the brother and sister, in a delightful way that is very much Jackson."
— L. KRAUCH, AUTHOR OF **THE 13TH ZO-DIAC**

"What a storyteller! Jackson spins an engaging story with haunting, lyrical prose steeped in creeping tension. And the dashing villain doesn't hurt either. Highly recommends for lovers of the genre!
— J.D. EDWIN, AUTHOR OF **HEADSPACE**

REVENANT

BY
JAMIE JACKSON

This is a work of fiction. Unless otherwise indicated, all the names, characters, businesses, places, events and incidents in this book are either the product of the author's imagination or used in a fictitious manner. Any resemblance to actual persons, living or dead, or actual events is purely coincidental.

Copyright © 2025 by Jamie Jackson

All rights reserved.

No portion of this book may be reproduced in any form without written permission from the publisher or author, except as permitted by U.S. copyright law.

No generative artificial intelligence (AI) technologies were used in the creation of this publication. Any use of this publication to "train" generative AI technologies to generate text is expressly prohibited.

ISBN: 979-8-9909837-3-1

ISBN: 979-8-9909837-4-8 (ebook)

For my husband, who inspired this one

CONTENTS

CHAPTER ONE

File V-2338

Item A: a cosmetic compact mirror encased in fili-greed metal, received by this office via post. Letter included was addressed by the decedent. Signature matches sample on file. Postmark could not be verified.

"We're only here for a cursory inspection. In and out. Confirm the subject's death, write up our report, and head on home," he said.

The carriage shuddered as it hit yet another rut in the road, jouncing again as one of the wheels rolled its way back over the edge. Droplets of water from the rain sluicing down outside splashed through the gap in the window frame. Across from me, Victor swore under his breath, wiping at the wet spot the spatters left on his trousers.

I snorted, shifting in my seat to find a position mildly more comfortable than the last. Surely, I already had a bruise on my ass in the shape of the springs under the cushion despite the layers of skirts and petticoats between me and the metal. It was hardly my only discomfort: a hairpin was digging into my scalp, and the beginning of a headache was building pressure behind my eyes.

"Vivian," he warned.

"Victor," I mimicked.

He gave up trying to save his pants, settling back into his seat with a grumble and a half-hearted glare at the window. He drummed his fingers on his knee as I sat silently, running my own fingers over the soft leather of my gloves. I could feel a spot along my index finger where the seam had begun to weaken. I would need to mend it soon.

"The Company is only paid to confirm her death," he said. "That's always the procedure in these insurance cases—"

"If they cared to confirm it, they wouldn't wait for the person to be missing for seven years," I insisted. "They don't want answers. They just want the money—"

"—and that's why they bring us in," he said, riding smoothly over anything else I had to say. "To be sure this isn't fraud."

I rolled my eyes. "Yes, because someone goes missing for seven years, severs all contact with loved ones, and never goes out in public again, just so their family can—"

"Vivian," he said again, and I relented, unsure where my argument had been going, to begin with. Instead, I looked down and began picking at the seam, a scowl on my face.

Victor cleared his throat, and I glanced up to meet his eyes: gray, as steely as the weather, and, to anyone who didn't know him well, just as cold. His sharp features only strengthened the impression of a frosty demeanor despite his short-cut, sandy blonde hair.

Two peas in a pod we were, with Victor the elder by several minutes, although my own features were considered elfin rather than pointed. I had also inherited our mother's mahogany hair instead of the blonde much of our family carried.

But we both had our father's eyes.

Victor cleared his throat again, and I waited, rubbing at the worn seam on my gloves as if I intended to hasten its deterioration.

"Do you expect to find anything different?" I finally asked after the quiet between us stretched unpleasantly.

"No," he said. "And I expect you not to look for anything more."

I looked back to glare directly at him. "I cannot help what the objects tell me."

"But you *can* help what you tell the client."

I tilted my chin up and narrowed my eyes, looking down my nose at him as best I could. "Are you telling me to lie?"

"That's exactly what I'm telling you to do. They don't need the details."

"That's not what I'm asking."

"Then what *are* you asking?" he said, stifling a sigh.

"What if the objects tell me that she's not dead, but that this is not a fraudulent case?"

"If the subject ran away, it's no business of ours," he said. "And if that's what it is, you keep it to yourself."

"How exactly are we supposed to report that?"

This time, he did sigh. "Nobody cares, Vivian. These cases are rare enough that all the Company wants is a nice, neat report to hand over to the client's insurance so they can finally dole out the funds and close the file."

"But the client—"

"Will take the money, say thank you, and walk out the door with a hefty check in their pocket."

"Then why do they care if it's fraud?" I insisted. "They could just sign off on the check in the first place."

Victor pinched the bridge of his nose. "You're asking me to fathom the procedures of insurance companies? The hoops they make people jump through so they can pay someone else to investigate and write up the report while pretending that they didn't stall for this long—" he took a breath, "—just to continue collecting the premiums required to keep the policy alive regardless?"

"But wouldn't they want to know if the insured was still alive?"

"You're going to give them yet another reason to deny the claim?" he asked. "Expose the poor woman for disappearing to begin with?"

"The Company—"

"Doesn't care," he repeated. "They've got their money, and they've given us our assignment. And we won't see a single penny more than what they're paying us to do."

"Why wouldn't they just send any old employee to say 'yes, she's dead' if that's the only result they want?"

"Because that would also be fraud, Viv. And while there are many untrustworthy things the Company does, committing fraud themselves is not one of them."

The carriage rocked again, and I leaned with it as we rounded a curve.

"If we're only meant to be in and out," I said, "why did they tell us to pack for three to four days?"

Victor's brow furrowed, his head tilted. "They what?"

I reached into the pocket of my skirt and pulled out the envelope. He snatched it from me, pausing as he saw the Company's red wax seal on the envelope's flap before tugging the letter free and flipping the folded paper open, eyes flicking back and forth as he read.

Miss Tailor: You have been assigned to case 1888-11-MP-001436 per the file received. The client has requested our expeditious assistance with an on-site investigation into the disappearance of one Lady LeVerre. Per our policies, you are approved to verify the subject's death. The client insists that the circumstances surrounding the subject's absence are suspicious, and related affairs continue to be unusual. Your presence will be required for a minimum of three to four days. Appropriate attire to suit the client's status on the initial call is expected.

When he was done, he flipped the letter over as if expecting to find more information on the other side.

"Suspicious circumstances," he muttered. "But in regard to what? Her initial disappearance or the events thereafter?"

I wasn't sure if he required a response, so instead, I quietly waited for him to come to his own conclusions.

He looked up, eyes locked on mine. "When did you receive this?"

"Two days ago," I said. "It came to the door shortly after you sent a note to tell me we had an assignment. I assumed you had gotten a similar one."

"I did not," he said. He scanned the page again. "They don't elaborate on what the circumstances are."

"I suppose," I said, reaching for the letter, "we will find out when we get there. Perhaps they thought the answer was obvious. Although, I'm surprised you said nothing when you met me at my house. Did you not wonder why I brought an entire trunk and not merely a bag?"

"I thought perhaps you had intentionally over-prepared."

I smirked. "I'm assuming you do not have clothing to last you through three to four days?"

"I'll make do," he said. "Especially as I doubt we'll be there that long. Five minutes, in and out. We'll be done before the carriage has gotten turned around in the drive."

The rain abated by the time we reached our destination, and I flung the curtains back to let in what meager light remained from the setting sun.

I caught glimpses of the manor through the trees' skeletal gray branches, dismal veins across the amber, aged parchment of its hulking mass. I lost sight of it as the road dipped below the horizon until the carriage trundled to a stop in front of its columned face. Not so brilliant without the light of the sun's retreating rays bouncing off its walls, the sprawling edifice was grimy and smeared with caked dirt kicked up against its foundation. Gray-green algae clung to every visible surface, seemingly embedded in the wood, which itself showed signs of decay, pieces crumbling away to reveal blackened, rotting boards beneath the paint.

The many windows were dark, staring eyes. And no one stood beneath the shadows to welcome us in.

"I thought the client was aware we were coming," I said.

"That's what the Company told me," Victor said, scooting forward to the edge of his seat to peer past the curtains. He drummed his fingers on the wood as he studied the house. "Well, nothing for it. We'll just have to rouse them."

"I hardly think they're sleeping," I said. "It can't possibly be later than half-past four."

Victor pulled his pocket watch from his waistcoat, glancing down at the glass face. "You would be right." He tapped his fingers again. "Come on then—we're wasting what light there is." He shoved the carriage door open and slipped out to land with a grunt, the squelch of mud sucking at the soles of his boots. His lips were pursed, his nose wrinkled in distaste. "Damn thing didn't extend the steps again," he muttered before he gave it a hard thump with his fist. They unfolded and extended outward with a clacking groan.

Victor held out his hand, eyeing my voluminous, trailing skirts. "Watch your step," he warned.

"I'll just send the Company the cleaning bill," I said. "They're the ones who insisted we 'dress to impress.'"

Victor cast a glance at the house before us. "I certainly prefer when they call us in to work with the beetle crushers."

This time, I wrinkled my nose. "Must you call them that?"

"Why?" he asked. "Have you gone sweet on one of the detectives?"

"Hardly," I said, inching my way off the seat to poke my head and shoulders out the carriage door to look around before emerging. There wasn't much to see, only a sloping lawn to my left and the trees we had wound our way through off to the right. The air outside the carriage was much cooler than the air inside had been—a chill like fingers sliding along the skin to sweep loose strands from my face before crawling down my spine, a trickle of ice water.

"Viv," Victor said. "I've still got to get the luggage, as I doubt you'll assist in that get-up."

"I got the trunk out my front door on my own," I retorted but placed my gloved hand into Victor's palm and made my way carefully down the carriage steps.

Once I stood firmly in the mud, doing what I could to lift the hem free of the clinging slop, Victor scaled the side of the carriage to tug his case free and set it on the interior floor. Then he clambered back up to slide my trunk off the roof. It caught on the rungs, and he gave it a yank. It tipped and fell, and he fell with it, landing with a stagger and a yelp.

"Fuck," he swore, brushing at the mud now splattered on his trousers. "Of fucking course."

"Language," I said mildly from my spot by the carriage as I tried to ascertain the best route to the manor's front steps.

"Yes, *mother,*" Victor half-teased. "If you could please manage my case while I wrestle this behemoth you call a trunk, I would appreciate it."

I bundled my skirts scandalously high into one arm and picked the case up with my free hand before starting toward the front door.

Victor followed, dragging my trunk behind him, and I grimaced at the scraping, sucking noise it made as he pulled it through the mud and rock.

We trudged up the stairs, the trunk thudding against the stone, until we stood within the portico, staring at a heavy wood door with an embellished metal knocker set into its surface.

It looked like the gaping maw of a beast.

The temperature seemed to plummet further where we stood in the shadows, the kind of cold that skittered and burrowed into the muscle. Victor dropped my trunk with a thump while I set his case down much more gently and released and smoothed my skirts.

A creaking behind us had both of us turning, but it was only the spelled carriage moving itself to face back the way we had come. Once it was seemingly content with its positioning, it stilled, waiting for Victor's next command.

"In and done before the carriage turns around?" I asked, arching an eyebrow at him.

He ignored my comment and motioned to the knocker. "Would you like to do the honors?"

"Not particularly," I said as I took a step forward to grab the ring and rap it hard against the plate. I half-expected the thing to clamp down on my hand and withdrew as hastily as possible, listening as the echoing shot of metal upon metal died away.

We were greeted only by silence.

Victor shifted from side to side. "Prompt service here."

"You could try the door this time," I said. I twisted to look over my shoulder at the carriage in the deepening gloom. "Unless the carriage brought us to the wrong manor?"

"Can't have done," he said distractedly, trying to peer in through the windows to either side of the door. "That's never been a problem, even when the spells begin breaking down."

"First time for everything."

"And it would be just our luck, wouldn't it, that it would happen now?" He half-bent, his face practically pressed to the dusty glass. "We should try the—ah, there's a light!"

He straightened and hastened away from the window, tugging at the hem of his waistcoat and lapels of his jacket. "Let me do the talking, for once."

"Don't I always?" I asked sweetly.

"No, no, you do not, or I wouldn't need to remind you," he said.

I brushed at the folds of my skirt, squared my shoulders, and settled my hands demurely at my front.

The door swung open with a groan, revealing an elderly man in trousers and a frock coat, armed against the encroaching darkness with an old-fashioned lit lantern. He said nothing as he assessed us.

The flame bobbed with his movements, flickering across his craggy features, creating shadows where there should have been none and leaving his eyes lightless voids before it steadied.

He blinked owlishly before he said, "Yes?" His voice was rusty and hoarse, crackling like a seldom-used mechanism.

"I believe we're expected," Victor said. "Tailor and Tailor, from the Company." He reached into his waistcoat pocket and pulled out his own letter—a certified writ of our assignment with the Company's seal embossed into the paper and signatures from at least two managers.

"Ah, the soul reader," the man said, his brow furrowed as he studied the paper in Victor's hand. "I believe his lordship was not expecting you until morning."

"Our conveyance made exceptionally good time," Victor said, a polite smile on his face, his tone apologetic. "But we don't intend to be long—"

"You can come back tomorrow when his lordship is expecting you," the man said.

There was a tick in Victor's jaw, his smile fixed and barely more than a grimace. "As much as we hate to intrude on his—*lordship*, we truly will be just a few moments' time, and then we can take our leave without causing any further inconvenience."

"As I said," the man said sternly, "you will have to come back tomorr—"

"John, who's at the door?"

The velvet soft, smooth baritone voice asked—no, *demanded*—and all three of us turned to see its owner standing at the edge of the glow cast by John's lantern.

"The Tailors are here a full day early, my lord," John said acidly, raising the lantern so that I was forced to turn my head to the side and squint against the glare.

"I hardly think we need to stand on formality, John," the man in the shadows said. There was the steady tread of footsteps on a wood floor, and in my periphery, I could see his shape bloom more solidly beside John. He appeared casually attired, dressed only in tight trousers, a vest, and a white shirt with billowing sleeves. It seemed we had interrupted his nightly preparations rather than dressing for dinner.

Despite his proximity, I could not catch his visage with the lantern's light boring into my eyes.

"Your father—"

"Is dead," the man said. "And it's painfully old-fashioned to call me by anything but my name when you've known me since I was a boy barely as tall as your knee."

John only grumbled and lowered his lantern.

"Sir," Victor said, "as I was telling your John here—"

"My John?" The man's voice sounded amused.

I turned back to face him, blinking away the aura left by the lantern light.

His lips were curved into a small smile, dark hair swept back from a lean face and narrow chin, and the initial impression I got from him was one of warmth and a quiet kind of studiousness. His eyes were a golden russet in color that one could spend hours staring into, trying to pick out all the tones and shades the flickering flame suggested were hidden within.

"I don't know what else to call him, sir," Victor said. "As I was saying, we'll be in and out, no more than five minutes total, and then we can be on our way without any further hospitality on your part. I'm sure you're busy and would like to get this whole ordeal over with."

"Which one of you is the soul reader?" the man asked.

If Victor was at all thrown by the man's skip past the expected reciprocity of polite conversation, he didn't show it. He merely waved a hand at me. "My sister, Vivian Tailor, sir."

"Vivian Tailor," said the man, sounding pleased at the way my name rolled off his tongue. He took a step forward, one hand extended. "A pleasure, Ms. Tailor. I am—"

Behind him, John cleared his throat.

There was a flash of something in the man's eyes, a momentary darkening perhaps not altogether caused by the guttering lamplight, that disappeared just as quickly, and all that remained was pleasant curiosity.

"—Lord LeVerre," he finished.

I reached up and shook his hand; his grasp was firm and warm through the leather of my glove. "The pleasure is all mine, sir," I said.

He didn't release my hand immediately. There was a pause, a hesitation, before he loosened his fingers.

"I will admit, I expected something more just now," he said, breaking the tentative silence among us.

"Ah, the gloves, sir," Victor said. "The reading requires skin contact."

"Does it now," Lord LeVerre said as if we had confirmed something he suspected. He shifted a step back. "John, I believe we've kept the Tailors waiting on the doorstep long enough. Surely we can at least offer them some refreshment in the drawing room?"

John muttered to himself as he turned. He shot a look back at the two of us. "Follow me, please."

"In the meantime, I will go fetch an—item? Of my mother's," Lord LeVerre said.

"Something she used often," I said as I stepped through the doorway.

Victor followed closely enough to tread on the train of my skirts, and I quickly swept the fabric out of his way. Mud on the hem, I could easily argue the Company into cleaning, but a shoe print on the cloth, I could not.

Lord LeVerre nodded and strode off in the opposite direction from where John seemed to be leading us.

"Try not to touch it yourself!" I called after him.

He paused, twisting halfway to look back at me.

"Contact between you and the object will make it harder for me to read her presence, especially with the length of time that's elapsed since she last used it," I said, almost apologetically. "If you could pick it up with a handkerchief, or perhaps a hand towel, to prevent the effect of your touch—"

"Certainly," he interrupted. "Far be it from me to make this more taxing than necessary."

I wasn't sure if he was being courteous or curt, but the shadows beyond the foyer swallowed him before I could reply.

Victor nudged me with his shoulder. "John's glaring at us."

Belatedly, I fell into step behind the man.

He wheezed as he walked, despite the short distance from the front door to the drawing room—barely twenty steps away.

A blazing fire crackled on the hearth, flooding the room with flickering light. Several lamps stood on various side tables—not oil like the lantern that John carried, but spelled, indicated by their bluish luster and unwavering glow. The curtains were drawn closed, which would explain why the windows had appeared dark from the outside.

"I will see if Cook can put together tea," John said stiffly, shutting the door with a snap behind him.

"In and out?" I quipped at Victor as I tugged at my gloves, sliding the leather off my hands while I studied the room.

The walls were boldly painted plaster and dark-stained oak, the couches and chairs a deep burgundy, trimmed in dull gold. The curtains were much the same. But what seized my attention were the mirrors framed in heavy, gilded wood on each of the four walls; I could watch us move about the room from every angle. It had the air of a brothel, and I wrinkled my nose at the whole gaudy affair.

"This is certainly more...attention than I would have expected from someone like him," Victor said.

I ran my fingers along the wood of one of the tables. All I felt was an air of disuse, the aftertaste of impatience, and the quick swipe of a cleaning rag to clear the dust. "I believe this room gets very little use," I said.

I caught sight of my image in the glass with a thin, shrouded figure behind me at the door. I glanced over my shoulder, but the wood was innocently blank of any such creature. When I turned back and stepped over to the mirror on the wall, the shape resolved into nothing more than a smudge, a smeared blemish on the aging surface. My distorted reflection stared back at me.

"Stop being nosy," Victor said.

"I could have come to that conclusion by simple observation," I said, gesturing at the room.

"But you didn't," he said. "Or did you think I wouldn't catch you poking at the furniture?"

"I hardly tried to hide it," I said, drifting toward the fireplace to study the mantel. It was crowded with items: a heavyset clock with unmoving hands, vases empty of flowers, and little figurines. One of them had a chipped face, a blank white surface where an eye used to be.

The door swung back open with a clatter, and John stomped in carrying a tray laden with a teapot, tea cups on their saucers, and a platter of little cakes. He set the whole thing down on one of the tables with a thump, turned on his heel, and walked back out without a word.

"Friendly fellow," Victor muttered. "No, allow me," he said sternly when I started toward the tray.

"I'll have to pick up the cup to drink from it," I reminded him. "And contact with my lips will have the same effect as if I touched it with my hand."

"I feel sorry for any man who ever tries to kiss you," he muttered. "At least let me dull it first."

"I only wanted one of the cakes anyway," I said, intentionally sliding past his first comment. "I've only ever encountered focus and love in baked goods. I doubt this time will be any different."

I couldn't say the same for porcelain dishware. The sense of every person who had ever used the item clung to the material; I would be sifting through dozens of emotions and events, sometimes hundreds, perhaps thousands, if I ever tried to dine at a restaurant without Victor there to blunt them.

"I'm not so sure it won't be," he said, shifting as he peered about the room.

"What makes you say that?" I asked, leaning over the tray to look at the cakes. They had been cut into circles and decorated with flowers of golden yellow buttercream. Small enough that one could eat them in two, perhaps three bites.

"The air feels stale," Victor said.

I twisted to look at him from my half-bent position. "That could be because the house needs a good airing out."

"Old and thick, and full of dust," he continued as if I hadn't said a word.

I straightened.

"It chokes off his breath. Leaves him gasping in the dark."

"Vic..." I said warily.

He blinked at me. "Like I said, the air is stale."

The door creaked open, and I jumped.

It was only Lord LeVerre in the doorframe, carefully holding a hairbrush with a handkerchief wrapped around its handle. He set it down on the table next to the tray, his arm nearly brushing against my skirts.

"My apologies," he said. "I hope this will do. There are other...*mementos* that I believe meant more to her, but this she would have used daily."

"This will be perfect," I said.

"Before we start," Victor said, "I am required to inform you that Vivian is only authorized to provide confirmation of your mother's passing."

Lord LeVerre paused, hovering near me before he stepped back to open the space between us. "Understood," he said. "But I don't believe my mother is dead."

"Then—" Victor cleared his throat. "Never mind, not our business." He waved at the hairbrush. "Vivian, if you would?"

"Why the insurance claim?" I asked.

"Viv," Victor hissed.

Lord LeVerre waved him off. "I'm hardly that easy to offend with questions. I have no insurance claim."

We stared at him in silence.

"Right," Victor said as he rocked back on his heels. "Right," he repeated. "Right then. Vivian, your gloves; we're leaving."

Lord LeVerre and I responded at the same time:

"What?" I asked.

"Wait," Lord LeVerre protested.

"I said, get your gloves; we're leaving," Victor said.

"Wait," Lord LeVerre repeated.

"Why should we?" Victor demanded. "You've filed a fraudulent case with the Company, and my sister and I will have no part of that—"

"It's not a false case," Lord LeVerre argued.

"Then what is it, pray tell?" Victor snapped back. "The assignment we received was quite clear: a woman has been missing for seven years—"

"And she has been—"

"And the insurance company has done all it can to repeatedly delay a payout on the assumption of her death when she did not return within the first five—"

"Also true—"

"Then why would you state there is no claim, to begin with?" I threw in the question before Victor could.

"I said *I* have no claim. That claim died with my father," Lord LeVerre said. "He was the main beneficiary listed on the policy, and with his death six months ago, the funds were paid out instead to the contingent beneficiary, a theater my mother patronized—"

"Then why are we here?" Victor asked. "If the policy is defunct—"

"Because the Company offered it," Lord LeVerre retorted. "Your Company had already been paid, the wheels set in motion, and by the time my father was buried and all the paperwork waded through, the final decision from the insurance issued, there were all of two weeks left before you were to arrive. They said you would be informed."

"Oh," was all Victor said.

Lord LeVerre stepped back, gracefully collapsing onto a chair beside the table where he'd placed the hairbrush.

It was a movement I intensely, immediately envied. Grace, under the right circumstances, I could manage, but grace under pressure, I could not.

"You are here," Lord LeVerre said, "because, unlike my father, I am certain my mother is not dead. And I want to know where she is."

There was a long pause, the silence growing until it loomed over us.

"What makes you think she's alive?" I asked.

"I—have you ever just known something to be true, deep in your bones?" Lord LeVerre asked. "You have no evidence, no way to prove it, but you know it? I know she's alive because there is no other explanation. She may not have returned, but not because she's dead. She's gone for a different reason."

"So, a missing person's case?" Victor asked brusquely.

"Yes," Lord LeVerre said. "A missing person's case."

Victor was silent, the muscle in his jaw jumping again. "Viv, I leave this decision in your hands."

"Viv?" Lord LeVerre asked.

"Miss Tailor to you," Victor said sharply.

"Miss, is it?" Lord LeVerre asked, his eyes on me.

"Yes," I said shortly.

We lapsed back into strained silence.

"Miss Tailor," Lord LeVerre said at last. "Please? I want—need—to know what happened to my mother."

I hesitated and then settled back into the chair, posing myself at the edge so I could lean forward. I picked up the handkerchief and gently folded it back. There was only a faint impression left in the fabric, the fleeting thought of being plucked up from somewhere nearby—not the feeling that would come from an item in daily use. There were little roses embroidered on the corner closest to me.

"The handkerchief was also hers," Lord LeVerre said quietly. "I thought perhaps if I wrapped the hairbrush in something solely hers, it would be the least likely to cause any contamination."

"An unnecessary but considerate precaution," I said. I took a breath as I steeled myself, then reached forward to press the tips of my fingers to the handle of the brush.

Music came first—soft notes that floated in the air and rang in my ear, the hum of a voice before the lilt of song. Next were murmurs, reassurances in the dark, the broken sobs of a frightened child, and the flash of an image too quick to catch more than a glimpse of sloping wood. I chased after the moonlit memory, and found a woman in skirts, gentle hands, and a soft pair of eyes, whiskey gold and russet-toned in the fading light. My breath caught, but that was where it stayed, wavering, not solid enough to be sure, but not the sinking darkness that came with death.

The lid of a trunk slammed shut, and I jerked. My fingers came away from the handle, the vision lost. I blinked as if I could see the cause of the noise through solid walls.

Neither Lord LeVerre nor Victor were looking at me. Both were turned toward the door of the drawing room, Lord LeVerre's hands clenched tightly to his knees, his knuckles bloodless and pale in the steady glow of the lamps. He rose to his feet, crossed to the door, and peered out into the hall. "John, if the luggage is too heavy, get the porter to move it."

There was a grunted reply in return, muffled by the walls.

"I can get the luggage back on the carriage," Victor said.

"I am having John move it upstairs to your rooms," Lord LeVerre replied cautiously as if he expected Victor to begin arguing again.

He wasn't wrong to be wary.

"Why?" Victor asked.

"It is—" Lord LeVerre shot a glance at the unmoving clock on the mantel. "Well, the hour is growing late. With as dark as it gets in the country at night, if your conveyance were to break an axle on the road with the condition it's in, you'll have a hell of a time trying to find your way. I recommend staying at least the night and leaving in the morning if your sister has found no answers to give."

The two of them turned back to me, expectation on Victor's face and hope on Lord LeVerre's. He kept trying to smooth his features, but it would return—that shine to his eyes, the upturned corners of his lips.

"Well?" he asked. "Did you...find anything?"

"I can't confirm she's deceased," I said carefully, determined not to tread on his optimism. "But I could not get an impression beyond that."

"Could we try again?" he asked.

"The Company only paid us for the confirmation of death," Victor put in. "We cannot afford—"

"Whatever your rates are for further work, I'll pay them," Lord LeVerre said.

"That will hardly cover the cost of the jobs we'll lose for being out of the city for this long."

"Seven pounds a day."

"We can't—"

"Eight."

Victor opened his mouth, closed it, and opened it again. "Eight-fifty."

"Deal—"

"Each," Victor finished.

"Deal," Lord LeVerre repeated. "If you'll follow me, John will show you to your rooms. We can pick up this task again in the morning."

CHAPTER TWO

Lord LeVerre entered Station 163 of District 238 to report that no one has seen or heard from his wife. He requests a missing person report be filed.

Our rooms were across the hall from one another, although mine was connected to a sitting room. The furniture was more feminine, the wood stained a far lighter color, the fabrics on the couch and chairs delicate rose pinks and pastel blues. The curtains were gauzy white lace, and a full-length mirror was positioned between the windows. I found more of the spelled lamps that John was sorely missing, dainty things crafted from curved wood and stained glass shades with blooming flower patterns.

I had pulled my gloves back on as we followed John up the stairs, and now I trailed my fingers along the surface of the vanity in one corner, the leather a barrier between my skin and the wood.

Victor, having checked that his case was in his room, was back, hovering in my doorway.

"You might as well come in and sit down," I said. "You've obviously got something on your mind."

He hesitated briefly before stepping in and closing the door with a soft click. "I think we need to be cautious."

"Of what?"

He gestured vaguely behind him. "Of our host and his intentions."

"His intention seems to be finding out what happened to his mother."

"On the surface," he said. "We don't yet know what lurks beneath."

"You doubt his motives?" I arched a brow at him.

"Yes," he said. "He is—best guess, how old would you say he is?"

Instead of answering immediately, I settled in one of the chairs. I called to mind images of Lord LeVerre's face, the timbre of his voice, and his movements, trying to pick out some clue that would aid me in an accurate guess. "Thirty," I said.

"Thirty-five," Victor replied. "I asked John while you were exploring your rooms."

"And what does this have to do with his motives?"

"Do you not find it odd that a man who was twenty-eight when she disappeared would be so determined to discover what happened to her, and yet—" he said and held up a hand to forestall any argument on Lord LeVerre's behalf, "and yet, made no move to hire anyone to look for her when it occurred?"

I shut my mouth, looking at my hands, where they rested in my lap. "That is indeed curious," I murmured.

"Unless he is a waste-about," Victor continued, "leeching off his inheritance and therefore on a fixed stipend, making hiring anyone unaffordable, how worried was he?"

I ran a finger along the worn seam of my glove. "Surely, if he were that concerned, he would have set aside the funds he was being given until he had saved up the necessary amount."

"Exactly," Victor said. "It's what you and I would have done."

"So what do you think it is that he's about?"

"I don't know," Victor said, coming around the couch and settling onto its cushions directly across from the mirror and his reflection. "My guess is it ties back to his inheritance. Both—supposedly—of his parents are dead. How is the will written? Is—was—he the only heir? Is his determination to find her alive only because if he doesn't, the estate passes to another relative? Was it put into a trust to prevent him from accessing the funds or selling off the land to spend himself into debt so large everything his father built is forfeit?"

"Why not just hire someone to play the part of Lady LeVerre in that case?" I asked. "Wouldn't that be simpler?"

"The Company would see through that ruse in a matter of minutes. And they would be called if the case took such a turn." He tapped his foot and went silent, brooding as he stared at the floor. "Greed is one of the oldest motivators."

"I do not know that is all it is," I said. "Or at least, it doesn't feel as uncomplicated as that."

"How often has money driven people to choose to do monstrous things?"

"Often," I acknowledged. "But if that's all it was, wouldn't it be easier for him to go after those he *knows* are alive to ensure his inheritance if it's otherwise tied up?"

Victor jiggled his knee, the heel of his shoe scuffing against the floor. "We'd have to get ahold of the will to be sure, and I don't see any chance of that."

"So what do we do?"

"What we've already agreed to. In the morning, you'll read another of her items and find the answer we both know is the only possibility. We'll collect our money and be on our way home before lunch."

"It is not always so cut and dried," I said.

"For this, it needs to be," Victor said seriously. "It would be foolhardy to trust this man."

"Perhaps," I said, the most I would concede.

"Thank you," he said.

"I'll admit I'm surprised you agreed so readily to this," I said. "Even with convincing him to pay."

"If it weren't for the fact that the Company already expected us to be gone for three to four days according to their letter, I wouldn't even have attempted it. We would have been back out to the carriage and down the drive before he could cry 'foul.'"

"And you?" I asked.

"And me what?"

"What of your vision? Is the air still stale?"

He drummed his fingers against his thigh. "Yes," he said as he rose from the couch. "And I do not think anything we discover will relieve it." He shifted from foot to foot with a quick glance around the room. "Is there another door?"

"There is a door in the bedroom that opens into the hall, yes," I said.

"Lock them both."

"The bedroom door already is."

"By you?"

"Yes," I said. "And the key is on the bedroom dresser."

"Good. Lock the door behind me." He stepped out into the dimly lit hall and shut the door.

I got up and turned the key in the lock. "But will you lock your door?" I said to the air.

A latch clicked, and a weight settled on the bed next to me. Someone tugged at the blankets and set a hand on my arm, ice cold through the fabric of my sleeve, a chill trickling down through the muscle and into the bone.

I jerked awake.

I stared into the darkness of an unfamiliar room, watching the vague shapes and humps of hulking, leering shadows that surely were only the dresser and the wardrobe.

The weight behind me shifted.

My breath caught in my throat, my heart beating frantically in my chest. I didn't dare move, afraid to alert this person that I was awake and aware of their presence.

I had locked the doors, hadn't I?

I stayed as still as a rabbit spotting a predator while my skin crawled with the need to turn on a light and face whoever was in my room.

Slowly, achingly, the seconds turned to minutes, yet neither of us moved even an inch. I fought to keep my breathing even, which sounded loud and rasping to my ears. That made me realize the only breath I heard in the room was my own. Surely I would hear theirs with them pressed against my back?

I laid still, gathering my courage, before I lunged for the spelled bedside lamp, my fingers scrabbling at the knob. The light flared bright enough that I winced. I jerked my face to the side, blinking the spots out of my vision. Even half-blinded, I could see there was no one else on the bed. Cautiously, I leaned over to peer at the floor; it was just as empty as the bed. I slipped out from beneath the blankets and set my bare feet on the cold wood floor, grimacing at the way dozens of moments flooded my skin—a cacophony of footsteps drumming through my mind. I knelt, flinging the blanket over the mattress, and checked the space under the bed.

There was nothing there, although now that the light was on and the room empty, I didn't expect there to be.

I stood up, moved around the bed to the door, and set my palm on the handle, taking another breath at the memories crowding in: excited chatter, high-pitched giggles, the sharp command that followed. I gave the handle a jiggle, but the door stayed firmly closed. I released it and padded over to the sitting room door.

I peered into the space, reluctant to step into the shadows to reach one of the lamps.

After what felt like hours of debate, I lunged at the closest lamp, my fingers closing around the knob; with a click, light flooded the room. It, too, was empty, and, sense restored now that I had chased away the dark, I hastened to check the door to the hall. It was still locked, the key on the vanity where I had left it. A quick glance back into the bedroom showed that the second still rested on the dresser.

I left the light in the sitting room on with the door half-closed before I climbed back into bed. I sat there, running my fingers along the fabric of the blanket. Faded these memories were, blurred edges of dreams and nightmares, few and far between. Maybe the sensation of another person in the room had been nothing more than these fleeting impressions working their way into my own dreams.

I rarely, if ever, slept in a bed that was not my own, as much as I had teased Victor about not packing enough clothing for the trip. In truth, I had expected he would be right, and we would be halfway home by now, dozing in fits as the carriage rumbled down the road.

I drew the blankets up to my chin, fingers clutching the cloth, before I reached over and turned off the lamp.

The next time I woke, sunlight was streaming through the lacy curtains, bathing the room in a pale golden glow. A peek out the windows showed me a cold and clear day, with white frost settled over the landscape. I particularly noticed a garden of evergreen hedges directly below me with needles so dark they bordered on black. Shadows pooled on the ground beneath their boughs, a veritable labyrinth of living walls.

I set my fingers on the glass, savoring the feel of the chill in their tips, the blankness that came from the material: no memories, no impressions, no emotions to block out my own. Glass could only reflect—never absorb. The feel of people and animals passed right through it, the same as light.

I stepped away from the window to shove open the lid of my trunk, wrinkling my nose as John's emotions filtered up to me, bitter and irritated, an angry mutter. Victor's lay just beneath, a roiling bubble of exasperation, soothing and as familiar to me as my own.

I pulled out a split riding skirt of dark brown heavy wool, a long-sleeved white shirt, and my own tweed waistcoat and jacket. There was no reason to dress for first impressions this morning, but there was a need for warmth.

Once changed and with my gloves firmly in place, I carefully folded my gown from the day before and placed it in the trunk. Picking the key off the dresser, I unlocked the door and stepped out into the hallway, slipping the key into my pocket.

Victor's door was open, and upon peering inside, I could see that he had already made up the bed and repacked his case. It sat on the floor just inside the threshold.

I trotted down the hall to the stairs, following the scent of freshly brewed coffee and sizzling bacon.

Fortunately, that strategy landed me in the dining room, where our host and Victor had already beaten me to breakfast. Even this space contained mirrors lined up along one wall so the occupants were reflected, creating the illusion of a larger, more crowded room.

Victor was eating, elbows on the table, fork in one hand, and an empty, delicate porcelain cup cradled in his other.

Lord LeVerre appeared to be trying not to stare at this behavior, half-hidden behind a newspaper, although before either of them realized I was standing in the doorway, I caught him sneaking peeks over the top of the page, brow furrowed.

I shifted, and my movement caught his eye; he quickly laid the paper down, practically in his plate on top of his eggs, and rose to his feet.

"Miss Tailor."

Victor glanced up, placed his cup on the table, and picked up the silver coffee pot before him. "Coffee?" he asked.

"Please," I said, settling in the seat next to him.

Lord LeVerre hastily sat back down.

I picked up my now full cup and took a sip of the steaming coffee. Victor's strength and concentration of thought had drowned out the other emotions to the point where I would have to delve far past the surface to pick them out; the only memories crowding in were quiet, calm, and collected. "You've been practicing," I said.

"I don't have much else to do with my nights," he said.

Lord LeVerre watched our exchange silently, even as he picked his paper back up, his gaze surreptitiously fastened on us as he pretended to check over the food on his plate.

Victor took the time I spent quietly drinking to gather up my knife and fork and hold them in his hand.

"I doubt the knife is necessary," I said.

He shrugged. "Can't hurt."

"I suppose not."

Lord LeVerre could contain his curiosity no longer. "What exactly are you doing?"

"Replacing the surface memories," Victor said. He set down the fork and knife next to my plate. "Should be clear now."

"Why?" Lord LeVerre asked.

I took another sip of my coffee, deciding how best to explain. "It is—taxing to have the feel of many people crowding in every time I touch an object. Victor will hold the items long enough that casual use won't affect me more than a passing familiarity."

"Ah," he said.

I dished out eggs from one of the covered platters, snagging bacon from another in relative silence.

"You'll stain your gloves," Victor said mildly.

"Not if I take them off," I said, mimicking his tone. "Are you going to?"

I merely smirked at him and took a bite of my eggs.

"I was thinking—" Lord LeVerre began.

Victor and I turned from our quibbling to look at him.

"I was thinking after breakfast I would go fetch another of my mother's items for Miss Tailor to try to read?"

"You could go fetch it now," Victor said. "The sooner she can give you an answer, the sooner we can take our leave."

"I should—wrap it again?" Lord LeVerre asked.

"Please," I said.

He pushed back from the table, setting his newspaper down more carefully this time along with his own untouched cup of coffee, and hurried from the room.

Victor watched him go, then leaned toward me. "I recommend that you find an answer."

"And if I don't?"

"I recommend you pick the most expedient one."

I arched a brow at him. "Are you suggesting I lie, brother dear?"

"That is exactly what I am suggesting," he said.

I set down my fork. "Have you had another vision?"

"No," he said. "But the air is thicker today. I can taste the ash coating my tongue."

I propped my elbows up on the table. "I do not think he will be satisfied with a simple answer."

"He'll have to be."

I shook my head. "He'll want to know more."

Victor sighed. He was jiggling his knee; I could feel the vibration of it through the table. "And if you truly cannot give him the answers he seeks?"

I shrugged. "Then at least we will have been honest?"

He slouched in his chair, scowling down at his own plate. "I do not like it."

"You do not like the dearth of communication from the Company initially," I corrected him. "If you had been forewarned, you may have approached this differently."

"No," he said, "I don't think I would have. And my approach would also be no different if I hadn't received that vision."

Clicking footsteps interrupted us, and Victor straightened in his seat.

I picked my cup up, took a sip, and grimaced. The coffee had gone cold.

Lord LeVerre sailed back in, the item in his hands completely obscured by a slip of a pashmina. He set it in front of me, the elegant shawl half-sliding to land in my lap, the rest of it pinned beneath the object.

It was a book, the cloth-bound cover frayed at the edges, faded shades of cobalt from uneven bouts of time left in the sun. The pages were yellowed and brittle enough that I feared they would crumble to dust if I tried to open it. Pale gold gilt scrawled down its spine read *Where Honeysuckles Embrace the Thorn*.

Reverently, I ran my gloved fingers down its face, then looked up to meet Lord LeVerre's eyes with my own. "She loved this?"

He nodded. Hope flared in his gaze. "My father often complained that she loved that book more than she loved him." He paused, the light in his eyes dimming, their gaze growing distant. "I wouldn't be surprised if it was true."

Slowly, I pulled the glove off my right hand, setting it down on the table beside the book. I placed my palm on its surface, the cloth beneath my fingers smooth and worn.

What came first was the breath of spring, the sweet scent of blooming flowers, the stinging cold of retreating snow, and quiet days spent lazing about in the noonday sun. The rustle of turning pages, hours of nothing but whiling away time with reading and the pursuit of peaceful activities.

It shifted to biting winds and frost, breath fogging up windows, heated blankets, and hot drinks. The blue-tinted glow of spelled lamps to chase away the dark of winter. Crackling fires and stone hearths, clocks ticking on the mantel.

It was sight and sound, the weight of pressing memories with no urgency. They were as solid as if their patron still lived, with no tears, no holes or rips, no deep sinking into quiet, numbing waters that would tell me they had passed. But it lacked depth—the currents of emotions, the taste of them that someone left on all the things in life they encountered. This one should be rich with them, flooded to the point that I would be drowning in their joys and sorrows.

Instead, the impressions were echoes; something else lingered there. It crowded up against my back, breathed on my neck and my cheek, stirring loose strands of hair. Was I being watched, or was it the Lady LeVerre? They twisted together, these sensations until I couldn't tell them apart.

I drew my hand away, settling it in my lap.

"Well?" Lord LeVerre asked when I said nothing.

Victor leaned forward, brow furrowed. "Viv?" he asked. "What did you see?"

"Nothing," I said.

"Nothing?" Victor asked.

"What does that mean?" Lord LeVerre asked.

I hesitated. Between Lord LeVerre's hope and Victor's warning, I felt as though I was balanced on a knife's edge. One wrong step and I could plummet into consequences I had no way to foresee.

"How long has this book been untouched?" I asked.

"Since the day she disappeared," Lord LeVerre said. "My father closed up her rooms; I've only recently had the servants go in to clean."

I looked down at the book. I'd noticed no competing voices to contend with, but I had to ask. "Did they touch or move anything?"

"No," he said quickly.

I twisted to look at him, catching his gaze with mine; he flushed and looked away.

"I don't know," he admitted. "I only asked that they air out the rooms and remove the dust. It felt like too much of a mausoleum to demand they leave every item in its place."

I pulled my glove back on and ran my fingers down the length of the cover one last time. "It doesn't have the feel of an item handled by many people."

"But you got nothing from it?" Lord LeVerre asked.

"Nothing that would give you answers," I said.

"So what do we do next?" he asked.

"Next," I said, pushing my chair back from the table, "*I* go for a walk. After that, we can discuss which steps you wish to take."

It did not take me long to find the rear of the house. I stepped onto the stone veranda and descended the stairs to a meticulously manicured garden. Straight gravel paths lined with empty flower beds, dormant for the coming winter, were hemmed in by closely trimmed evergreen hedges.

The air was cold enough that every breath was a white cloud, and I would not want to be outside long, even standing in full sun. The earlier frost had melted away, the gravel crunching under my feet.

I followed the trail to the left, directly next to one of the towering hedges. It took me mere moments to lose sight of the house once I was inside the maze.

It was a relief to be out here, away from people and their expectations and the constant need to shield my skin from the majority of day-to-day interaction.

It was no one's fault that I had to be mindful of what I touched. The ability was a sense like any other. I could not will myself *not* to experience the memories any more than I could will myself not to see.

A shiver crawled up my spine, and I glanced at the top edges of the dark branches. I could see nothing of the manor, not even the peak of the roof. Yet the feel of watching eyes stayed, pressed into my skin. A remnant from the book unwilling to release its hold.

Footsteps crunched behind me; I turned, resigned, expecting Victor to have followed in escort.

Lord LeVerre came around the bend, stopping short when he saw me. I caught the flash of a brown leather glove as he brushed a hand down the front of his thick gray overcoat.

"Are you not cold?" he asked.

"No," I lied.

"Do you mind if I join you on your walk?"

I shrugged and turned back to face the direction I had been going. "They're your paths."

Stones skittered as he hastened to catch up with me. "Mine they might be, but even I understand the value in time spent alone."

"You can be alone in a crowd," I said. "The only requirement is that no one speak."

"Is that your way of asking that I not talk?"

I shot him a sideways glance. "If I say yes, will you remain quiet?"

"I would hardly deny such a request from you."

"Then yes."

True to his word, he did not reply to that, staying silent. We strolled forward with our hands in our pockets, our breath puffing out into the air and the pebbles grinding beneath our shoes.

The quiet only lasted so long.

"When you aren't dealing with nonexistent insurance claims," he said wryly as if he considered the whole thing an inconvenience, "what else do you and your brother do?"

"Prove fraud," I said. "Help the police with difficult-to-solve crimes."

"Oh?" he asked. "Any in particular that stand out?"

Blood pooled and congealing on the floor, a dented candlestick holder dropped next to it, splattered in the sticky liquid. Jealousy and rage twisted up in black spikes that prickled under my skin, left a film smeared on my fingers.

"No," I said.

"None?" he asked. "No cases that have stuck with you?"

I stopped in my tracks. "None," I said firmly. "Consider the subject closed."

I started forward, and he fell into step with me.

"My apologies," he said. "For prying."

"Accepted."

"May I ask how long you've been employed in this capacity?"

"Eleven years."

"A well-established career then."

"If you want to put it that way."

"What else could it be considered?"

"A job, nothing more."

"You feel no—loyalty to it?"

"I would hardly be heartbroken if I was informed of my immediate retirement if you must know."

"And what would you choose to do instead?"

"I would open a flower shop," I said the words as if they were a throwaway—a plan thought of in the moment, not something I had been dreaming of for the past five years or more.

"You enjoy all things botanical?"

I snorted. "Hardly. The choice is entirely practical."

"How so?"

I pulled a hand out of my pocket and wiggled my fingers at him. "No one, not even my employees, would think to ask why I always wear gloves. They'll assume it's due to the arranging and handling of the blooms, particularly roses. And they're lucrative, provided the proprietor has the right kind of connections."

"And you have those right kinds of connections?"

"If I did, do you think I'd be here with Victor, *indulging* you in your request?"

At my words, his steps faltered, and I cursed my tongue that I would unwittingly trample his hope.

"Do you know what would cause it?" he asked at length when the silence between us lengthened.

"Cause what?"

"The nothing, you sensed."

I shook my head. "Nothing was a poor choice—a poor way to phrase it."

"Then what was it?"

"It was...half of what it should have been."

"Half?"

I stopped, one hand raised, fingers pressed to my brow. "Bland," I said. "Normally emotions, memories—they have a flavor to them. I can taste it on my tongue, feel it under my skin. This was lacking."

"How could it be lacking?"

"I don't know," I admitted. "Even casual contact will impart something, a sense of one's mood from the moment they held it, touched it, or even brushed up against it. Items that were loved provide even stronger sentiments. Like the difference between a simple soup stock and a hearty stew."

His only response was thoughtful silence as if he was turning what I had said over in his mind.

"This an ability your brother shares?" he asked.

"No," I said.

He left it at that, and I was grateful. I would not explain the extent of what Victor could or could not do to a relative stranger.

I was not sure the Company even informed their clients of what we, and the others like us in their employ, were truly capable of.

"Is Victor your only sibling?" Lucien asked.

"No," I said.

"And no one else in your family is likewise talented?"

"No," I repeated.

We lapsed into reticence.

"Do you have any siblings?" I asked, venturing forth when it appeared we had truly run out of anything to discuss.

"No," he said ruefully. "I am an only child."

"What about your parents?" I asked. "Did they have any brothers or sisters?"

"My father was also an only child," he said, and the flash of the smile he gave me appeared strained. "From what I understand, my grandmother died early, and her husband never remarried. Familial history was often a...discouraged topic in our household."

"That seems odd, from what I know of those who belong to high society. Isn't pride of ancestry generally the standard?"

"Generally," he said; the bitter tone in his voice did not invite further inquiry into the subject. I let it go, unwilling to probe into something that appeared to be of a sensitive nature.

I paused on our path, wiggling my toes in my shoes, which were beginning to go numb from the cold. The chill was biting at my nose. If we didn't go inside soon, it would begin to run, and I hadn't brought a handkerchief with me.

"Are you cold now?" he asked.

"A bit," I said.

"I—" he hesitated before continuing. "Would you like my coat?"

"No," I said, turning to head back toward the house, and he hurried to follow after me.

CHAPTER THREE

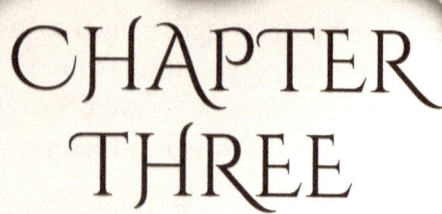

Case 1888–11–MP–001436
November 12, 1888
Interviews with household staff conducted. Lord LeVerre was kept absent as per regulations.

W e found Victor in the drawing room, brooding by the fire. One arm was resting on the mantel, and his other hand held his pocket watch, thumb brushing back and forth across the glass face. He snapped it shut when we came in.

"Did you enjoy your walk?" he asked.

"As much as could be expected," I said, drifting past him to settle in an armchair by the fire.

"Well," he said after neither of us said anything else. "Should we be taking our leave?"

"I would like Miss Tailor to try again," Lord LeVerre said. "Perhaps the problem is the length of time since my mother has been in contact with any of her items."

"Then I would choose the next one with great care," Victor said.

The two of them sized each other up—two dogs with a meaty bone between them; the only thing holding them back was the polite veneer of society. I wasn't sure what it was about Lord LeVerre that set Victor on edge.

"Perhaps Miss Tailor can accompany me to my mother's rooms instead," Lord LeVerre said. "I believe it simplest to give her full access in the hopes she finds an item that provides the information she needs."

Victor's eyes flicked between us. "Viv?" There was a warning in his tone, caution in that simple word. And I ignored it.

"I am amenable to that," I said.

"Excellent," Lord LeVerre said, a smile blooming across his face. "Let's go, then."

I followed him out of the drawing room with Victor close behind. He snatched at my arm before I could go far, pulling me to a stop as he leaned in to murmur in my ear. "I do not know that this path is the best one for us to pursue."

"I am not so sure myself," I admitted. "But I do not feel we can leave him wondering if there is any chance we can give him some form of an answer."

Victor hadn't yet released my arm.

"I urge you to be careful," he said, "not to leave him with false hope. These cases..."

"...generally do not end well," I finished for him.

He nodded, and we moved to catch up to Lord LeVerre. Rather than turning to the left at the top of the stairs, toward the wing where Victor and I had spent the night, he turned to the right into shadowed halls. Having caught sight of him, we were content to stroll side by side.

A door creaked open ahead of us, sunlight filtering into the hallway. Lord LeVerre's shape flashed as he slipped into the room.

I stepped through the door, and Victor paused on the threshold. When I turned back, his mouth was twisted in a grimace, and he leaned with one hand on the doorframe, the other pressed to his chest. "Vic?" I asked, taking a step toward him.

"I'm alright, Viv; the air is stale."

"Yes," Lord LeVerre said, busily shoving the curtains farther back from the windows. "We can't seem to get rid of the sense of—decay?" He shook his head. "The word feels too strong."

"The word feels right to me," Victor muttered.

I set a hand on his arm.

He pulled his hand off the doorframe and patted the back of mine, his palm warm through the leather of my glove. "I'm alright, truly."

"Are you sure?" I asked, glancing over my shoulder at Lord LeVerre. Discussing Victor's vision would need to happen away from listening ears.

"Quite sure," Victor said, lowering his other hand and straightening up.

"Quite sure of what?" Lord LeVerre asked.

"Just a passing fancy," Victor said smoothly. "It's nothing, really."

For half a breath, I thought Lord LeVerre would pry further from the way his brow furrowed. But the expression was there and gone in an instant, and I thought perhaps I had only imagined it.

"Shall we get started?" he asked. He motioned at the room—a vague, encompassing gesture. "I don't quite know where to begin."

I pulled my gloves off, stowing them in my skirt pocket. "The room will tell me where," I said, drifting over toward a settee and running my fingers along the curve of its back. The wood was cool to the touch, the memories distant, fleeting things. The only lingering sensation was darkness, the impression of continuously sinking. I drew my hand away, frowning. It didn't have the same feel as the other items his mother had touched. But there was a likeness there, someone akin to her.

"Who died on this couch?" I asked.

There was a long, expectant pause. When I looked up to meet Lord LeVerre's eyes, his gaze flicked to the floor. "My aunt," he said quietly. "Mother said she laid down for a short nap and never woke up."

"We're sorry for your loss," I said, the words tripping off my tongue automatically.

"Thank you," he said. "I would not say I knew her well." He gave me a wan sort of smile. "But it is reassuring to see that your abilities work."

It was my turn to be the one with a furrowed brow, and I narrowed my eyes, but he simply stared back innocently at me. Rather than be baited by the implied insult, I turned away and studied the remainder of his mother's sitting room.

The furniture was stiff and high-backed despite the curving wood frames of the couches and chairs. Their upholstery was a dusky rose and faded mauve, a nod toward femininity juxtaposed against the cold and calculating air the pieces held. The nearby tables were much the same, their corners pointed and sharp.

A pair of heavy mirrors hung above the cold, empty fireplace, the metal of its grate blackened from use. They looked like staring eyes above an open maw. I turned away from them, every inch of me aware that my reflection's eyes could be fastened on my back, a silly superstition I had never been able to shake.

A quill and paper were still on the top of the small writing desk in the corner, although I suspected the ink had long since dried out. The beginnings of a letter were written on the top page, stopped mid-sentence as if the writer had been called away in the middle, and never returned.

I peered at the faint lines of text, the brown ink that didn't quite blend in with the discolored surface. I leaned over, slowly picking out the shapes and the way the writing flowed. I reached out, then hesitated, the tips of my fingers hovering over the letter.

"The day your mother disappeared," I said, "where were you?"

"In the city," Lord LeVerre said. "I was learning the business of trade, and as my father said, I had wasted enough time on the pursuits of country life."

"Wasn't your father a countryman himself?" Victor asked.

I turned my head to watch their exchange.

"Yes," Lord LeVerre said tightly. "And so was his father, and his father before him. He felt it was high time we rose in the ranks of society to match the status our wealth implied."

"And after your mother vanished, was your father still interested in pursuing higher social standing?" Victor asked, his tone bland curiosity, but anyone who knew him would spot the way his eyes narrowed and the twitch of his fingers.

Lord LeVerre's eyes hardened, flecks of cold flint in his face. "I fail to see how that's relevant."

"What was done in the wake of your mother's disappearance is exceedingly relevant," Victor said.

Lord LeVerre hesitated a moment longer before sinking onto one of the chairs. "My father sent me a letter—more of a note, really. He said there was no reason for me to come home but that no one had seen my mother in two—*two*—days."

Victor and I exchanged half-startled glances. "Was your mother prone to disappearing?" he asked, his tone taking on a gentleness I was familiar with.

"No," Lord LeVerre said. "She rarely went *anywhere*. She hated to travel, always had."

"Then why are you so convinced that she simply left and never returned?" Victor asked.

"This place is stifling," Lord LeVerre said. "Surely you can feel it? You've said it yourself. The air is stale. No one would stay here, given another opportunity."

"So why do you stay?" I asked.

Lord LeVerre fell silent. "I would like a moment alone."

"Certainly," Victor said. "Come on, Viv. We'll be downstairs in the drawing room when you're ready for Vivian to try again, Lord LeVerre."

The latter nodded, and I followed Victor, leaving Lord LeVerre brooding behind us.

Once on the stairs, I caught Victor's arm and tugged him to a halt. "Your vision?" I asked quietly.

He shot a glance toward the landing, but as far as I could tell, we were the only ones standing in this shadowed space. "There isn't much to tell, Viv," he said. "Just a sense of looming pressure and unease." He continued down the stairs, and I hesitated, unsure if I should push the issue.

In the end, I let the silence endure.

The drawing room was hardly the most exciting place to sit and wait. There was nothing to entertain ourselves with, and John had left the curtains drawn. We were forced to light the lamps or uncover the windows ourselves if we wanted something other than the closeted dark pierced only by the ever-present, crackling flames in the fireplace.

I perched on the edge of one of the spindly chairs while Victor continuously checked his pocket watch.

"It must be close to noon by this point," I said, tracing my fingers over the worn seam on my glove.

"It is," Victor said.

"Do you think they'll call us for lunch, or are we expected to intuit when it will be served?"

"As I've not seen hide nor hair of John since last night or any evidence of the other servants, we'll likely need to seek it out ourselves."

I looked up from my hands. "No one?"

"No one," Victor confirmed. "Although I've not explored any farther than our rooms, the dining room, and this one. Did you happen to see anyone on your way to the gardens?"

"No," I said almost absently as I retraced my steps. "They're quite adept at staying out of sight."

"Could be he's reduced the staff to only John and the aforementioned porter and cook," Victor said, running a finger down along the mantel itself. He made a face as he attempted to wipe off the grit clinging to his skin. "Has some of the local village girls come in and dust when it gets to be too much for him to endure."

"If he despises it here so much, you would think he would engage a solicitor to sell it for him." If he could sell it. But it appeared that our current Lord LeVerre was all that was left of his family, so a contentious inheritance seemed unlikely.

"He may very well be," Victor said. He turned away from the fireplace and sat on the couch across from me, fingers drumming against the dark wood. "I hate these kinds of cases."

"Which kinds of cases?" I asked, examining my gloves.

Victor waved a hand at the room. "The ones for the wealthy."

I looked up and arched an eyebrow at him. "You have something against those with money? He is paying us a salary in addition to what we will be paid by the Company."

"The speed at which they move," he said. "Everything is done with propriety when haste and efficiency are needed." He snorted. "The Company often suffers from the same problem."

"I hardly think haste will help us with this one," I said. "Seven years is a long time to wait to seek out answers."

"You and I are of one mind there." He tapped his fingers again and jiggled his foot. "I still do not see why he did not seek assistance sooner unless his father intentionally put a stop to any and all attempts to request police assistance at minimum." He shifted in his seat. "And I can only think of one reason why his father would actively discourage an investigation."

We were quiet, mulling it over—this knowledge that it was often those closest to the victim who were guilty.

"Maybe we should ask John," I said.

"Ask him what? Why no one had opened an investigation before now?"

"Yes," I said. "Maybe they did open one, but the police were incompetent."

"Always a chance of that," Victor mused. "And if the police insisted there was no reason for Company involvement, perhaps no one questioned it."

"I want to know if they noticed immediately when she went missing," I said. "What were her steps before her disappearance?"

"We need the initial reports," Victor said. "If we're going to do this, we can't do it by halves."

"I thought we were already doing this," I said. "Surely we're not lollygagging about our investigation?"

Victor flashed me a knowing grin. "I'm not the one dawdling. Are you already partial to the denizens in the shadows here?"

"I've no idea what you're talking about," I said, pushing myself up off the chair. "We should go secure our coats and either find John or some paper to leave a note for Lord LeVerre, so he knows where we've gone and haven't simply run out on him."

"Without being paid first? Banish the thought."

We left the drawing room and checked the dining room first, though breakfast should have long since been cleared away. It was empty, the curtains redrawn across the windows.

"No wonder our host finds his house so stifling," I muttered, "if they always leave the windows covered. It's like living in a cave."

"If he hadn't gone out for a walk with you," Victor mused, "I would think he was allergic to sunlight or a creature of the night."

"We might still discover he is," I said as I turned away from the dining room and headed down the hall toward what I hoped was the kitchen.

"I would think he wouldn't have gone outside at all if he was either of those."

"Perhaps he has a brief immunity," I said. "Or painted his skin with a thick layer of makeup to protect it."

"Did he appear to be wearing makeup?" Victor asked, amused.

"No," I said. "But then he may have been wearing it since we arrived, and neither of us would be able to tell the times he is or isn't."

"Artfully applied, we shouldn't be able to tell at all."

"Since when have you acquired so much knowledge about it?"

"Since the theater case," he said. "Curiosity spurred the rest."

"Ah." I paused with Victor close behind and peered through an open door into a study. Once again, the curtains were drawn over the windows, but there was a blazing fire on the hearth, and lamps lit on the heavy-set desk that dominated the space. A mirror hung directly across from it, reflecting back its empty image, although I could have sworn I caught a flash of movement in the glass. The shelves up against the walls were packed with books, their spines marching in neat rows of varying heights.

Paper, ink, and quill were set up tidily on the desk's surface, and unerringly, I headed there. Victor leaned back against the doorframe, arms crossed, while I pulled a piece of paper toward me. I dipped the point of a quill in ink and scrawled a note.

"He's a bit old-fashioned, don't you think?" Victor asked.

"Hmm?" I said, more an acknowledgment that he had spoken than anything else.

"The quills," he said. "Surely he could afford a pen set instead."

"Why fix what isn't broken?" I asked, gently blowing across the ink to dry it. "Besides, he would still have to fill them with ink to begin with."

Note secured, we headed back to the drawing room, finding it just as empty as before. I left the paper hanging noticeably from the mantel, and we headed out the front door, the hinges creaking as we shut it behind us.

The chill in the air had deepened; we hurried across the muddy yard to the carriage where it stood waiting. We didn't bother extending the steps; we simply hauled ourselves up.

Victor pulled a piece of paper out of his pocket, looking over the information he had noted. "Village of Sparrow Oak," he announced.

There was a pause while the spells that made the conveyance work registered the command; with a shudder, the carriage rocked forward and began trundling its way down the drive. We settled in our seats, huddling against the hard back for the duration of the ride.

The village was quaint, to put it lightly. The buildings I spotted from behind the curtains were low-slung stone cottages, plaster and timber, with a fountain seated in the middle of the town square. Our carriage paused, parking itself directly next to the fountain.

Victor climbed out first, waiting while I hopped down before shutting the carriage door, and we took a moment to orient ourselves.

The village appeared relatively lively, with people out and about running errands. While quiet compared to the city, there was still a buzz in the air. Victor stopped a man in the street to obtain directions to the local police station.

It wasn't far from the center of town—just a couple of streets down and over—and we were standing in front of one of the more modern buildings the village contained. Its façade was brick, with steps leading up to the black-painted door in the center. A bronze plaque with raised lettering was set firmly in the wood, informing us which district and station we had the fortune to visit.

The interior was modern, with thin, dark-stained wooden floorboards, a chair rail along the walls of the lobby, cream-white paint, and sturdy chairs. The desk sergeant sat before the door leading farther back into the station, scribbling away in a ledger.

"Visitors must sign in," he said without looking up from his work.

"Vivian and Victor Tailor, with the Company," Victor said, pulling out our assignment sheet. The paper was beginning to look rather worse for the wear from the time spent in his pocket. "We've been hired to look into the disappearance of Lady LeVerre and would like to see the original case notes, please."

The sergeant used the top end of his ink pen to point at the empty sheet of paper on the desk in front of him. "Sign in."

Victor picked up the extra pen on the desk and scrawled our names out across the top of the sheet of paper.

"State your business," the desk sergeant said.

"Vivian and Victor Tailor, with the Company," Victor repeated, a bite in his tone. "We've been hired to look into the disappearance of Lady LeVerre and would like to see the original case notes, *please*."

The sergeant motioned at the door behind him. "You'll want the evidence locker down the hall, third door on the left. Tell Tilly I sent you."

"Thank you," Victor said, and we moved past the desk and into a hallway just as bland and modern in appearance as the lobby.

The third door on the left brought us to a set of stairs. With a shrug, we followed them up to another hallway. Here, we found Tilly, her nose in a book, seated at a small desk beside a closed wooden door with another bronze plaque fastened to its front.

It was blank.

"Miss Tilly?" Victor asked.

She looked up from her novel. "Yes?" she asked, irritation in her voice.

"We're sorry to interrupt," Victor said, "but the desk sergeant sent us to see you. Vivian and Victor Tailor from the Company. We need any notes you have on the disappearance of Lady LeVerre and a chance to speak with the detective who worked the case, if possible."

She sighed and set her book aside. Pushing her chair back, she stood and bustled to open the wooden door. Victor and I leaned in that direction, peering into the shadowy space.

She was back within moments, placing a large, packed envelope meant for official documents on the desk in front of us. "There, case notes. You'll want Detective Brant, but he's away today."

"Do you know when he'll be back?" Victor asked, picking up the envelope.

"No," she said and pointed at an open door just down the hall from us. "You can use examination room ten, but leave *those* in the room when you're done." She jabbed a finger at the envelope.

"Of course," he said. "Thank you for your assistance."

We headed into the room she indicated, shutting the door behind us. He pulled the papers out, set the notes on the table in the room, and pulled out a chair to sit down before he picked up the topmost sheet.

"Well?" I asked, settling into the chair across from him. "Anything useful?"

"Police were called to the residence of one Lord LeVerre—I'm assuming that's our host's father—at ten o'clock in the morning on April the tenth, where he informed the responding officer that his wife had been missing for *four* days."

"So even after he sent in a letter to his son, he didn't bother bringing the police in for at least two more days?" I asked, leaning across the table to try to read the notes upside down.

"See for yourself," Victor said and set the paper before me.

I read through the initial report, my eyes narrowing with every line. "Has our Lord LeVerre—"

"*Our*?" Victor asked.

"Oh hush, how else are we to differentiate between the two? Has our Lord LeVerre seen this information?" I asked. "Do you think he's aware his father took so long to report his mother's disappearance?"

Victor leaned back in his chair. "I would wager he at least suspects."

"Do you also have a guess as to why the elder Lord LeVerre didn't report her missing immediately?"

"Yours is probably much the same as mine." He tapped a finger against the surface of the table. "He needed the time to hide or destroy any evidence."

I lifted the paper, reading back through the initial notes once again. "I suspect our client will not rest until we can at least provide him with a body, and not just my word that she has passed."

"I suspect you're correct," Victor said. "Have you considered checking the attic?"

"Don't be crude, Vic," I said, reaching for the next paper. "Hiding bodies in attics."

"Is it any worse than a shallow grave in the garden?"

"Doubtful," I said. "The end result is the same."

"They've a list of—witnesses if that's what you would call them," Victor said, picking up another piece of paper and scanning the page. "I would *wager* a guess that they all still live in the area." He pulled a worn pocket-sized notebook from within his jacket, along with an old, nubby pencil that had seen far better days, flipped the cover open, and began copying down the witnesses' information.

I tugged off one of my gloves and cast a glance back at the door.

"I highly doubt they'll know what you're about," Victor said absently, still scribbling.

I laid my palm against the paper.

Whispers, a gruff voice, a sense of curiosity followed by growing concern, and a stern kind of judgment swiftly swallowed up by determination. I blinked and lifted my hand. "Someone other than us has handled these papers recently," I said.

Victor looked up from his notes. "Did my handling of them not blunt anything?"

"Were you attempting to?"

"No, but I know how it is." He leaned forward, studying the page my fingers still hovered over. "Unpredictable at best, depending on the emotions at the time." He tucked his notebook and pencil back in his jacket pocket. "What did you sense? Did it feel anything like our host?"

"No," I said slowly. "At least, not the kind of read I would expect to get from an object he had handled, based on his mannerisms." I hesitated, considering picking the paper up as if further contact would let me glean anything new. "I certainly got the feeling that our Lord LeVerre is not the only one dissatisfied with the current *status quo*."

"Ah," Victor said. "A bulldog." He settled back in his seat, scooting closer to the table. "Well, in that case, perhaps we'll have an ally." He paused and drummed his fingers on the table, head tilted to the side. "Or a block in the road."

"I suppose that depends on how possessive he is of his case," I said lightly, pulling my glove back on.

Victor shuffled through the pile and set aside three separate pages, running his finger down one as he read, his lips moving. He moved on to the next one, and curiously, I tugged the first one free.

A witness statement from Anne Worthy.

Victor was finished with his third page before I was done reading through the interview. "They all say the same thing," he said, rubbing his eyes. "The wording might differ, but from what I can tell, they found absolutely no answers in questioning the staff."

"The elder Lord LeVerre had time to make sure everyone's story matched," I murmured, looking over the next page, but Victor was right. I could gather no new information from this, or the third one either. "They all say she went upstairs to write a letter to her—" I paused, reading back through it. "Her sister?"

Victor rose and came around the table to look back down at the papers. "Is that what that awful handwriting says?"

"I could be entirely misreading it," I said. "But it looks like this—" I poked a finger at the letter, "is an s."

"That one is obvious," Victor said. "At least choose a hard one to puzzle out."

"It could be a shorthand note for 'solicitor,'" I said, picking up the page, holding it aloft, and squinting at it. "The letters are all crammed a bit closely together."

"She may have had more than one sister," Victor said. "And the one the letter was meant for was not the one who died on her couch."

"I suppose we'll need to ask Lord LeVerre if he has any other family members to be sure."

"Indeed," Victor said as he moved back to his chair and picked up yet another page.

CHAPTER FOUR

November 13, 1888
A search of the house and grounds resulted only in disappointment and aggrava-
tion of dust.

T he ride back to Lord LeVerre's manor was un-
eventful, although it took the carriage a moment to respond to Victor's command.

"The thing is on its last legs," he had muttered and
then spent the entire drive pressed to the side, curtain
flung out of his way, the window opened wide, head
practically hanging out the frame, despite the way the
conveyance jolted and shuddered its way down the
road.

"Are you alright?" I asked when he finally sat back,
settling into the seat cushion with his head slumped
against the back wall.

"The air is stale," he murmured.

I chanced a peek out the window and saw the flash
of columns before the carriage came to a creaking halt.

"Stale, how?" I asked, edging the curtain back a bit
more, checking for a presence on the front steps. No

one was there—only the dark eyes of the house stared back at me.

"It's in his throat," he said. "The dust and grit."

I hesitated, fingers digging into the fabric of my riding skirt, unsure which question would lead him down the path this vision sought to show us. "Whose throat?"

"Lord LeVerre," he said. "It chokes off his breath, and he has none left with which to scream."

"A tad melodramatic," I said cautiously. "He could leave the house any time he wishes to, couldn't he?" I had to be careful, or Victor's vision would pop like a soap bubble, leaving us with only the bare surface of what he had seen. The information he received and gave may be useless—nothing more than white noise and chatter—but I would rather all of it than half, even if it told us nothing important.

"Can you?" he asked.

"Can I what?" I asked. "Leave?"

"Leave?" Victor said. "Why would we leave? We've only just arrived." He shoved himself forward, scooting off his seat and pushing the carriage door open.

"In time for lunch, it would appear," I said warily, watching him before following after and landing on the now-dried mud with a thump. "Are you quite alright?"

"It's only a vision, Viv," he said, shutting the door behind me. "And a poor one at that. What sane man yokes himself to a home he hates?"

"One that cannot let go of the past?" I suggested. "Or one that thinks he has no other future."

Victor snorted. "He's old enough to know better."

"I certainly agree with you there," I murmured. "He strikes me as far younger than he is."

"Emotionally or physically?" Victor asked.

I tilted my head, considering. "I would wager both. He's one of those rare few gifted with an ageless countenance."

"Do I detect a hint of envy, sister dear?"

"Certainly," I said. "Eternally flawless skin? Most would give their right arm for that privilege."

Victor chuckled. "And that would make both of us no different from the rest of them."

He pushed the door open, and we stepped into the shadowed hall.

"Do you think he'll be in the drawing or dining room?" I asked.

"We should check first to make sure he got our note," Victor said. I followed close behind, loathe to be left in this darkened space alone.

Lord LeVerre was indeed in the drawing room, sitting in one of its many chairs. He rose to his feet, brushing his hands down his pants at his thighs as he stood. "Did you find anything?"

"Witness statements only," Victor said. "So we would like a chance to speak to the staff to see if there's any new information they recall about that day."

Lord LeVerre hesitated. "I'm afraid that won't be an easy task. All but John and Cook are gone, you see."

"Gone?" I asked.

"Left," he said. "They've been trickling away from our employment since the disappearance."

"How curious," I muttered. The porter must have been a recent loss if he had been here to help with the luggage the night before.

"I'm sorry, Miss Tailor; I didn't quite catch that."

"I asked if they were still in the village," I lied, and there was a moment where he fastened his eyes on mine and I was sure he wouldn't let the lie go.

"I believe most are," he said, and the muscles tensing all along my shoulders relaxed.

"A job for tomorrow, then," Victor said. "In the meantime, could we try speaking with John?"

"I'm afraid he's indisposed," Lord LeVerre said. "And at this moment, is resting. Perhaps once he's feeling better and is back on his feet?"

"And Cook?" Victor asked.

"Was away visiting her family when my mother vanished and won't have anything to tell you."

Victor opened his mouth, then shut it as if he thought better of what he was about to say, and shuffled his feet. "She will be an important piece of the puzzle in helping us understand the interactions between your mother and father and might help explain the reason for her disappearance."

Lord LeVerre stood there, brow furrowed and mouth puckered. I couldn't be sure if he was thinking through Victor's words or trying to think of some excuse as to why we couldn't speak to his cook. Although, why he would block us from finding out where his mother had gone made little sense, considering his previous claims?

"She's in the kitchen preparing lunch," he finally said. "I'll thank you not to get in her way while you speak to her."

"Of course," Victor said. "And the kitchen is located...?"

"Down the hall from the dining room, left-hand side," Lord LeVerre said, settling back in the chair and picking up the book on the side table. I caught the flash of gilt lettering on its spine and front but wasn't close enough to pick out the title from the curling, curving letters. He opened it, his long fingers, pale and bloodless in color, spread across its cover.

"Viv," Victor said from the doorway. With a start, I turned away from Lord LeVerre and hurried after him, back into the hall and down its echoing length, the sound of our footsteps bouncing off the walls.

"They serve lunch late here," I said. "If it's not already prepared."

"Two o'clock does seem late," he said. "But I'm afraid we're on country time and not city while we're here. Noon must be a strange concept to them."

"It feels as though it should be the opposite with how early in the day they've shuttered the house."

"Not for the aristocracy," Victor muttered. "Certainly, it's the other way around for everyone else. Up with the sun and in bed shortly after it disappears beneath the horizon."

We reached the kitchen door, its heavy wood form closed to other entrants, and Victor tried the handle. Fortunately, it gave way with a click and groaning hinges into a space as dim as the rest of the manor.

The majority of the light came from the lamps positioned along the walls, their glow casting a blue pall over the room. The curtains pulled over the windows seemed at odds with what the space was meant for. Surely, this would be the one room one wouldn't want stray bits of fabric at risk of catching fire. A single mirror stretching nearly the length of the room hung on one side, the reflected light making the space brighter than it would have been otherwise. A neat trick to brighten the workspace for any late-night preparations, but hardly necessary during the day if they would just pull the curtains back.

The woman within was gangly, tall, and thin, her face pinched and sour as she put together equally slim sandwiches. Her bony fingers moved swiftly to remove the crust from the bread, slap some spread on the remnants, and add in slices of cucumber and bits of watercress.

She caught sight of us hovering in the doorway; with a sharp jerk of her chin toward the table where she stood, she motioned us to come inside. "If you're after food," she said, her voice sweet and calm despite her obvious flurry, "I'm sorry that it's so late. Lord LeVerre was unsure if you'd be back for it, and we didn't want it sitting out getting stale."

"We weren't sure ourselves," Victor said apologetically. "Our time in town didn't take us quite as long as we expected."

"If the two of you would like to go sit in the dining room, I'll have it out in just a jiffy—"

"Actually," I said, "we came to speak to you."

"Oh?" she said, looking up and catching my eyes with a quick flick of her own, dark and wary before her gaze moved back to the sandwiches. "What about?"

"The Lady LeVerre and her disappearance," Victor said.

"Ah," she said.

"Could you tell us what happened that day?" I prodded. I was trying to ascertain if there was a subtle way I could remove my gloves, run my fingers along the dishes on the table, or find an excuse to brush across the knife she had set to one side. A way to read her mood and emotions while we spoke.

"There isn't much to tell," the cook said. "From what I've gathered, it was a normal day when it began. Nothing untoward from either her, anyone on the staff, or his lordship."

"No arguments in the days leading up to it?" Victor asked. "Quarrels of any kind?"

The cook shook her head, lips pressed tightly together. "None," she said. "I would remember if there had been any arguing, as she wasn't the arguing kind. You could blow her about like she was a leaf. What his lordship said went, and she simply followed along with it." She set her palms flat against the table, pausing as if she had something more she wanted to say, then shook her head again before she went back to preparing the sandwiches.

"Nothing from the servants, perhaps?" I asked. "Someone who tried to take advantage of her meek manner and found more than they bargained for?" I lowered my hands so they were hidden by the edge of the table, tugged off a glove and then pressed the tips of my fingers to its underside. There was irritation there, spiky and grating, impatience with the whole affair, and nothing else. No sense of guilt, no secrets or the clinging ooze of lies, no sharp points of nervousness.

I dropped my fingers away from the wood and slipped my hand back into its glove.

"Never," she said firmly. "The staff adored her, and his lordship would have come down on them like a hammer if they made her shed so much as a single tear."

"Would you say his lordship loved her?" Victor asked.

"With all his heart," she said, pressing together another sandwich.

Victor and I exchanged glances, and he shifted, his fingers twitching again.

"It seems odd, then," I said, "that he would wait four days to report her disappearance."

"Well, she'd begun vanishing for hours at a time around then," the cook said casually. "So he didn't begin to worry until the second day."

There was a pause while Victor and I digested this statement. "Did anyone ask her where she was going during those times?" I asked.

"Why would we?" the cook said. "She never left the house, so we always assumed she was in one room or another."

"Was his son aware of this new habit?" Victor asked.

Her hands slowed, hovering in the air, a slight tremor to the fingers as she glanced up at Victor. "Well, he wouldn't be, would he? Away in the city like he was," she said, picking up the platter of sandwiches she had been piling up together and thumping it onto a tray.

"And no one ever thought to mention it to him?" I asked.

The cook paused, her movements jerking to a halt as she stopped and stared at the wall behind us. Both Victor and I half-twisted to see what had arrested her attention, but there was nothing there, only our images reflected back at us in the glass. We turned back, but she hadn't shifted, her eyes unfocused and glazed.

"Cook?" Victor said cautiously when the seconds crawled by, but she still hadn't pulled her gaze from whatever it was that had captivated her.

She blinked and caught up the empty teapot, placing it and several cups and saucers onto the tray next to the food. "It seemed like such common knowledge; it wouldn't surprise me if no one thought to inform him."

"But none of this was in the reports given to the detective who came to interview the staff," I said gently. "Surely someone would have thought to mention it to him?"

The look she shot me this time was cautious, narrow-eyed. "You trust those big city coppers of yours?"

"Is the detective not local?" Victor asked.

"He wasn't at the time," the cook snorted. "I'm sure he's ingratiated himself by now."

"So none of you were willing to speak openly to him despite the apparent danger a woman you purport to adore was in?" I said heatedly. "Because he was a transfer?"

"We take care of our own," the cook shot back. "We didn't need some beetle crusher coming in, telling us how to do things, what questions to ask." She hefted the tray up, the dishes rattling with the movement. "I've your lunch ready for you city folk," she said stiffly. "And if I were you, I'd ask my questions of someone else." She marched around the table and out the kitchen door with her nose in the air.

Victor sighed.

"Are you on her side?" I demanded.

"No, Viv," he said. "You know, I think you're right. They stalled it out before a real investigation could even happen. But let's not make our job any harder than it needs to be by casting judgment where they can hear it." He patted me on the shoulder, then followed in the silent wake left by the cook and her sandwiches.

Lunch was a quiet, awkward affair. Lord LeVerre had left his drawing room to sit at the dining room table with his nose still in his book. He lounged there, a sandwich dangling from his fingers, the pages rustling when he turned them.

Victor dropped a couple of the squashed sandwiches onto my plate before he picked up my cup, turning it around in one hand, the ceramic sliding over his palm.

I waited, unsure if I wanted to try eating the food that may have absorbed the cook's mood.

Victor poured me some tea from the now-steaming pot.

My stomach rumbled, and I gave up on avoiding the food. I picked up a sandwich, took a bite, and was relieved when I experienced nothing more than the sharp, peppery taste of the watercress. I took a sip of tea, my eyes darting between Lord LeVerre and Victor, the former seemingly determined to ignore the two of us and the latter contentedly eating his lunch.

I had yet to see Lord LeVerre take a bite of his own sandwich. It was as if he had forgotten it, and his cup of tea existed.

"Are you not hungry?" I asked, and his eyes—black, swirling, yawning pits—flicked up to meet mine. I teetered on their edge, balanced on that whispering void. I blinked, and there was only Lord LeVerre looking back at me, his russet eyes dark in the dim room—but studious, serious, and calm.

"I am not *fond* of watercress," he said. "My mother was, and Cook often forgets that preferences do not always span the generations." He set his sandwich down and sipped his tea, grimacing. "But don't let my reticence prevent you from enjoying your own lunch," he said, settling back with his book.

I was still trying to catch the faded gilt title but was distracted by the frayed corners of the cover and the wear along its spine, where it had been cracked open and laid flat more than once. "Is that a favorite of yours?" I asked.

Victor poked my foot with the tip of his own. I nudged him back, shooting him a look with a raised eyebrow and a tilt of my head. He narrowed his eyes at me.

"Hmm?" Lord LeVerre said without looking up from the page.

"I asked if that's a favorite book of yours," I repeated, raising the volume of my voice only the slightest as if it needed to be heard down the length of the table.

Lord LeVerre tipped the book so the cover closed over his fingers, his gaze raking along the lettering. "I would not say so, no."

"Oh," I said.

But now that I had his attention, he seemed loathe to return to ignoring us. He set the book down on the table, his fingers between the pages. "I am enjoying it, though, which I suppose speaks volumes for going to the library and picking one up at random."

"You have a library?" I asked.

"Yes," he said. "I can show it to you after lunch if you wish."

I smiled hesitantly. "That would be lovely."

Victor's prodding my foot was less gentle this time. I blinked innocently at him while he narrowed his eyes into an outright scolding glare.

Lord LeVerre swept his book back up. "Then I'll wait for you to finish."

"No need," I said, pushing away my plate and cup. "I'm quite finished now."

Lord LeVerre hurriedly placed his book back down, pages splayed to mark his place, and pushed his chair away from the table.

Victor caught my hand against the wood surface. "If you would give me a moment with my sister."

Lord LeVerre paused halfway up from his seat, then gave Victor a curt nod. "Certainly," he said before heading out the dining room door, where I assumed he lingered somewhere in the hall.

Victor leaned in toward me. "Do not get nosy," he warned. "We're not here to poke around in his business."

"I won't," I promised. It was a half-truth, and Victor didn't fall for it.

"I'm asking you, Viv, not to go looking where you have no right to go looking," he said. "There are some things we shouldn't be privy to knowing, and his life outside this investigation is one of them. His choices are none of our business."

I sighed and settled back in my seat so I could meet Victor's eyes face to face. "I won't," I repeated.

He squeezed my hand. "Thank you. I don't blame you for your curiosity, but there are times when you should not, and cannot, exercise it."

"I know," I said churlishly. "I don't need a lecture on it."

"Were you going to go poking into things you shouldn't be poking into?"

"Maybe," I muttered.

He gave my hand another squeeze and then let go. "Go, pick out a book to read. I'll go through the list of witnesses and decide which order to speak to them in."

I got up from my chair and left the dining room to find I was right: Lord LeVerre had been hovering in the hall, hands in his pockets, the absolute picture of innocence as if he had attempted to listen in on our conversation but hadn't quite managed to catch the words.

"So…" he began as we headed down the hall, not quite side by side. "Is your investigation proceeding well?" He sounded hopeful.

"As well as one can hope with so little initial information," I said honestly.

We were silent for a moment as we walked, turning down a hallway I hadn't noticed previously. We stepped farther into the dark, and a chill crept up my spine at the way the shadows pressed in around us.

"Would it help if you attempt the items in her rooms again?" he asked quietly.

"It may," I said. "Did no one mention to you that she had been vanishing for hours at a time prior to her disappearance?"

He started, stumbling before he recovered, half-turning to face me. "No," he said. "No one has ever told me that."

"You may wish to speak to your cook in that case," I said. "Any knowledge we can gather may tell us where she would have gone."

"So you think she still lives?"

"I cannot give an opinion on that," I said.

"I'm not asking for your professional, reportable opinion," he said. "I'm asking for what you yourself think or what you hope to discover."

I stopped in my tracks, and he stopped with me, the two of us facing each other in the dim blue glow of the lit sconces on the walls. The light flickered eerily across his features, a pale wraith in these shadows. "I don't know what to think," I said.

He stepped closer to me, and if I had been wearing one of my dresses, his legs would have brushed up against my skirts. All I could feel was the need to back away.

"But you haven't encountered results like this before," he said, his eyes empty hollows, his face drained of all color, white as a skull.

I blinked, swallowed, and took that step I longed for back and away from him. There was only Lord LeVerre, staring down entreatingly at me.

The lights and the dark were playing tricks on me.

"I haven't," I said, my voice barely above a whisper, but I wasn't so sure I wanted to follow this man any farther into his house, library or not. Fear skittered at the base of my neck, sinking talons into the muscles of my shoulders and back—that animalistic instinct that something was here, lurking in the shadows, just beyond the edge of where we stood.

He merely nodded and turned away from me to throw open a door I hadn't noticed, and light flooded the corridor. The tension in my body sagged as if I were a puppet with cut strings while he motioned for me to come forward. "Perhaps later, we can try my mother's rooms again."

"I believe we already determined that," I said, moving slowly toward him and the door. I caught a glimpse of shelves crowded with books and deep armchairs with little round tables beside them. I hesitated, caught between caution and curiosity.

It was the only room I had seen brightly lit. The curtains on the windows were shoved as far back as they could go to let the sun in, with numerous lamps placed throughout.

"Oh," I said, lingering on the threshold to stare at the multitude of books. The massive shelves were lined up against the walls, and stood sentinel throughout the room, tall enough that a ladder would be necessary to reach even half of them.

Lord LeVerre leaned into the doorframe, close enough that I could feel his presence hovering at my back, and I hurriedly took a step into the room. "You would need an eternity to read all of them," he said.

"Well, then, I suppose I should get started," I said with a laugh.

"Indeed," he said, and I half-turned, catching his smile in the second before it disappeared from his face, a hint of a toothy grin that left me feeling unsettled and off balance. I waited a moment, but his face remained smooth, bland agreement etched across it. He motioned at the room. "I would recommend you start somewhere in the middle; the ones on the right side of the room are textbooks."

I turned to face the books he had mentioned, soldiers all the same height marching down the shelves. I headed toward them first, ignoring his advice. "What kinds of subjects?" I asked.

"The usual," he said. "History, medicine, maths, sciences, mechanics, magic..."

"I don't believe most people have a university in their house," I said, wandering down the shelves, running my fingers along the spines of the books I could reach, studying the titles, as dry and dull as most of the text would be. "Most won't have a use for the repair and charging of lamps."

"Ah, but out here, we've got to be self-sufficient," he said, coming up beside me and tapping one of the books. "We don't have a shop down the street that can diagnose why our carriage keeps jerking to a halt halfway to our destination."

"Do you have a carriage?" I asked. "I didn't see one beside ours in the drive."

"We used to," he said. "It stopped taking a charge ages ago, and we've never bothered to fix it. When the materials wouldn't absorb the spells, we pulled it around to the side and left it there to rot. There was no one in town capable of diagnosing the problem, and anyone with the ability to cast such a large spell was too far away to make it worth the expense. The lamps, on the other hand, are simple enough; all they need is a charge to keep going."

"Victor could take a look at your carriage for you if you wish," I said. "He's talented at understanding what needs fixing with that kind of situation."

"Can he charge it for us if he gets it repaired?" Lord LeVerre asked curiously.

"No," I sighed. "Sadly, his talents do not run in that direction. If they were purely mechanical, I would say yes."

"A travesty," he said, seriously enough that I turned to face him, eyes narrowed. There was nothing in his expression that would tell me he had been intention-ally mocking me or my brother, so after a brief con-sideration, I turned back to the books, following the line of shelves down the wall.

Lord LeVerre stayed where he was, his eyes on my back as I wandered.

"You haven't said much about the rest of your family," he said.

I shrugged without taking my eyes off the books. "There isn't much to tell. We're a quiet, average family living quiet, average lives and working quiet, average jobs to scrimp and save for a quiet, average retirement."

"I would not say you and your brother are working quiet, average jobs."

"Maybe we would prefer to be," I said.

"You mean your flower shop?"

It was perhaps the one thing that would draw my attention from the shelves, and I twisted to face him. "Yes," I said. The word floated in the air between us, that unvoiced longing given form. "But I don't know that it is ever meant to be." I turned back to my meandering search through the stacks.

"Do you keep those on constantly?" he asked.

I paused, looking away from the spine of a novel labeled *Dreamtaker* in bold, gold letters to catch Lord LeVerre's gaze. "Do I keep what on constantly?"

His hand twitched as if he had clamped down on the impulse to motion at me. "Your gloves."

"Generally," I said.

"Even when sleeping?"

"That would depend," I said. "But I don't believe you've earned the right to that kind of familiarity."

He flushed. "My apologies," he said. "I've gone about my curiosity in the wrong way."

My fingers were loath to remove themselves from the book they were resting against, on the edge of pulling it free of its spot. "Your curiosity?"

He cleared his throat and looked down at the floor. "I understand that your abilities are—constant."

"Yes," I said slowly.

"And the fabric between you and an object prevents you from being subjected to whatever remains with it?"

"Yes," I repeated. "I believe we've been over this, so where exactly is your line of questioning headed?"

"Do your own objects affect you?"

I relaxed and pulled the book free, cradling it in my arms. "They do not."

"So at your home..."

"I am free to leave my gloves on whatever table I wish," I said, moving down the shelves with every intention of extricating myself from our current conversation.

He followed along behind me, trailing like a lost, eager puppy, although we had the full width of the aisle between us. "Have you ever attempted to read a person?"

I halted, turning around quickly enough that I caught how close he was before he jumped back.

Tension crawled its way up my spine as I realized I hadn't known how near to me he was, silent and stalking. I clutched the book to my chest, a useless shield between the two of us. Heavy as it might be in my arms, it wasn't thick enough to make a satisfying weapon. "I prefer not to," I said stiffly.

"But you have?" he pressed.

"I've read the dead," I said.

He blinked, and the blanching I expected to see there didn't pass over his features. Instead, his curiosity seemed to deepen, a light glimmering in his eyes. "For a case?" he asked. "They brought you in that quickly?" He stepped closer to me, and I had to tilt my head back with my chin up to keep my gaze locked on his. Other than that one small movement, I felt frozen, as if my legs were not my own and would not, could not, obey my command to step away.

"It was not quickly," I said. "And it was not a pleasant experience."

"No," he mused. "If the rot had set in, I would think not." He turned, and whatever force of will his eyes held went with it. I slid away from him, intent on setting the novel I had claimed down and running from the room. "Miss Tailor," he said.

I paused in my steps and half-turned to face him again, unsure why I continued to linger. "I hope you enjoy the book," he said. "Once you've finished it, you're more than welcome to select another."

"Thank you," I said and practically fled the room as he turned back to the shelves.

CHAPTER FIVE

Sparrow Oak Gazette
November 2, 1888
Ms. Anne Gale was found deceased on the floor of her home. Police have stated that a cursory examination of the space indicates she died of natural causes, and no further investigation shall be performed. She leaves behind no one.

I headed straight for the drawing room, hopeful I would find Victor immersed in his list-making.

I was correct: Victor was indeed there, seated in one of the armchairs, leaning toward one of the side tables as he made his notes, that nub of a pencil in his fingers trailing down along the page as he read. He shifted to jot down whatever thought he had on the paper next to it. He looked up when I entered, a brief flick of his eyes as I hustled over to the chair across from him and flopped into it, flushed and clutching the book to my chest.

I wasn't even sure what I had been so frightened of. It was only a library, and it was only Lord LeVerre.

"Did you find a novel worth reading?" Victor asked mildly. He set his pencil aside, and although his tone of voice was unconcerned, the sharp look in his gaze implied otherwise.

I tilted the book back to glance at the title. "I'm not sure."

"Well, there's only one way to find out," he said as he picked his pencil back up and made another note.

Instead of opening it, I set it on the table. "Have you made any progress?"

"We'll have to do quite a bit of asking around town to locate the people who were interviewed."

"Unless the detective is back," I said. "He can lead us right to them."

"I don't think we want to depend on his cooperation," Victor said distantly. "We will need to plan for someone who insists on standing in our way."

"Plan for who to stand in your way?" Lord LeVerre asked, and I jumped, jerking to turn toward him where he stood in the doorway. I would have sworn he had made his entrance without any noise, ghosting into the room on silent feet.

The soft scrape of Victor's pencil stilled; after a moment, I heard him tap the tip of it against the page. "The detective who worked the case." There was an undertone to his words, a hint of condemnation and concern, and I twisted back to look at him. His eyes flicked between me and Lord LeVerre.

I shook my head, and he relaxed.

Lord LeVerre came around the chairs to select another near us, settling his armful of books on a separate table before he sat. He leaned back in his seat, lounging the same as he had at lunch, those whiskey-toned eyes focused on Victor and me. He patted the pile of novels. "I brought you a few additional texts to consider," he said, a small smile pulling at the corners of his lips.

"Thank you," I said, surprised by the courtesy. Whatever misgivings I had now felt increasingly uncharitable on my part, leaving my footing even more uncertain.

He turned his attention back to Victor. "You think the police will attempt to impede your investigation?"

Victor shifted, shuffling his feet as he moved his papers back and forth, taking a moment to examine the contents. "They don't, generally. Occasionally, we get a stubborn one."

"What do you have there?" Lord LeVerre asked curiously, leaning forward in his chair.

"Interviewee list," Victor said. "If you happen to know their whereabouts in town, that information would be appreciated."

Lord LeVerre picked it up, eyes scanning the paper. "I don't, but John may have their addresses."

"If he's willing to share," Victor said congenially, "we would be indebted."

"Rather, I think *I* would be indebted," Lord LeVerre said. "May I bring this copy to him?"

"Certainly. If we can have any information back before the morning, that would be most expedient."

Lord LeVerre nodded. As he headed back out the drawing-room door, I half-turned to watch him go until he disappeared past the frame and down the hall.

"What's going on?" Victor asked.

"Nothing," I said.

"You don't come rabbiting into a room with that look on your face for nothing, Viv."

"It's truly nothing," I said. "An overactive imagination on my part and unintentionally insensitive questions on his."

Victor laid his pencil down on top of the remaining pages and settled back in his chair, legs crossed at the ankles. "Sensation seeker, you think?"

"I believe that's all it was," I said honestly. "Curiosity on his part, harmless in his opinion."

He rubbed at his chin, fingers sliding along his jaw. "If he does it again, let me know. Someone will need to tell him that line of questioning is inappropriate."

"I'm quite capable—"

"I know you're capable, Viv. The question is: will you?"

"I already have," I said shortly.

He waited a beat, the quiet between us stretching. "Alright," he said. "If you're sure. But you tell me if you want me to come in swinging."

There was a long stretch of time between Lord LeVerre leaving with the list and when dinner would be served. Since he had yet to return to discuss further examination of his mother's rooms, I scooped up both the book I had chosen and the ones he brought me and headed to my rooms. I unlocked the sitting room door, slipped inside, and then stopped there, the door still gaping behind me.

On the surface, everything appeared to be exactly as I had left it. The curtains were still pulled back to let what light there was into the space, and nothing in the room looked any different than it had earlier.

But something felt off.

I inched into the room, leaving the door open as I moved toward one of the side tables to set down the books I held. I peered about, eyes narrowed.

Nothing had been disturbed, yet I couldn't shake the feeling that something was altered. I stood there, trying to spot what it was that was causing my unease.

When I couldn't find it in the sitting room, I headed for the bedroom door, hovering in the frame as I studied the space.

Here there was also nothing out of place: the curtains were open, the bed made, and my trunk of clothes was exactly how I left it.

I hesitated, staring at the blankets and pillows.

Had I made the bed?

I couldn't remember if I had. I knew I had seen a bed with the covers pulled back up and pillows straightened—but had it been mine or Victor's?

I was sure I had locked both doors when I went down for breakfast, although I had only taken one key with me. With a quick glance at the dresser, I spotted the bedroom door key immediately, sitting right where I had placed it, gleaming against the wood.

Surely I was overreacting to something misremembered.

I shook it off, headed to my trunk, and threw the lid open. Nothing inside was askew—the clothing folded and undisturbed.

Although why anyone would go through my things, I wasn't sure. I carried nothing of value with me. I supposed a thief wouldn't immediately know that, but it seemed odd that John or even the cook would have gone pawing through my trunk looking for money or jewelry.

I closed the lid, my hand lingering against the surface before I pulled off my glove and set my palm against the worn leather surface.

There were no new emotions swirling through it, merely John's grumbling and beneath it, the cool, collected sense of Victor, the same as before. I waited there for another breath, not entirely sure what I was expecting—or hoping—would float upward for me to detect, but there was nothing else. I pulled my hand away and put my glove back on before I rose and went back into the sitting room.

I could sit and read one of the books I had brought up to my room with me or wander out to the gardens in the chilly afternoon weather. I moved over to the windows, peering out the glass, nose practically pressed to the surface as I examined the sky and the dark clouds gathering above.

A drop of rain hit the pane.

That decided for me. I turned away from the windows and clicked on the spelled lamps to flood the room with as much light as possible before I settled into one of the armchairs and picked the topmost book up off the pile. It appeared close to new, the fabric of the cover smooth and undisturbed by use and age, the gilt letters clear and easy to read—*One Mournful Winter* scrawled in curling script. A surprisingly appropriate choice with the approaching season. I ran my fingers along it, hesitating while I decided just how nosy I was willing to be when it came to our host.

I had to admit to a curious nature.

I set the book in my lap and pulled off my gloves. Taking a breath, I picked the book back up, turning it over in my hands. The emotion drifting up to me was *consideration*. The gentle thoughts of someone running over the information they had and deciding if this was something that would fit the person they had in mind. I furrowed my brow, staring down at the book, then set it aside and picked up the next one.

More of the same, but this time, a sense of hesitation, as if they were unsure that this selection would be the right one. Or even close to being appreciated.

I set it on top of the first book and picked up the last one Lord LeVerre had picked out for me. It was flooded with regret and a nagging sense of doubt. It swamped me, left my heartbeat tripping over itself, caught my breath, and stole it.

I dropped the book.

It tumbled to the floor, landed on its spine, and fell open, pages rustling as it settled. I sat there, staring at it, waiting patiently for my heart and breathing to resume their usual pace. They were hardly the worst emotions I had experienced, but his were strong. He must have stood there with the book in hand for several minutes before he made the decision to bring it to me as a sort of peace offering.

I rubbed at my chest as if that would convince my heart to slow sooner. I took a deep breath, then another. I pulled my gloves back on before I bent and scooped the book off the floor and put it aside, its own embossed title, *Shadowed Gilt and Glass,* staring balefully at the ceiling.

I wasn't sure I would read that one at all.

By the time Victor came to fetch me for dinner, the dark of night was upon us, and the storm that had only just been beginning was raging in full earnest with rumbling thunder and flashes of lightning.

I had taken the time to renew the fire in my sitting room, so in addition to the glow of the lamps, I had its cheerful crackling as the backdrop to the story I had been reading.

The dining room, in comparison, was dim and shadowed, with real candles lit in the chandelier above us and set in candelabras on the table. Their glimmering reflected around the room from the mirrors on the wall—the only reason the space wasn't swathed in the dark.

Lord LeVerre had beaten us there, which certainly wasn't unusual in and of itself, but unlike Victor and me, he had dressed for dinner—barely a step down from the jacket, waistcoat, and breeches that one would wear to a ball. A cravat graced his throat, a darkly gleaming jewel set in the snowy white folds.

Victor and I paused on the threshold when he rose from his seat, taken aback by the unexpected formality.

The three of us stood there until Lord LeVerre smoothed down the front of his waistcoat. "Are you both well?" he asked.

"Quite," Victor said. "I believe we're underdressed, however."

Lord LeVerre looked down, eyes widening in the gloom, and examined the edge of his sleeve. "I suppose it would be more apt to say I am overdressed. Old habits."

He looked back up and smiled, the candlelight glinting off his teeth, which seemed to elongate with the way the flames flickered and shifted.

Victor's smile back was tight. "Then I suppose we should stop hovering in the doorway and determine that we are all appropriately attired for the occasion." He stepped to the side. "Viv, after you."

I hesitated for one more breath and then headed toward the table. The shadows felt as though they were gathering at my heels and shoulders, the silent anticipation of walking straight into the maw of a beast.

Lord LeVerre waited until we claimed our seats before he smoothed out his waistcoat once more and resumed his place in his own chair. "Cook has prepared roast beef, potatoes, and, I believe, some form of squash for us tonight," he said. He picked up the glass set beside his plate and swirled the crimson liquid within it. "Wine?"

"We don't partake while working," Victor said, our fallback for refusing liquor in all its forms. Rather, we never drank.

"Ah," Lord LeVerre said. "Well, there is water available as well." He took a sip from his cup and settled back in his seat, lounging as much as one could in these stiff-backed chairs.

I looked down at my plate, avoiding his gaze. Even with how dim only candlelight made the room, he would surely pick out the way my eyes narrowed if I attempted to study him.

I couldn't quite get a bead on his mannerisms—he seemed to flow from uncertain and conscientious one moment to a lascivious kind of confidence in how he moved and presented himself. And I wondered which was the true him.

The flavor of his regret sat at the back of my mind.

Victor picked up my silverware and cup, cradling them in his palms, his elbows and forearms resting on the table.

"Would anyone be able to learn to do that?" Lord LeVerre asked. "Clear the items of emotion?"

"They're not cleared," I said. "They're replaced."

"I misremembered," Lord LeVerre said apologetically, leaning forward to place his wine back on the table, and this time he did manage to catch my gaze. "Could anyone learn to intentionally replace the emotions?"

"No," I lied.

He stayed in that position for a long moment, eyes on mine, before he sat back. "Ah. A kind of special talent, then?"

"You could call it that," I said.

Victor, for his part, remained silent, although I was willing to wager that he didn't like where this line of questioning was going any more than I did. He set my cutlery and cup back beside my plate. "Have you decided if you would like Vivian to attempt reading any of your mother's items again?" he said.

"Yes," Lord LeVerre said. "Certainly, do you think there's anything in there that might be of particular use?"

"I would like to try the letter on her desk," I said. "The one she was writing to her sister."

Lord LeVerre hesitated before he shifted forward in his seat, forearms and elbows flat on the surface of the table, the image of a predator before it leaps forward to catch its unsuspecting prey. "Her sister is deceased," he said slowly, evenly, entirely at odds with his poised position.

"The witness statements disagree," Victor said. "As every one of them said, that's who the letter was being written to."

"That can't be possible," Lord LeVerre said. "Everyone knows my aunt is dead. My mother had no other siblings."

"You could accompany us back to the station and see the statements for yourself," Victor said calmly. "But they all say the same thing. She was writing a letter to her sister before she vanished."

Lord LeVerre stood and shoved his chair back too quickly; it rocked on its heels, and I was astonished that it didn't topple over. "Then the detective wrote it down wrong." His tone was harsh, his voice thick, and both Victor and I stared at him.

It seemed a rather emotional reaction to such a banal remark.

"Perhaps he did," Victor said. "But it's quite a large oversight to have made that note on every statement." He drummed his fingers on the table. "It is also feasible," he said nonchalantly, as if entirely unbothered by the possibility, "that all the witnesses lied."

"That—" Lord LeVerre started heatedly, then stopped. If I wasn't mistaken, there was a flush to his skin, redness gathering in his cheeks. "It would mean my father insisted they lie."

"We could go find out if Vivian can tell who the letter was truthfully intended for," Victor said. "I doubt any of us will mind if our dinners get cold if it can move your case along?"

"Yes, let's," Lord LeVerre said, and he stalked out of the dining room, leaving Victor and I to scramble to our feet to follow after him.

He turned the corner and bounded up the stairs, requiring Victor and I to take them two at a time to keep up, regardless of the shadows that swallowed us up.

Upstairs, the thunder seemed three times louder, its rumbling growl rattling the walls. I could only guess which door led to Lord LeVerre's mother's room, thanks to the brilliant flash of lightning that spilled across the floor through the open frame.

"I wish I understood what they have against lights," Victor muttered. He slipped through the doorway first, with me directly behind, practically pressed against his back in my hurry not to be left behind alone in the dark.

Lord LeVerre had lit a single lamp in his mother's room, the solitary blue glow only heightening the gloom. The shadows loomed, our reflections shifting wraiths in the mirrors over the fireplace. The light reflected off his face, making the hollows beneath his eyes larger, his chin longer, and conjured the flash of fangs in his mouth when he spoke.

"I can turn on more of the lamps if you need," he said.

"Not necessary, but certainly appreciated," I said, still half-hidden by Victor's bulk. "I can see well enough to make my way to her desk." I pulled off the glove on my left hand as I carefully skirted past the other furniture.

My fingers hovered over the paper, and though I couldn't see the remnants of the words pressed to it, I placed my palm flat against the page.

Whispers, pale and insubstantial, floated up to me, a general sense of unease that all was not as it seemed. Thin intentions that swept past, buoyed by the taste of grief. It coated my tongue, blood and ash, a thick iron carpet.

The firm belief that all was lost and she was lost with it.

Which had come first: the letter or her sister's death?

I blinked and pulled my hand back, confusion settling like a physical weight on my shoulders. The age of one should preclude the other; instead, it felt like the moments came at the same time, one on top of another.

"Well?" Lord LeVerre's voice startled me, and I jerked, twisting to face him. "Well," he repeated, more gently this time, as if he had caught the frightened look that flickered across my face. "Have you sensed anything of use?"

"Your mother," I said slowly, considering how to ask my question in a clear yet inoffensive manner. "Had she begun to—drift?"

"Drift?"

"Her mental acuity," I said. "When last you saw her, how strong was it?"

"Are you implying that my mother lost her mind?" He said it as carefully as I had, each word solid and heavy.

I licked my lips, my fingers centimeters from brushing against the letter. "I could try again," I said. "But the emotions I got were that she believed her sister to be alive and dead at the same moment."

"That—" he started, then paused. "You got solid emotions?"

"Yes."

"So she's alive?" There was hope in his voice, bursting through like sunlight filtered through tree leaves. He stepped forward, crowding in toward me; the only thing that kept him from coming closer was Victor standing in his way.

"I cannot verify that," I said hesitantly. "But I suspect she may be."

"Then we can find her." He rubbed his hands down the front of his waistcoat as if he longed to grab my hands and press them back to the surface of the paper.

"With luck and more information, we may be able to." I spoke the words slowly, aware with every passing moment that I was only encouraging him in his conviction.

Victor's gaze bored into me—his disapproval a palpable weight in the air. "Was there anywhere your mother ever spoke of?" he asked. Although he managed to keep his tone neutral—that ever-present brusque, business-like cadence—the glare he shot me did not bode well for our discussion once we were in private. "A place she mentioned as having always wanted to visit?"

Lord LeVerre shook his head, the shadows shifting and elongating, the blue light from the lamp dancing across his face with his movement. "No. At least, not to me. Perhaps one of the previous servants will know."

"Then I suggest we all reconvene for our dinner," Victor said. "And then get some rest, as Vivian and I have several people to interview tomorrow."

I was restless.

I could not settle in my bed, even with the sheets and pillows cool against me and the storm outside slowly abating, the thunder growing ever distant and quieter in its grumbling.

I left every lamp in my sitting room blazing, the door between it and my bedroom cracked open enough that the light easily crept in, spilling across the wood floor.

Still, it felt like something lingered in the corners of my room, a darkness even the lamps could not drive back.

Surely it was merely the product of too-heavy food too close to bed. An overactive imagination and the effects of nightmares imbued into the mattress itself.

I could not rid myself of the sense of being watched.

I threw back the covers, intending to go to the sitting room and read until my lids grew heavy, when movement caught my eye. I froze, waiting.

When nothing else occurred, I half-laughed to myself—I was jumping at my own shadows. I leaned to the side and switched on the lamp on the bedside table, turning the light up just enough that while the room was still dim, it was not cloaked in night.

It was just as empty as it had been when I had laid down: there was merely me, myself, and I.

The previous owner of this room must have been prone to nightmares to leave such a lasting impression of an ever-present threat. It would have sunk into the mattress, the pillows, the metal frame, even the floor and the rugs, the bedside tables, and the walls—completely permeating the space—to still be so strong.

They haunted it and, therefore, haunted me.

I got out of bed and scurried away from it as if I expected a hand to sweep out from under the frame and grab me by the ankle. I turned back once I was safely ensconced in the doorway; there were no grasping fingers, no talons or claws scrabbling at the floor for something just out of reach.

I shook my head and ducked into the sitting room. Those kinds of monsters didn't exist.

Now that I was in the well-lit sitting room, I considered stepping back into the bedroom to snag the blanket to wrap around myself and settle in on the couch, but the chill shivering its way up my spine decided for me. I thought it would be better to suffer the cold while my imagination was still in full swing. The last thing I needed to do was give myself enough of a scare that I shrieked and woke the house. I curled up on the armchair, out of view of the mirror and its reflection of the rest of the room, and picked a book up off the pile on the table beside it without considering which one I chose.

Regret hit me directly on the nose, and I dropped the book with a thump. It landed off kilter—half on the rest of them, half on the wood. I nudged it with my arm, placing the fabric of the sleeve between me and the spine, and it slid the rest of the way off the other books.

The second time I chose a book, I took more care to read the words on the spines before I selected the one I wanted. Quiet contemplation drifted from its surface through my palms. I settled with it braced against the arm of the chair, one leg tucked up under the other, and read until the words began to blur together. When my head nodded, I wedged my cheek and chin against my shoulder as if that would keep my heavy eyelids open.

CHAPTER SIX

November 15, 1888
There are too many mirrors in this house. Were I Lady LeVerre, I would have left too, if only to have a moment's peace from my own reflection.

I woke with a crick in my neck, one leg numb beneath me, and sunlight streaming past the lacy curtains. At first, I could only blink blearily at the room, stuck in my position with the strange sensation of having been held fast to the chair by something that loomed over me, as much as the feeling that my muscles had simply gotten stuck, a venom that crawled and paralyzed its way through them. It was as if I had gotten no sleep at all, exhaustion sucking at my body as if I were mired in mud and tar.

I had dropped my book at some point in the night; it stared up at me, silent and judging from the floor. With a groan, I unfolded my legs and bent enough to retrieve it, setting it gently down on the side table. I had lost my place, but I suspected I would need to start the book again; I couldn't recall any of the events or characters. They were a blank spot in my mind, swept away by my dreams.

My stomach was attempting to eat itself, a spot on my neck itched like a wound freshly healed, and a headache was forming at my temples. My mouth was dry, my tongue and throat parched, and the first thing I wanted to do was seek out the pitcher of water in my bedroom. A tremor in my hands had me wondering if I was beginning to fall ill. A wave of dizziness and nausea swamped me when I pushed myself off the chair and to my feet. I caught its arm, half-bent at the waist, one hand pressed to my stomach, sucking air in through my teeth until the feeling passed. Perhaps the beef Cook served at dinner had been too far on the rare side for my intestines to handle.

I staggered past the bedroom door, each breath harder to pull in than the last, and leaned against the dresser, afraid that if I sat down on the floor, I wouldn't be able to get up again.

After a long moment, my breathing and trembling eased.

It took both hands to heft the heavy pitcher and pour myself a cup of water while *brusque, business-like, in a hurry, move, move, move*, crowded up against me from the porcelain pressed between my palms. I braced myself against the furniture once I set the pitcher down, and it was here that I began to get irritated with myself at having such a pronounced weakness when all I had done was fall asleep in an armchair.

There was a knock at the sitting room door.

"One—" My voice came out as a whisper, and I had to pause, take a breath, and add strength to it. "One minute!" My tone was harsher than I meant it to be, a combination of the dragging need to lie back down and sleep and my current inabilities.

It certainly took me longer than a minute to retrieve the sitting room key from its spot on the dresser and get the door unlocked. I practically had to cling to the heavy wood once I pulled it open to stare confusedly at the cook on the other side, who had a tray piled with a covered plate, a coffeepot, cup and saucer, and a small, separate glass carafe filled to the brim with orange juice.

She hustled past me, near enough to shove the door open that I almost tumbled to the floor to set the heavy tray on the coffee table by the sitting room couch. "Lord LeVerre thought you might want to take breakfast in your rooms this morning so there's no delay in making your way into town."

"Oh," I said, and then belatedly, "Thank you."

"You're quite welcome," she said shortly, bustling out the door without another word. A moment later, I heard her knock on Victor's door across the hall. The creak of the hinges and the rattle of dishes, the murmur of voices.

I left my door open and made my careful way over to the couch, gratefully sinking down onto its surface. I picked up the carafe first. I didn't even bother trying to pour myself out a cup of it; the carafe was small enough that I could drink straight from it. The juice hit my tongue, a burst of sweetness. I was sure that I was about to regret it, and it would come straight back up. That didn't stop me from draining the vessel dry. I set the carafe back on the tray and slumped against the back of the couch.

Nothing happened. No surging nausea, no bile rising in my throat, no need to fall to my knees and retch it all up.

Emboldened by that success, I leaned forward and plucked the cover off the plate to find neatly spooned scrambled eggs, sausage links, and toast. I hesitated—the smartest choice would be to begin with the toast to ensure my stomach would keep food down, regardless of its current insistence that I find it a meal before it withered away into nothing. I bypassed the fork and snagged one of the sausages with my fingers and bit down on it, juices immediately dribbling down my lips and chin. I caught them with my other hand.

Footsteps accompanied the rattle of dishes as Victor came around the corner of the couch, settled in beside me, and put his tray next to mine. Unlike me, he was already dressed for the day, although I caught sight of the wrinkling of his trousers, which made me wonder if he had slept in his clothes.

He picked up my fork, rolling it between his fingers, waiting for the surface memories to be replaced with his own. "You look like shit, Viv."

I swallowed the mouthful I had been chewing. "I didn't sleep well."

"I can tell. Do we need to push back the interviews a day?"

I shook my head and took another bite of the sausage.

"If you're certain," he said. He set my fork back down to pick up the coffee cup.

I wasn't, but the sense that we needed to finish our investigation and quickly take our leave of Lord LeVerre and his manor nagged at me. As if there was more at stake than merely finding answers.

"I am," was what I said.

"Alright," he said, placing the cup back before lifting the coffee pot and pouring out a stream of dark liquid. "Once we've eaten and dressed, we'll head out."

Victor leaned back, drumming his fingers on the arm of the couch the way he did when there were words sitting on the tip of his tongue. "We need to discuss your findings from last night."

I picked up the cup, took a sip, and sighed as its warmth worked its way through my chest. And this time, I used the fork to spear the next sausage.

"You cannot get around the conversation by ignoring it," he said pointedly.

"What would you like me to say?" I asked, trying and failing to keep the bite out of my tone.

"I thought," Victor said, his voice heated, "we were going to avoid offering him hope."

I sat silently, fiddling with my fork, my appetite lost.

Victor scooted forward, leaning toward me as though it would make the urgency in his words more apparent. "I don't know that we want to encourage him when we know what the answer is likely to be."

"It didn't feel like she was dead," I said.

"Then where could she be?" he asked. "If she's not deceased, then what happened?"

"I don't know," I said. "But I do not know that I can leave him without answers." It prickled at my skin—this need—as if I wanted nothing more desperately than to know, but I couldn't quite bring myself to face it without understanding why. It felt as if the house and its mirrors already lingered beneath my skin. The sooner we were done and gone, the better. "I do not think we are going to agree on how to approach this one," I said, as close to an apology as I was capable of giving.

"No," Victor sighed. "I do not think we will." He pulled out his watch, checked the time, and put it back away. "I suppose we will do this your way, but I beg you to err on the side of caution. This case is an odd one, and I do not like it."

"I will," I promised, although I only half meant it.

Victor patted my shoulder and got off my couch with a groan and a stretch.

"Did you sleep well?" I asked.

He rubbed his fingers along his jaw. "Not exactly," he said. "A sight better than you did, I would say, but my dreams were odd."

"Odd, how?"

He shrugged. "I can't really recall them now that I'm awake—just dust and mazes."

"Sounds like the house is getting to you," I said lightly.

He chuckled. "I don't know that either of us has liked this place since we arrived."

"No," I said. "We haven't." I took another sip of coffee. "So I suppose we shouldn't delay any further."

"I'll leave you to it, then," he said as he left the sitting room, shutting the door behind himself with a click.

I sat for a moment more, considering the leap in my energy level from something as simple as some juice and food, before I pushed myself off the couch and headed for my trunk. I chose a walking skirt that ended at the ankles and left the low-heeled boots I wore exposed to anyone who cared to look. A white blouse with extra strips of fabric tied into a bow at the neck and a fitted jacket that skimmed along the shape of my chest, waist, and hips completed the look. And, of course, my ever-present gloves.

I finagled my hair into a coiled bun at the nape of my neck, leaving loose some strands to frame my face. I craned my neck to the side with one last glance into the mirror located between the windows to catch a glimpse of the back of my head, hoping I had managed a decent job of it. Satisfied, I plucked the sitting room key back off the dresser and met Victor in the hallway.

I took the time to lock the door behind me, and we both headed down the stairs.

"Do you think *our* Lord LeVerre will need us to leave a note that we're heading out?" Victor asked.

"I would think he would assume we would be leaving since he sent breakfast up to us," I said, ignoring his emphasis. "And I wouldn't want to disturb his meal simply to poke our heads in with a goodbye."

"Fair enough," he said, and we went out the front door and down to the carriage. Once we were seated within, Victor gave it our destination, and it paused, rocking on its wheels before lumbering forward with a shudder and a moaning creak.

The town was much the same as the day before—a bustling hive of activity and people—and the carriage again parked itself beside the fountain.

Victor pulled his notes out of his pocket and smoothed the crinkled paper. "I would say we want to start with Lady LeVerre's personal maid as the person most likely to have been closest to her the day she disappeared."

"If you're waiting for my agreement, you certainly won't get any argument," I said when he looked up from the pages.

In response, he shoved open the door and hopped out of the carriage, leaning back in long enough to assist me down. He shut the door behind me, consulted his notes one more time, and gave my hand a tug.

We wove our way through the crowd, which dwindled once we were out of the main square. We headed up a street with houses standing shoulder to shoulder in long rows, a mixture of white-washed and bare-faced brick. Our destination was a rusty red house with empty window boxes hanging forlornly in the front, their images reflected in the glass. The door was painted a cool blue.

Victor knocked—three sharp raps of his knuckles.

After enough time without response, he raised his hand to knock again.

The door creaked open a crack, accompanied by the rattle of a chain lock.

The face staring out at us was older and wrinkled, but clear-eyed and currently holding a frown. "I wasn't expecting any visitors today," they said with a note of wariness.

"Ms. Edwina George?" Victor asked.

"Just Edwina or George is fine; I don't use the honorifics," they said. "But you are?"

"We apologize for disturbing you," Victor said. "Victor and Vivian Tailor from the Company. We're investigating the disappearance of Lady LeVerre and would like to ask you some questions if you have the time."

"That's a name I haven't heard in a spell," they said. "Took them long enough to get off their asses—pardon the language—and do something about it."

"Did you feel they delayed unnecessarily?" Victor asked, jumping on their attitude before I could.

"Well, of course—didn't everyone?" they scoffed. "You'd best come in; one moment." They shut the door, and I could hear a clink and scrape as they slid the lock free. They stepped back so Victor and I could slip past them and shut the door behind us, then turned, heading into a sunny sitting room crowded with soft couches and armchairs.

Edwina perched on the edge of one of the chairs, their skirts swirling about their ankles, hands in their lap, and peered up at us. "Well then, you said you have questions?"

Victor moved before I did, claiming the couch closest to them and pulling out his little notebook and the stub of a pencil. I chose one of the armchairs near the edge of the room, though it placed distance between us.

They had offered no refreshments, which left me without a way to read any of their items while Lady LeVerre was at the forefront of their mind, the surfacing memories imparted on cups and saucers. I could hardly lunge for their chair: propriety insisted I remain where I was rather than take a turn about the room, running my fingers along their belongings.

Still, I tugged off my gloves and set my palm on the arm of my chair.

The only thing that filtered up to me was an air of disuse. The brush of skirts going past, a hand laid briefly on the back as they ignored it in favor of their preferred spot by the fire, even in the midst of summer. It seemed we would be relegated to the realm of conversation for the time being.

"You said everyone felt there was an unacceptable amount of delay?" Victor asked, the point of his pencil poised above the paper.

"Oh, of course," Edwina said. "Her ladyship goes missing from her rooms and no one sees her leave, then his lordship waits four days before contacting the police? He was insistent she would show back up, but of course, she didn't."

Victor scribbled down their words even as he spoke. "From what we understood, this had become a recent habit of hers? She would disappear for a few hours at a time then return, none the worse for the wear?"

"Recent?" they said. They paused, tapping one finger against their cheek. "I don't recall if it was a recent development. It certainly seemed to me that she would often pop up unexpectedly in rooms you could have sworn were empty."

"Why don't we move on to the day of," Victor said. "From the statements, everyone said she had gone up to her rooms to write a letter to her sister."

"Yes."

"Were you aware her sister was deceased?" Victor asked.

"Oh, we all knew," they said. "It seemed to be something that brought her comfort after her sister passed. She would write her letters weekly. She would give them to me, sealed up, of course, and tell me to go store them in the attic."

"She didn't leave them at the gravesite?" I asked.

"Oh, no," they said. "She never left the house beyond the exterior gardens if she could help it. I would have sworn she was tied to it and the grounds because she wouldn't step one foot past the end of the drive. It was odd, really."

"How so?" Victor asked.

"Well, she loved the theater—that's how she and Lord LeVerre met, by the way—and even though she talked about how thrilled she was for the new shows opening in the city, they never went to see them. She used to get pamphlets about them, along with letters thanking her for her generous donations to their facilities and how pleased they were to have her patronage."

"Could it have been a form letter?" I asked.

"Perhaps," Edwina said. "I'm sure most of their donors probably insisted on seeing what their money had purchased, so I wouldn't be surprised if they had a script they used."

"So she went to her rooms to write her weekly missive," Victor said, still making notes. "When did you notice she wasn't in her room?"

"She had sent me to go get her tea and cakes while she wrote, so I couldn't have been gone for more than a quarter of an hour," they said. "When I returned, she wasn't at her desk, although the letter was started."

"What did you do at the time?"

"I set the tray down on one of the side tables—there was never room for it at her desk—and prepared her cup of tea the way she preferred it, two sugars and a dollop of cream, and left it on the desk for her with a cake alongside it on the saucer before I checked her bedroom. That was empty as well."

"And then?"

"I left her rooms," they said. "I had other duties to attend to and assumed when I checked back in an hour or two, she would be at her desk as if nothing had happened."

"Did you check to see if she needed use of the facilities?"

"She had a bathroom attached to her bedroom. If she had been in there, the door would have been closed, but it was open."

Victor made another note, a quick swipe of the pencil across the paper. "And when you went back?"

"She wasn't there."

"When you discovered that she hadn't returned, what did you do?"

"I went straight to his lordship, and he dismissed it. He said he was sure she would be back shortly or that I had merely missed her return." They fidgeted in their chair, shifting from side to side. "She didn't. It was four days of my insisting that this was different before he finally went to the police and reported her missing." Edwina paused a long, silent moment. "And even that felt—well, he still seemed unconcerned, and of course, the police found nothing, and no one could give the detective who came out any further details although he searched the house from top to bottom."

"Did she have anyone else she communicated with?" Victor asked. "Other than the letters to her sister?"

"No," they said. "She had no friends I was aware of; certainly, no one ever came to visit. It was only her and his lordship."

"How long had you worked for them?" he asked.

"Only a year or so," they said.

"So you never met her son?" Victor asked.

"I wasn't even aware she had a son," they said, their eyes widened. Victor, on the other hand, narrowed his. "She never spoke of him. At least, not to me. I would not say I was close to her ladyship, although I know some personal maids and butlers become quite close with their employers." They tapped their cheek again. "I was not prone to doing so. It was always just a job."

He shot me a look—the barest jerk of his chin. "How long had the other servants been with the LeVerres?"

"Only a year, maybe two at the most."

Victor paused in his note-taking, his pencil hovering over the page. "Was that kind of turnover common for them?"

"I wouldn't know. This was the first they had hired anyone from the village."

Victor leaned forward, eyes narrowed. "I thought it was general practice for those with lordships to hire local help."

"Usually," they said. "No one from town had been hired recently because his lordship had been absent until he brought home his wife. By that point, he had a retinue with him from the city."

Victor sat back, fingers drumming on the page. "When was that?"

"Oh goodness, forty years ago now?"

"No announcements in town when her ladyship bore him a son?"

Edwina shook their head. "Not that I recall. Bless, I may not have cared a whit at the time. They tended to keep to themselves, so there wouldn't have been any opportunities to see her with a babe in arms out here in the village."

"What happened to the servants they employed before you?"

"Retired, I assume."

"And John? He's a local, correct?"

"Goodness, yes, is he still there? I would have thought he would have quit by now. He always was cantankerous and now he's the only one taking any orders?"

"Him and the cook," I said.

"Bless them both," they said. "I wouldn't have had the wherewithal to put up with his lordship alone like that."

"What was his lordship like?" Victor asked.

They hesitated then, regarding us like a bird perched on a branch. "Too quiet," they finally said. "You'd be working in a room, door closed, and you wouldn't even hear it open. He'd be right behind or in front of you, and you'd have no idea when or how he approached you to begin with."

A similar habit, it appeared, our Lord LeVerre shared with his father.

"A bad habit of sneaking up on people?"

"If you want to call it that."

"Did he ever harm any of the servants?"

"Not that I'm aware of," they said. "I would've heard if he had. Those are the kinds of rumors that spread."

Victor tapped his pencil against the paper, leaving little dark dots on the page. "I think," he said slowly, "that is all for now. If I come up with any other questions, do you mind if we stop by again?"

"You're more than welcome to," they said. "Although I'm not sure how much help I'll be."

Victor flashed them a grin. "Any information is better than no information." He got to his feet and held out his hand toward them. "Thank you for your assistance."

They shook his hand, the merest press of their fingers to his. "You're more than welcome."

Victor headed for the front door, and I rose from my seat and followed after him, pulling my gloves back on as I went. It wasn't until the door was shut firmly behind us and we were back down the front steps and standing on the sidewalk that he said anything. "I have the distinct feeling that we won't get any deeper detail from any of the others."

"Perhaps not," I said. "But maybe we can find out more about his lordship and what other traits he's passed on to our Lord LeVerre."

Victor looked up from the page of addresses he was consulting. "Does ours have a bad habit of sneaking up on people?"

"He managed to end up directly behind me in the library without my noticing," I said. "I don't believe he meant any harm, but it was...disconcerting."

Victor motioned toward my right with his list, the corner edges of the paper fluttering with the movement. "Next address is up the street and two over." We fell into step with each other, breath puffing out into the cold morning air.

The next two interviews were more of the same. They were relatively short in comparison, merely confirming the events we were already aware of, including the elder Lord LeVerre's habits of moving silently throughout the house and often unintentionally surprising the servants.

By the time we finished with the most recent, the sun was at its zenith, and my stomach was clawing at my backbone.

"I suppose we should find a restaurant or a pub," Victor said at one particularly loud, long growl.

"Or a grocer?" I suggested. "I'm not averse to getting cheese and some apples and sitting in the carriage."

"I'll handle your dishes," he said. "I'm sure they'll have fare as simple as a sandwich, so you won't need to touch the utensils at all."

I wrinkled my nose but followed him down the street, as he appeared to have a destination already in mind.

The pub he had chosen was called *The Dripping Bucket*, and below the curling script on its wooden sign was the raised image of a man desperately bailing out a sinking rowboat with a hole in the bottom of his pail. Half the water he was tipping out leaked back into his vessel.

I eyed it warily. "I do hope you haven't chosen a location that offers seafood so far from the ocean."

"I believe our erstwhile companion is on a river," he said as we stepped under the sign and through the door into warmth and golden, dim, flickering light.

It also appeared to be a "seat yourself" kind of establishment, with a bar lined with stools along one edge, deep booths against the opposite wall, and scattered tables between the two. We settled into a booth and waited to be noticed.

The waiter who bellied up to our table seemed unflappable and unhurried, a nub of a pencil stuck behind his ear and a small notepad in the pocket of his apron. "What'll it be for you?"

"Tea, if you have it?" Victor asked.

"Served cold in a glass, if it's not any trouble," I inserted.

"Hot for me, if you please," Victor said.

"We can do that," he said, making no moves to retrieve either the pad or the pencil. "Special today is potato soup: nice and filling, warms you up, served in a crock."

He said nothing else.

Victor and I looked back at each other. A quick examination of the surrounding surface of the table and the wall revealed no paper menus.

"I suppose...two of the potato soup then," Victor said hesitantly.

"Excellent," our waiter said. "Be right back with those drinks and your meal."

"I suppose we can't expect much more in terms of service?" Victor mused once the waiter had left.

"How does a restaurant survive offering only one dish a day?" I asked.

"I get the feeling it's less a place to eat and more a place to drink. Perhaps I've chosen poorly."

"Next time, you'll have to let me decide where we dine."

"We'd be eating in the carriage."

"You say that as if this isn't any less discomforting."

Victor settled his arms on the table, crossed in front of him as he leaned forward. "You say she's alive."

"I suspect," I clarified.

"For all intents and purposes," he said, "she's alive if we can find no evidence of her death."

"I want to know how she got out of a house full of people without a single person seeing her," I said.

"Secret passageways."

I rolled my eyes. "That's always your answer."

"And one of these days, I'll be right."

I rubbed at a spot on the table, the leather of my glove sliding over and back along a bump in the wood. "Perhaps, in all seriousness, we should examine her rooms for such a thing."

Victor drummed his fingers on the table, that steady *tap, tap, tap*. "If she did leave, what was her reasoning?"

"Maybe she was tired of her husband popping up unexpectedly around corners," I said lightly.

Victor rubbed at his jaw. "There has to be more to it," he said. "Three separate people, and none of them mentioned her being afraid of him? Or that she had some sort of longing to see the world? Something, anything that would give her cause to step out that door and not return."

"Maybe the cause was her sister," I suggested.

"None of this makes sense," he said. "A devoted husband, a loving son—"

"That she spoke of to none of the servants, which in itself, I find curious," I interjected. "He may have loved her, but did she love him?"

We were both silent as our waiter returned with a steaming teapot and an empty cup and saucer for Victor, and a glass, dripping with condensation, filled with ice and golden brown liquid for me. He disappeared again shortly, and Victor craned his neck, examining the room before turning his attention back to me.

"It doesn't appear to be the actions of a doting mother, no," he said. "You would think she would speak of him to any and all with pride."

"Maybe she wasn't proud of him."

Victor poured tea into his cup and watched the fluid swirl for a moment. "Do you think they had some kind of falling out before he left?"

I took a sip of my tea, the glass cold against my lips, but the taste was bland, more of water than actual tea. I grimaced and set it down. "It might explain why she didn't mention him."

"It might also explain why his father waited two days to let him know she had gone missing," Victor said. "If they were already on the outs, he may have been hesitant to alert his son if he wasn't sure how her would respond."

"It explains why our Lord LeVerre is so determined to find out what happened to her," I said. "He feels guilty."

Our waiter returned, this time, bearing two small cauldrons of soup that he set down in front of us, along with two metal spoons.

Victor picked up my spoon; his fingers wrapped around the handle while he counted to himself. "I think after lunch, we should see if we can speak to the detective who originally worked the case and get his viewpoint on the family."

CHAPTER SEVEN

Case 1888-11-MP-001436
As no new information has come to light, we are stopping all investigation at this time. Victim's husband has been informed.

The soup turned out to be much better than the tea, and both Victor and I emptied our bowls. Before long, we were back out in the cold, headed to the police station.

The desk sergeant was the same person as before, and he eyed us lazily, a bored expression pasted across his face. "Sign in, please," he said before either Victor or I had a chance to speak.

"We'd like to see Detective Brant if possible," Victor said while picking up the pencil lying next to the sign-in sheet.

"Third floor, last door on the right," the desk sergeant said without so much as a flicker of his eyes.

We eased past him, heading down the hall and up the stairs to another hallway.

The last door on the right was shut with a plaque that read *Edward Brant* fixed to the front.

"Well regarded, at least?" Victor said before rapping on the wood with his knuckles.

We stood in silence, listening to the heavy tread of boots before the door cracked open. Detective Brant stuck his head out to regard us with narrowed pale blue eyes and furrowed brows. His hair was a nondescript shade of brown, left surprisingly long for a detective, the locks nearly brushing at his eyelashes. "Can I help you?" he asked curiously, his voice a friendly kind of tenor. He was, in a singular word, disarming.

"Vivian and Victor Tailor from the Company," Victor said. The words had begun to take on the tired cadence that oft accompanies information consistently repeated. "We've been hired by Lord LeVerre to investigate the disappearance of Lady LeVerre and perhaps shed some light on what happened to her."

The curiosity on Brant's face cleared, replaced with a wary understanding as he stepped back and pulled the door to his office wide open. "Ah," he said. "You might as well come have a seat in that case."

He headed back behind his desk and sat in the chair behind it. It creaked disconcertingly, and he pulled a face. "Damn thing will collapse on me any day now," he said conversationally, waving at the other two chairs in front of the hulking surface between us. "Those two are in better condition, so I leave them for visitors."

"You get visitors often?" I asked, perching gingerly on one of the chairs, expecting it to make the same kind of groaning noise his other had. It remained silent, as solid beneath me as any other piece I'd had the pleasure of parking my ass on.

"Often enough, Miss—Tailor, was it?"

"It is," I confirmed.

"Forgive me the curiosity—occupational hazard," he said, "but you and Mr. Tailor are—?"

"Brother and sister," Victor said, settling in the chair next to me.

"Ah." Brant leaned back, his chair emitting a wooden moan with the movement. He paused, seemingly ready to leap to his feet, but at the same time frozen, as if sure the next breath would be too much for the chair to support. When nothing happened, his shoulders eased down from their tense position. "From the Company, you said?"

"Yes," Victor said.

"And you're here to look into where Lady LeVerre hared off to?"

"So you think she left of her own accord?" Victor asked.

Brant shrugged. "To be honest, I don't know what to think. I've spent a lot of time going back over my notes from that case, and I'll be damned if it isn't one of the few that stuck with me over the years."

"Why?" I asked.

"Why what?" Brant countered.

"Why has it stuck with you?"

"True mystery, isn't it?" he asked. "You've got a houseful of people who insist she would've had no reason to leave, there's no evidence as to where she went, and no one saw her exit, not even for a walk in the gardens? Wouldn't that be the kind of case that

would stick with you? The sheer number of unan-
swered questions?"

"Yes," I said honestly.

"Well then," he said, in a tone that implied the matter was entirely settled as far as he was concerned.

"We've spoken to a few of the servants employed by
the LeVerres at the time," Victor said.

"And they've all given you the same story, haven't
they?" Brant said shrewdly. "No new information
coming to light?"

"Did you know they have a son?" Victor asked.

Brant shifted upright in his chair, surprise flickering
across his face. "Do they?"

"A couple of the servants were shocked by this
information as well," Victor said calmly, pulling his
notes from his waistcoat pocket. He flipped through
the pages, paused on one, shook his head, and serenely
tucked them back away.

"Lord LeVerre never mentioned him," Brant said
musingly.

"He was, apparently, away in the city at the time of
Lady LeVerre's disappearance, and according to him,
his father didn't mention his mother was missing until
two days had passed."

"And then didn't report it for another two past that
because it took him four to come forward," Brant
muttered. He shifted, the chair groaning again. He
cleared his throat. "What exactly about the case can I
help you with?"

"Is there anything that might not be in the case
notes?" Victor asked. "Any information or theories
that didn't seem relevant at the time?"

"No," Brant said. "Every scrap of paper, every thought related to it went into that file." He tapped a finger on the desk. "I'm afraid that this is one mystery that is likely to remain unsolved unless a body turns up."

"How much of the house did you search at the time?" Victor asked.

"Every inch," Brant said. "Even the attic. Opened every trunk and crate up there, but considering it smelled only like a dusty old attic, we weren't going to find anything anyway."

Victor was silent, his brow furrowed, before he sighed and shook his head. "I suppose we won't be finding any answers here, in that case."

"Sadly, no," Brant said. "I'm sorry I'm not more help, but as you've seen, there isn't much to go on. Most I could recommend is checking the records to see who owns the house now, but I'm not sure how much help that will be either."

"Thank you for the suggestion, but I'm not sure that will be necessary," Victor said. He stood, and both Brant and I rose with him.

Brant held out his hand. "Feel free to come back if you think of any further questions."

Victor shook the offered hand. "I appreciate the offer. We're sorry to have taken up your time."

"Oh, no bother at all," Brant said. The words sounded automatic, but they at least missed the tone of relief that meant we *had* been a bother, and he was glad to see the back of us. "Miss Tailor, a pleasure," he added hastily.

"The pleasure was all mine," I said ruefully, as I had hardly contributed anything to the conversation, content to let Victor lead unless my input was needed. I turned and slipped past Victor, where he waited at the door, ignoring the additional murmured pleasantries until Victor caught up to me in the hall.

"I quite think you charmed him," Victor said.

I scoffed. "I hardly spoke a word."

"Perhaps he likes the strong, silent type."

"Then I suppose you've already lost your chance there."

Victor chuckled. "I'd be a fool to get involved with someone in our business."

"Arguments about who's interfering in whose jurisdiction over the dinner table?"

"Precisely," he said. "I'm not involved in interdepartmental squabbles, and I'm not about to start with it at home."

"What I would like to know," I said, "is this lack of curiosity from everyone we've spoken to about the fact that the Lord and Lady LeVerre had a son they never mentioned. Surely there would be some interest in who the property and title passed to since they're both...considered deceased?"

Victor shrugged. "Perhaps they are curious, and the only thing that's stayed their tongue is propriety."

I snorted. "All of them are oh-so-proper?"

"They were servants for the peerage."

We were quiet as we headed out of the station. The sky was beginning to darken—thick, gray clouds swirling together on the horizon.

"I think we're in for another storm tonight," Victor said as we headed back toward our carriage.

"I think—" I started slowly, paused, and then continued, "that if we do not find anything in her ladyship's rooms to suggest where she's gone, we'll have to admit defeat."

Victor didn't respond at first; when I spared a glance at his face, he looked as if he was chewing over the words. "It's not often we come across a case where you cannot locate the answer."

"I'm of the opinion that she doesn't want to be found," I said. "Otherwise..." I sighed, unable to articulate exactly what my sense of *otherwise* was.

"We'll spend one last night with our Lord LeVerre," Victor said. He pulled the carriage door open and waited for me to settle inside before he followed. He shut the door behind us and tapped on the wall of the carriage with a mutter. It jerked, rocking, then began trundling forward.

"You should have this thing examined when we arrive home," I said.

"I will," he said absently. "No point in the expense of having one if it doesn't work correctly to begin with." He paused. "To continue my earlier thought—one last night to give you a chance to read the items in her room and see if we can pick up her scent. If not, we'll deliver him the bad news and head home in the morning." He flicked one of the curtains aside, peering out the glass. "I would say head home tonight, but we risk the carriage getting stuck, or worse, in the storm."

"I think we can handle one last uncomfortable night," I said.

The wind was gaining strength when we pulled into Lord LeVerre's drive, the branches of the trees groaning with their movements. The carriage stopped in front of the manor steps—an unusual consideration from the conveyance—and Victor and I tumbled out to reach shelter as the first fat raindrops descended, one of them plopping directly onto the tip of my nose.

Fortunately, we made it inside before the deluge truly began.

"Do they never lock the door?" Victor asked as he shut it behind us, leaving us in the dark but for the glow coming from the drawing room.

"Perhaps only at night?" I suggested. "To be fair, they were expecting our return."

Victor grunted as we made our way toward the square of light creeping out from the open doorway. Inside, the lamps were lit, a cheerful fire crackling on the hearth, but the room was empty.

Victor sighed, settling into one of the chairs, his legs splayed outward. "As usual, our host is a ghost."

"We did tell him we would be gone for the majority of the day," I said, sitting across from him with my hands demurely positioned in my lap, my back ramrod straight.

The chair didn't allow for much else. Perhaps I should have chosen the settee instead.

Victor rubbed at his chin, brow furrowed. "We can hardly take one last try at his mother's things while he's off haunting the rest of the manor. Procedure and all that."

"I suppose we'll have to practice patience," I said sweetly, running my fingers along the worn seam of my glove.

"Are you about to go poking around?" Victor asked, one eyebrow raised.

"Not if you are," I said, catching his gaze and imitating his expression.

He huffed, rolling his eyes. "You know mine doesn't work that way, much as I wish it would. Visions on demand."

"Have they told you nothing of her?" I asked quietly.

"No," he said. "Not even shadows, and were it not for all the people who had met her, I would think she never existed to begin with."

"It's quite a strange case, isn't it?" I murmured.

"I think it's a case with a very logical end," Victor said. "They all have logical ends, even if we can't solve them."

"And what do you think the end is?" I asked, looking back up.

"Someone here is lying," he said. "They're lying about having seen her go. In fact," and his voice warmed with enthusiasm as he chased down the weavings of his theory, "I would say they helped her. It's the only possibility that makes sense. Her disappearing for hours with no one the wiser as to where she had gone; someone was helping her practice sneaking out." He leaned forward, gaze locked on mine. "And they helped her when it was time for her to truly leave. Helped her and lied about ever having seen her."

I peeked over my shoulder at the drawing room door, but it was empty, not even the hint of a shadowed form listening in on us. I shifted, matching Victor's positioning so that I could keep my voice low. "You don't want to find her."

"I don't think she wants to be found," he said gently. "And that is the difference."

"Not even by her son?"

"Not everyone views family the way we do," Victor said as he sat back with a sigh. "We grew up loved, treasured. How do we know their relationship had any familial warmth to it? Has he confessed all his motives to you?"

"No," I said quietly. "Nor have I even attempted to suss those out."

We were silent, sitting in the glow of the flames and lamps.

"I feel sorry for him if that is the case," I said finally. "That we cannot give him more than this limbo."

Slow, measured footsteps echoed in the hall. We twisted to look at the door, but it was only John at its threshold. The flickering flames cast a strange pall across his face, shadows and hollows under his eyes and cheeks; he looked drained, as if whatever illness he had seemed to have sucked the life from his body, the weight from his almost skeletal frame. "Dinner is served," he said, his voice a whispered croak.

"So early?" Victor asked, surprise coloring his tone. "I thought it wasn't for at least another hour."

John apparently still maintained the power to cast withering stares because that was exactly what he did before he shuffled away with a haughty sniff, leaving us sitting in the drawing room.

"Well," Victor said, rising from his chair, "I suppose we should go dine with our Lord LeVerre and speak to him about one last try."

With a groan, I got up and followed after him. I found I was longing for my bed more than I typically did at this point in the day. If I could have, I would have pardoned myself and sought out my rooms. Instead, I trailed along in Victor's wake to the dining room, where we found Lord LeVerre already seated, a half-empty glass of wine in front of him.

"Ah," he said when we entered, the remnants of a smile playing about his lips. "I was not entirely sure you would return with how long you were gone today."

"Interviewing witnesses takes time," Victor said, pulling out my chair and waiting until I was seated before claiming his own.

"Quite a bit more than I expected," Lord LeVerre said, and I found myself studying him—the flush in his cheeks, the warm glow that seemed to extend down even to his fingertips.

The man was drunk.

"Did you come across any useful information?" he continued, and I snapped my eyes back up to his face.

"Unfortunately, no," Victor said. "Their stories remain the same, but both Vivian and I find it," he paused, searching for the right word, "questionable that positively no one would have seen her leave any of those times she vanished."

"You think one of them lied?" Lord LeVerre asked, his tone taking on an icy, deadly quality—claws hidden in snow.

"We suspect," Victor said slowly, "but we cannot prove it."

Lord LeVerre motioned at me. "Why not have Miss Tailor touch them and ascertain that?"

"We would need a warrant, sir," Victor said, and it was his turn for his tone to become cold. "There are steps, procedures that must be undertaken before we subject anyone, let alone a witness, to my sister's touch."

I glanced at him when he stopped there and failed to mention that I had never read the living before and didn't even know if I could.

"Ah," Lord LeVerre said, settling back in his chair with his glass, swirling the crimson liquid within before he took a sip. "And how would one go about obtaining said warrant?"

"The detective who worked the case must first consider whether such a warrant would be deemed necessary."

"I think we would have that easily," Lord LeVerre said.

"He has to bring his reasoning to a judge, who will review the case and will make a determination as to whether he will grant the warrant. And, I'm sorry to say, this can be affected by several factors, including but not limited to the age of the case."

Lord LeVerre clucked his tongue, one quick click, and then he licked his lips. "The first stumbling block."

"Indeed," Victor said stiffly.

"And if I were to get the detective and the judge to agree that such a warrant is crucial to solving my mother's case?"

"They submit it to the Company and then wait," Victor said. "To be approved or denied."

Lord LeVerre narrowed his eyes, staring down the table at us. "Why does the Company have the final say in this? A matter of the law?"

"They will determine if they have anyone capable of obtaining the information you require," I said. "A denial would mean no one of that skill is currently available."

Lord LeVerre froze, head cocked to the side, his gaze locked on me as if he could hear my heartbeat and know by its speed whether I was lying. "Is no one of that skill available?" he asked.

"I've never read anyone living," I said. "If that's what you're asking."

"And you know no one else employed by the Company who might have?"

"We don't often have time to socialize with our—peers," Victor said wryly. "And discussing case-work is frowned upon."

"And why would that be—discouraged?" Lord LeVerre asked.

"The information, the evidence we gather, is turned over to the police," I said. "They use it to make an arrest and present it at trial. To gossip over what we found would increase the risk that the perpetrator hears what evidence is known and makes their escape before they can be found."

"Seems a small risk," Lord LeVerre said.

I shrugged. "A risk nonetheless, although that would be why discussions aren't outright banned. But the atmosphere around the Company means we all comply regardless."

Lord LeVerre took another sip of his wine. "So, what are our steps for now?"

"I'm afraid," Victor said, "that other than Vivian attempting one last time to determine where your mother may have gone by reading one or more of her items, we are at an end."

"That," Lord LeVerre said with a sigh, "is disappointing."

"For us as well," I said. "I—we do not like leaving a case unresolved."

Lord LeVerre set his glass down. "I would imagine not."

The three of us sat there, the silence lengthening, growing, until it was looming in the room the same as the shadows that crept their way up the walls, crawling toward the ceiling.

"If Miss Tailor makes this attempt and discovers nothing to help us any further," Lord LeVerre finally asked, "what are my steps then? To seek out a warrant? Will that be my only recourse?"

"You will need seven of them," Victor said. "One for each witness, including John and your cook."

"As we don't know which of them is the liar," Lord LeVerre murmured. "And that is seven chances to be denied, correct?"

"Yes," Victor said. "Each warrant comes with its own risk that you will be turned down. I would recommend you attempt them as a packet. A singular request sent in to the Company, even as seven warrants, will increase the chance that they will be able to approve it."

"And if I am approved, will they send Miss Tailor back again?"

"We don't know," Victor said. "That will depend entirely on our own availability and what the Company determines concerning her abilities."

"So I could receive someone entirely unfamiliar with the case, and I'll be back at square one catching them up to speed."

"I'll submit copies of my notes to the Company," Victor said. "They'll go into the case file, and anyone who is sent out will be provided that information."

"Then I suppose I am out of arguments against it," Lord LeVerre said. "And it is just a matter of determining which of my mother's items gives you the best chance of discovering anything, no matter how small." He shifted in his seat before shoving his chair back and getting to his feet. "Miss Tailor, if you'll come with me?"

Victor and I rose from our seats at the table and followed him to his mother's rooms where we hovered by the door while he lit the lamps.

Lord LeVerre must have spent quite a bit of time among these rooms to know where each piece of furniture was, even in the dark. Once the room was bathed in the pale glow of what lights there were, he stepped back and motioned me forward. "I'll be honest, I don't know where to start. What could possibly have been precious enough to her that she would have revealed her intentions to it, even accidentally?"

"It's conceivable she took that item with her," I said gently. Still, I tugged the gloves off my hands, slipped them into my skirt pockets, and stepped into the room.

The first thing I did was trail along its edges, slipping my fingers down the walls as I walked, but all that rose from them was dust and a vague sense of irritation. I slid them along the mantel, past the vases empty of flowers, and my reflections in the mirrors followed along with my movements, disappearing once I stepped past the frames.

She had touched the wood in much the same way, that brief sense of her fingertips swiping along its surface. I paused, my gaze locked on the glass and its shadowy figures, the dark shapes of the room beyond, a breath catching where I considered reaching for the frame itself.

"Miss Tailor?" Lord LeVerre's voice cut through my hesitation, and I turned away from the mirror, unsure of just what I thought I would find. They were hung too far above the hearth for her to have had any reason to press her hands to the heavy gilt, and the glass would be empty.

I set my hand with the palm flat against one of the side tables; there was nothing more than the rattle of teacups and the thump of a book being set down, but

I would never have expected a table to be her confidant to begin with. I went back over to her desk, curling my fingers along the top of the chair. She was sitting, stiff-backed as she wrote, stress roiling in waves just out of my reach—a longing for something, a hunger with no direction. She must have spent hours in this chair for the emotions to be so strong when they were so faded with everything else. I leaned forward, and placed my other hand on top of the desk itself.

It was blank. As if she herself had never touched it.

Hesitantly, I pulled my hand off and set it back down. But it was more of the same—only the brief interludes of the craftsperson who had created it, the shopkeeper who had sold it, and the mover who had brought it to the house. I shifted my hand and touched my fingers to the letter that sat upon the desk's surface. There was her grief, as strong as it had been the first time I had placed my hand upon the page.

"Anything?" Lord LeVerre asked hopefully from where he stood by one of the couches.

"Has any of the furniture in this room ever been replaced?" I asked.

"Not to my knowledge," he said. "I think every piece has been here since she moved in. Why? Did you find something?"

I took my hands away from the desk and the chair. "No," I said.

The remainder of dinner was only Victor and me in the dining room, as Lord LeVerre had pardoned himself, saying he wished to be alone.

I could not blame him.

Victor and I hurried through our meal before retiring to our own rooms, and I went to bed, sure that tired as I was, sleep would elude me, and I had been right. I lay there for a moment longer before I gave up and got out of bed, pulling the blanket with me and wrapping it about my shoulders as I padded into the sitting room. I attempted to settle into a chair and read, but I was just as restless there, the letters blurring together on the page. With a sigh, I set the book aside and stared blankly at the furniture and the walls before I cast a furtive glance at the door to the hall.

Lady LeVerre's maid had said they stored every letter she ever wrote to her sister in the attic.

I was on my feet before I had finished deciding, snatching the key up along with one of the smaller lamps off a side table. I ignored the nagging doubts as I stepped out my door and locked it behind me. The floor held a welcome blankness to it, merely the faded competence of workmen long since gone, a sure sign that the people of the house rarely tread this hall without footwear of some kind. I hesitated briefly, casting a glance at the bottom of Victor's door, but no light escaped from its space, and I could only assume he was sleeping.

I turned away from the direction of the first floor, choosing instead to head deeper into the manor, the pale blue glow of the lamp casting a small circle of light

just in front of me. The walls and ceilings were out
of reach of its wan halo, leaving the space around me
thick with shadows, the way back quickly swallowed
up by the dark. My ears were straining for any evidence
of sound other than the quiet tread of my feet, and I
looked back as often as I looked ahead, convinced that
there was something there, waiting in the gloom.

Whatever bravado I had was fading, the drive to
discover if Lady LeVerre's letters still existed steadily
dribbling away into uncertainty. The thought that
perhaps I should have woken Victor instead of haring
off into the night prickled at my skin, hot with regret,
and I paused, vacillating as I came to a crossroads of
sorts in this hall, the lamp lifted high as I attempted to
choose which of these voids I dared stumble towards.

"Miss Tailor?" Lord LeVerre's voice came directly
from my left.

I gasped, staggered into the wall with a thud, and
dropped the lamp. It tumbled to the floor, rolling
away from me and coming to a rest at Lord LeVerre's
feet, its glow cast over the tips of his shoes.

His hand seemed to emerge from nowhere, reaching down into the halo, its pale fingers wrapping
around its base before it was lifted, and his face swam
into view. The light reflected strangely off his eyes,
creating shadowed hollows in the sockets and beneath
his cheeks until he blinked and changed the angle of
the lamp so it no longer lit his face from below. "Did
I frighten you?" he asked.

"No," I lied, taking the opportunity to tug the slipping blanket back over my shoulders and gather the

fabric close together, a cover for my trembling hands and frantically beating heart.

"May I ask what you were doing wandering the halls?"

"Looking for the kitchen," I said, unsure of whether I should broach the topic with him at a moment such as this. "I believe I've gotten turned around in the dark."

"A common thing to happen in unfamiliar halls," he said. "I can lead you to it if you would like."

"I think I may actually prefer to go back to my room," I said, giving him a tentative smile. Now that I had company, I was loath to continue walking through the house. A trip to the kitchen would necessitate returning to the gloom-filled spaces between me and what comfort my room offered.

It triggered a matching smile on his face. "This way then—" he paused, hesitating, eyes on the lamp. "Would you prefer to hold this or have me continue to carry it?" His gaze flicked down to where my bare feet rested against the floor and, from there, to my hands and then to my face. "Does it not bother you?"

"Does what bother me?"

He gestured, the glow and surrounding shadows shifting with the motion. "Your soles touching the floor."

"It does," I acknowledged.

"And yet you chose to leave your room without shoes or your gloves."

"I admit I did not pause to think through the ramifications of seeking out a late-night snack. I suppose I was not fully awake when I made the decision."

"Shall I continue to hold the lamp in that case to minimize your discomfort?"

If I was being honest with myself, I was surprised by the thought behind the question. It was not something many people considered when confronted with my abilities, that their touch being unmasked, so to say, without the layers of fabric between me and the world would cause me substantial distress at times.

"I would appreciate it," I admitted.

He nodded and set off in the direction I had come from, and I fell into step alongside him.

His shoes clicked against the wood with each step, and I half-suspected he did so intentionally. Elsewise, the silence between us was lingering, the kind that needed filling before it became painfully awkward.

"A house this large—" I began, pausing for a breath when he glanced in my direction. The light was making strange shadows and shapes again, and I tamped down the desire to go no farther: if the man had meant me harm, he already had ample opportunity before I knew he was there.

Still, the uncertainty stayed.

"It must have storage of some kind. An attic?" I finally continued when he seemed content to wait.

"It does," he said. "Although it's empty of everything but cobwebs now."

I stopped. He took a step or two past me before realizing I was no longer following. "Empty?" I asked.

"Yes," he said. "It used to be crammed full of old furniture and boxes of things, but about two, no, three years ago, my father had all of it hauled off to be sold, given to charity, or left at the dump." He lifted the lamp and took a step toward me, and for once, I didn't give in to the desire to open the space between us.

"Why?" he asked curiously.

"Your mother's maid had said they used to take each letter your mother wrote to her sister up to the attic to store them away. I just thought if they were still there, perhaps those would give us one last chance at discovering what had happened to her."

The expression on his face wavered—hope had flooded it and then just as quickly drained away. "Oh," he said softly, so quietly I wasn't sure he had spoken at all.

"But if the attic is empty..." I left the remark hovering in the air—not quite an accusation between us, but it felt like one, a stab to the gut.

"Then they're gone, and we have no path left for us other than the warrants," he said, his voice strengthening with each word spoken. He motioned with the lamp toward a door I hadn't noticed in the gloom. "Here we are—safely delivered."

"Thank you," I said, unlocking the door and slipping inside. I hovered just past the threshold, reluctant to leave him alone with this one recent piece of misfortune. "I am sorry," I said, "I could not bring you a quick and certain resolution."

The smile he gave me was faint. "I appreciate that and all your efforts. Good night, Miss Tailor."

"Good night, Lord LeVerre," I said, at a loss for what else I could say or even do.

"Lucien," he said, and this time the smile making its way across his face appeared genuine, a soft entreaty.

"I suppose the least I can do is offer my name in exchange for all your efforts."

I hesitated, unsure of whether it was growing misgivings working its way upward or socially imposed discomfort with anything but addressing someone by their surname. "Good night," I repeated and shut the door, leaving him in the hall with only a single lamp to light his way.

I had assumed that after my small misadventure, I would once again have a difficult time falling asleep and been proven wrong. Now I was awake, I thought, with that presence at my back again. Frozen breath gusted at my neck, the touch of someone's lips just under my jaw. Ice that slid down along my arm, the delicate touch of hesitant fingers, my heart thrumming frantically in my chest, but I could not will myself to move.

Their hand wrapped around my wrist.

I jerked upright.

I sat there, gasping in the dark, shivering cold, and the presence I thought I sensed seemed to be still looming up and away in one of the corners of the ceiling. With shaking fingers, I reached out and flicked on one of the lamps, flooding the room with light, as I was forced to blink away the spots it left in my vision.

Cautiously, I peeked over my shoulder, but, as should have been expected, there was nothing there.

CHAPTER EIGHT

November 16, 1888
Unidentified body found in tenement house. Cause of death is undetermined.

Morning saw me hurriedly dressed and packed, both doors to the hallway flung wide as I dragged my trunk from the bedroom toward the stairs. I had no intention of waiting on John, who looked as if one good, stiff wind could blow him away. If anything, the man should still be resting, not fulfilling his duties.

With a click and creak, another door opened, and footsteps followed; then Victor was beside me, his case resting on the top edge of my trunk. I huffed out a breath. He had left the door to his room open, and through the gap, I caught sight of the yellow wallpaper, tinged a sickly green from the light of the still-lit lamp. I might have gone mad if I'd had to stare at that color for the entirety of our stay.

"I'll trade you," he said.

Carefully, I eased the trunk down, took the proffered case, and waited while Victor took over the managing of my luggage down to the front door.

"I'll be right back," he said, and he slipped outside while I waited, impatiently tapping my foot.

There were certainly people and places I had been glad to see the back of, but not quite as relieved as I would be with this one. I didn't often have nightmares, so to be subject to the same one for three nights running was too much.

"Ah, Miss Tailor, already packed and prepared to go, I see."

I twisted with a jerk. "Lord LeVerre," I said, pleased that I managed some semblance of calm in my tone. "We are nothing if not efficient when it comes to travel."

"I would say I was impressed, although it certainly leaves me questioning my hospitality."

"Your hospitality was quite pleasant," I said, the lie sliding easily enough off my tongue. "I've certainly endured worse."

He laughed a low chuckle. "I am not sure that I should take that as the compliment it was surely intended to be. That I'm being compared to your worst experience and not your best."

I opened my mouth, then shut it, tripped off balance by the departure from what should have been the usual pleasantries.

The door opened, and Victor stepped back in, grabbing the handle of the trunk. "I've moved the carriage up by the steps so we can get loaded in—ah, Lord LeVerre, apologies, I didn't see you there."

"It wouldn't have been entirely untoward for you not to expect me," Lucien said. He reached down and hefted up the opposite end of the trunk before either of us could protest. "I would not say I've been the most present host."

"We assumed you were a busy man," Victor said, backing out the door with Lucien and me following. He set the trunk down at the edge of the steps, and Lucien copied his movements. Victor held his hand out toward him. "I apologize that we couldn't be more help."

Lucien grasped his hand with a brief shake. "Understood. I'll be approaching that—Detective Brant you spoke of and see if I can obtain a warrant. As you've said, the story makes no sense unless one of them is lying."

Victor nodded, reaching back down to lift my trunk onto the top of the carriage and tie it down.

Lucien turned to me. "Miss Tailor, I suppose technically we've already said our goodbyes."

"I would say so," I agreed.

"I will, therefore, only close with the hope that it is you the Company sends back this way, should my warrant get their approval."

"Warrants," I automatically corrected.

"Right, warrants," he said.

The carriage creaked as Victor climbed off the side, retrieved his case, and set it down on the interior floor. "All set to go," he said, turning back toward me. "Viv, if you will?"

"Thank you both again," Lucien said. "For what help you could give. It's certainly more than anyone else has over the years."

"You're welcome," I said, slipping past Victor and into the carriage. The metal spring in the cushion was already pushing up against me; I pulled a face at the thought that the discomfort of the journey would start at the beginning rather than halfway through at least.

"Do feel free to keep us updated on any progress," Victor said. "If we can make any arguments in your favor, we'll put them into the right ears."

"Thank you," Lucien said with surprise in his tone, but the words were cut off as Victor shut the door and sat down across from me. He turned, rapped his knuckles on the wall behind him, and with a shudder, the conveyance rolled forward.

I leaned toward the window and swept the curtain back out of my way, watching out the glass as we lumbered down the drive. Lucien and his house quickly disappeared from my view, leaving me with only the gray trees and their reaching branches.

I wasn't sorry to see them go.

Victor left me at my townhouse with my trunk situated in my upstairs bedroom and the cash from Lucien's payment in my hand before he headed to his own home.

I placed most of the cash in a tin in the kitchen, hidden on top of the upper cabinets. Most people would look past something that appeared decorative out in plain sight. The rest, a couple of pounds at most, went into my pocket. That done, I headed upstairs to unpack.

I left my gloves on as I pulled out the skirts, blouses, and jackets and laid them carefully over the armchair in my little room. I would need to take them to be laundered.

Something thunked to the floor as I unfolded my shirt from the day we had arrived, and I paused, staring curiously down at it.

It was a hand mirror and not one I recalled packing or having even seen before, despite the smooth, gleaming maple wood that matched the interior of the trunk. I glanced over at the luggage, studying the inside of the lid and the sides, looking for a built-in pocket the mirror could have slipped out of at some point from the trunk being dragged around. I didn't spot one, but that didn't mean it wasn't there.

I bent and scooped the mirror up, turning it over in my hands as I examined it, but there was nothing beyond the simple wood and my reflection staring up at me. Holding the handle of the mirror in one hand, I gripped both it and the fingers of my other glove, wiggling my empty hand out of the fabric. Once it was free, I pressed my palm to the back of the mirror.

Brusque, quick swipes, a business-like attitude from whoever had constructed the mirror, and that was it. The same kind of emotions that had drifted up to me from when I had purchased the trunk years ago, which only seemed to reinforce the idea that the mirror had come with it, and I had simply ignored or missed it when I first opened the lid.

I was half-uncertain as I stared down at my reflection, the gray eyes and mahogany hair slipping free of its bun, the delicate features of my face. Surely, I would have noticed the mirror long before this point. I would not say that Victor and I were sent on overnight trips often, but I would think I should have spotted or knocked the thing loose sooner.

Still unsure, I set the mirror down on my dresser, where it reflected up against the full-size looking glass hanging on the wall. I pursed my lips, glancing back and forth between both of them, briefly entertaining the thought that perhaps I should move the mirror out of my room and to the hall where I wouldn't catch sight of my reflection in the middle of the night.

The feel of Lucien's manor and the mirrors there lingered.

I shook my head, tugged my glove back on, snagged my jacket off the edge of the trunk, and pulled it on before gathering the rest of my clothing and stuffing it haphazardly into a laundry bag. I was jumping at shadows again, thinking monsters were lurking in the dark. I checked to make sure I had money in my pocket, then went down the stairs and out the front door of my house, locking it behind me.

It was starting to get late; the streetlamps were already on, glaring blue orbs of light up and down the sidewalks full of people on their way home or on their way to get dinner at a local pub. I joined the stream of them, relieved that I wouldn't be headed down these streets alone with the sun setting. It was cold enough that our breaths were puffing out as mist and fog into the air, brief tendrils that faded as quickly as they appeared. I wove in and out among them, and it wasn't long before I was past the majority of the residential section of this neighborhood, out on the edge where the laundress I frequented was. She was still open—the sign on her front door declared it in cheerful, curling letters and colors, bright white flowers adorning the edges.

I slipped in through the door. "Kate!" I called. "It's only me."

Footsteps came thumping up the hall from the back of the house. "Bless," she said as she emerged into the front room. "I appreciate you, dear, always letting me know you're standing there." She snagged the bag of clothes from my hands before I could respond, setting it on the large side table she had positioned against the wall. She peered in at the clothes, pushing the fabrics to the side as if to delve deeper down. "Just a clean and press?"

"Please," I said. "The skirts may have collected some mud, as it had been raining when we arrived, and the drive at our destination was practically a pit."

She looked up, brushing her hands on her apron as she came back around to me. "Is everything well? You're looking a bit peaky."

"Quite," I said, giving her a small smile. "You know how it is. Traveling always seems to leave one out of sorts."

"It does," she said agreeably. "I can do the whole lot for a pound fifty. That mud is going to take some work to get off."

I paid her, and she wrote a receipt and handed it to me.

"They'll be ready by the end of the week," she said.

"Thank you." I stuffed the receipt into my pocket and headed back onto the streets, where the crowds had thinned considerably. I could either hurry home or dive into the fray at a packed pub. I turned to the left and headed for my house and whatever I had in the larder there. I didn't have the patience to wait for a pie or any other dinner I could pick up and bring home with me.

The walk back seemed to take less time than the walk there; before long, I was unlocking my front door and slipping into the warmth of the foyer. I locked the door behind me and headed for the kitchen. Everything was as quiet as I had left it, the two chairs pushed in at the small table by the window, the tin still displayed up atop the cabinets.

Nothing was amiss.

The first place I went poking was the icebox, but I had emptied it of almost everything perishable before we left rather than risk the food going bad while we were out of town. All I had in there was a wedge of cheese and a block of butter. I pulled the cheese out, grabbed an apple from the bowl of fruit on the counter, and checked the loaf of bread in the breadbox for any mold. Seated at my little table, I made a meal out of what I had found. I would have to make a trip to the grocer's in the morning.

My stomach as satisfied as it was going to get, I cleaned up and headed back upstairs. My steps slowed when I reached the hallway and peered into the gathered shadows. A lamp glowed faintly through the cracked door of my bedroom; I neither remembered turning it on nor pulling the door mostly shut behind me when I left.

But there were no signs of disturbance in my house—both the front and the door at the back were locked. I hadn't checked the parlor, but the windows in the kitchen were intact, and surely I would've noticed if the front windows were smashed when I arrived. It was unlikely anyone would enter via the second floor, as they would've had to climb a drainpipe and then inch their way along the gutters to reach a window at this height.

I was being silly.

I marched up to my door, shoved it open, and was greeted only by the sight of my bedroom, the trunk open on the floor as I had left it, the single lamp on the bedside table casting its light across the bedding and up the wall at its back.

"Humbug," I said, half-laughing like the word would chase away ghosts when there were none to be had in the first place.

I shut the bedroom door, pulled a nightgown from the wardrobe, and changed, carefully setting aside the clothing I had traveled home in to take over to Kate at the end of the week. I set my gloves on the dresser, my fingers brushing past the hand mirror, where I hesitated. I doubted touching the wood would bring any other emotions or clues to the surface, so I left it where it was and climbed into bed. I flicked off the lamp and settled down to sleep, certain that there would be no nightmares among these familiar sheets.

Pain seared through my wrist, shards of glass that sliced into the flesh, and a vise clamped around the limb at my forearm—a stark contrast to the gentle cradle of someone's palm at the back of my hand, their fingers curled lightly over my own.

The vise released, and now there was a hand pressed to the back of my neck; even as I registered its presence, it shifted once again, brushing loose strands away from my cheeks before the fingers burrowed into the tresses and tenderly pulled, coaxing the tilt of my chin upward so the long line of my throat was exposed to the cold air of the room. The sharpness in my wrist withdrew, left behind the searing ache of relief, and was followed by warm breath gusting along the side of my neck.

I tried to jerk away but found I couldn't move. It was as if the command I gave my body never reached it, lost somewhere between my mind and a yawning void that shouldn't have been there.

There were lips against my skin.

I woke, blinking groggily at the sunlight streaming through my bedroom windows. For a moment, I lay there, half-awake, my body and mind still out of sync. When I finally sat up with a groan, it was to find my legs tangled in the sheets. I managed to free my limbs with little trouble and set my feet on the floor, the cold seeping up my heels and calves like spreading ice.

My wrist itched.

I glanced down at it and smoothed my thumb over the spot. The skin was unmarked.

I was as tired as if I hadn't slept at all, and it took an effort of will to shove myself off the bed and stagger over to my dresser and the pitcher of water there, where I stared at the ewer, pondering if it would be too heavy for me to lift. I picked it up and drank straight from it rather than attempt to pour it into the cup. Some of the water slipped past my lips, dribbling along my chin to drip onto my chest. I drank until I was as desperate for air as I had been for the liquid, then set the pitcher down with a gasp.

My reflection caught my eye.

We stared at each other, the two of us, strands of hair slipping free from the braid it was woven into, ghostly pale skin, and hollows under our cheekbones. I looked as though something had been drained out of me.

I scoffed at the notion, turning toward the wardrobe, but after considering the closed doors, decided it was hardly untoward for a woman alone in her own house to go downstairs in her nightgown. Getting dressed at this point in the day felt like too much effort.

I made it halfway down the stairs before remembering I had no food left from the night before. I sat down where I was, leaning against the wall while seriously considering going back to sleep on the step until this wave of exhaustion passed. I must have caught whatever it was John was sick with.

There was a knock at the door. I raised my head enough to peer suspiciously at it. No one I knew would call so early in the morning.

Whoever was there knocked again. I stayed where I was, determined to ignore them until they went away. Instead, I heard a key scrape in the lock and the door creak open as Victor stuck his head inside.

"Viv?" he called before he spotted me, and his brow furrowed. "What are you doing on the stairs?"

He came the rest of the way in, and with him drifted the scent of sausage rolls from the paper bag clutched in one of his hands. "Did you sleep at all last night?"

"No," I said. "I suspect I didn't."

With a sigh, I pushed myself to my feet, one hand on the wall to help me keep my balance. "What's in the bag?"

"Sausage rolls," he said. "As if you couldn't already smell them. I saw the way your eyes lit up when I came in, and I dare say it wasn't for me."

"You would be right," I said, giving him a half-hearted smile as I made my way down the stairs. "Just as sure as I am that you did not come here this early to inquire after my health." I turned, and he followed me into the kitchen.

"We've got another assignment," he said, setting the bag on the table and shrugging out of his overcoat, which he hung over the back of one of the chairs.

"So soon?" I asked. "We've only just returned."

"We're the only ones without a case to give it to," he said, settling into the chair his coat hung on. "Is there any coffee?"

"I've not had a chance to brew it."

He climbed to his feet. "Sit; I'll get it. I know my way around your kitchen as well as I know my own."

I perched on a chair and watched him as he moved about, lighting the stove to heat the water as he filled the kettle. Neither of us spoke until he set a steaming cup of coffee and a sausage roll in front of me.

I picked up the cup and took a sip, Victor's calm, steady presence washing over me.

"Are you well?" he asked, taking a sip from his own cup before he took a bite of his food.

"I believe I caught John's illness," I said.

Victor drummed his fingers on the table. "I suppose any exposure is exposure enough," he said, although he sounded doubtful.

I shrugged. "Perhaps I picked it up somewhere else."

"Perhaps. Are you going to be well enough to work on this assignment?"

"What kind of case is it?"

He pulled a face. "Murder. To be honest, it sounded cut and dry to me, so I don't understand why we're being called in so early."

"We could plead off."

He shook his head. "No. We'll put in an appearance, point out the culprit, and give them a lecture for wasting resources when we should be the last resort, not the first."

I picked up the sausage roll and took a bite, the taste of thyme, pork, and buttery pastry bursting across my tongue. I took the time to devour the entire thing and finish my cup of coffee before I got up from the table. "I suppose I should go get dressed."

"Might be a reasonable thing to do," Victor said. "We can stop at the grocers on the way home. Are your cupboards always this bare?"

"Only when I've been out of town."

"I'm astonished you didn't use that as an opportunity to inform me that you live on a diet of nothing but air."

I snorted. "Feel free to clear the dishes while I dress."

"You're angry you didn't think of it, aren't you?"

I left the kitchen to head back up to my bedroom.

"You are, aren't you?" Victor called after me.

Victor had brought the carriage, which meant the crime scene had to be at least half the city away and not only a block's walk. Therefore, I wasn't the least bit surprised when I climbed out of the carriage to find myself in one of the poorer areas of the city with houses made up of crumbling brick, plaster, and rotting wood, steps away from being condemned. I wrinkled my nose. Of course, in this area, they wouldn't keep on top of ensuring the sewer system was operational. It made it even more surprising that the police had requested our presence and that the Company had agreed in the first place.

A uniformed officer stood outside the address with a distinctly bored expression on his face, his arms crossed as he leaned back against the wall beside the gaping front door that led into the sagging building.

Victor paused beside the carriage, an unexpected hesitation that had me lingering beside him as he grimaced.

"Dust," he muttered. "Dust and glass, ripples and shadows."

I shifted to block Victor from the officer's sight. As helpful as he might mean to be, it would be closer to a disaster if he stepped in.

"Where?" I asked.

"Nowhere, everywhere," Victor said. "He has no air."

"Who has no air?" I asked cautiously, treading that careful line between too little and too much in the hopes the vision didn't simply vanish.

Victor blinked and rubbed a hand on his chest.

I sighed, anticipation gone.

"Piss poor," he mumbled and cleared his throat. "Useless again," he said more strongly this time. "If I'm going to have visions, the least they could do is drop a brightly lit sign that screams, 'This is your culprit.'"

"Was there truly nothing useful there?" I asked.

"Yes," he grumbled. "It was more of the same, and I would thank our Lord LeVerre for keeping his ennui to himself and out of my head." He gave me a nudge. "Come on, I believe we're expected." He moved around me toward our destination.

"You the Tailors?" the officer asked as we approached.

"We are," Victor said.

The officer nodded and went back to watching the street behind us.

"Well then, I suppose we see ourselves in," Victor muttered, heading past the man and through the door. I followed after him.

The first thing I noticed was the smell—dank mold and the sickly sweet scent of rotting meat. The next was that the wood beneath my feet felt spongy, the floorboards straining to keep from collapsing into the foundation of the house. I paused while my eyes adjusted to the dim light, and it was Victor's hesitation that saved me from losing track of where he went.

Fortunately, he stepped into the parlor just off the entryway.

The room contained a faded couch, stuffing poking out of its worn fabric, the shine on the polished wood long since gone. A water-stained table sat beside it, along with an equally old armchair. A cold and empty grate held only ashes from a previous fire; the single candle on the table was barely more than a stub. A cracked and spotted mirror was on the floor, leaning against the wall, the shapes reflected in it blurred smears of movement.

The only other thing in the room was the body splayed across the floor, glassy eyes staring up at the ceiling.

As far as I could see, there wasn't a single mark on him. Were it not for the blank gaze, the eyes almost marble-like in appearance, and the pale, bloodless visage of his skin, I would have thought the man was merely lying there, suffering from a moment of unusual contemplation.

"Bless the Company," said a familiar tenor behind me, warm like ginger on the tongue. "They sent me their best."

"We would hardly dare to claim that," I said, turning with a smile.

Detective Morris smiled back at me, bright eyes in a rich umber face, but her grin faltered as she took in my pallor. "Shit, Vivian, you look as though you shouldn't be out of bed."

I shot a look over her shoulder, but none of the other officers had followed her into the room. "I appear to have caught some sickness on our last assignment," I said. "It'll pass within a few days."

"I told her she didn't look well," Victor said from where he was, peering down at the corpse. "The Company would've understood if she begged off."

"That wasn't the impression I got," I said acridly. "In fact, I'm quite sure you said *we* couldn't."

"I should've just had you wait in the carriage and told management you did come with me," he said. "You look worse than you did when we left."

"Well, either way, you're here now," Morris interrupted. "We might as well go over the facts so you can get to business."

Victor stepped toward the body, circling around it. "Hmm, yes. Why exactly did you call us in?"

Morris ignored his question, reached into her jacket pocket, and pulled out a notebook and pencil remarkably similar to the ones Victor carried. She flipped through the pages. "The victim, Thomas Edward, fifty-five years old or thereabouts, did not report for his work release program this morning."

"That explains why you found the body so quickly," Victor said dryly.

"I think we can debate how often this area gets patrols over a drink in the pub rather than over the deceased," Morris countered. "But you might keep in mind this is an area where people watch out for their own and would have noticed they hadn't seen him."

"They shouldn't have to be the ones doing the policing," Victor said.

Morris shot him a stern look with narrowed eyes and pinched lips. "As I was saying, the victim didn't report for his work release program. An officer was dispatched to bring him in for violating the terms of his parole and found the body."

"And you sent for us because?" Victor asked.

"He has a daughter," Morris said. "No one's been able to locate her. There is a concern that whoever killed him took her with them when they left."

"How old is she?" Victor asked.

Morris looked back down at her notebook. "Twenty-two, unmarried, living with her father for financial reasons."

Victor took a pointed look around the room and its condition.

"I didn't say their finances were in a healthy position," Morris said. "Even with the two of them contributing to their combined coffers."

"What was her position?" Victor asked.

I shifted, tamping down on the desire to tap my foot. We were wasting time while he sussed out details of their lives, though sometimes it was the information given that triggered his visions.

Morris flipped another page over, shook her head, and flipped back. "She was a shop girl, and she worked the cash register for a store selling ribbons."

"What did he do?" Victor asked.

"A little of this, a little of that. Last assignment on his docket was for moving boxes to and from the warehouses."

"Delivery?"

Morris shrugged. "As far as I'm aware, yes."

"Does his daughter have any favorite haunts?" Victor asked. "Anywhere she might have gone?"

"No," Morris said. "We've spoken with the neighbors who said she goes nowhere and knows no one else. Quiet, the two of them. Go to work, come home, not even out to the local pub."

"Odd then that she would go missing like that," Victor muttered. "Could she have had anything to do with his death?"

"Again, the answer we've gotten from the neighbors is no," Morris said. "They were adamant she wouldn't hurt a fly, and as far as he was concerned, she hung the sun and the moon. To all appearances, a loving, close-knit pair."

"That does seem to point to the only possibility being an outsider," Victor said.

"Now you see why we went straight to the Company instead of puzzling through this one ourselves. We need Vivian to read the room and give us any clues she can as to what happened here." She turned toward me. "Viv, if you could?" She motioned at the space, a grimace on her face. "I know there's not much to go on, but maybe the couch? A brush with the wall?"

I pulled off my glove as she spoke, settling into my glide about the room before she finished her last sentence. I ran my fingers down the plaster; it felt damp as if the substance would crumble apart and fall away at the slightest pressure.

They whispered to me, these walls. The echoes of dozens of voices who had taken shelter within this decaying building. Even the most recent ones were faded, the essence of them dribbling away alongside the slow withering of the house that held them.

I gave up there: there was no information that would help me. I drifted away from them, brushing past the mirror and its empty glass that would hold no answers for me either. I ran my hand along the back of the couch, noticing that the wood was pitted with little bumps and divots; the emotions that filtered up to me were those of exasperation, tired feet, and aching hearts. There were also spurts of relief, the feel of collapsing off sore legs, warmth, and welcome. But that was all. Nothing more than that quiet and constant trudging forward into a life that wasn't easy and the fear that there would be no end to this drudgery.

"Anything?" Morris asked.

I hesitated, taking that one precious moment I needed to work through what I had read and the way the moments swam through my mind, filtered by my own perceptions. "Nothing."

"Nothing?"

"Nothing to tell me what happened here."

"No arguments?"

"No?"

"Truly nothing?" she asked. "There had to have been something."

"Truly nothing," I confirmed. "From either the building or the items in the room," I said as apologetically as I could, resignation in my tone.

Morris sighed, rubbing a hand over her face before she looked back at me. "I hate to ask it of you, but I think reading the body may be our only chance at solving this one."

She took a step away from the corpse at the same time I moved forward, sliding into the space she had so recently exited, my skirts pooling around me as I sank to my knees beside the body. I hesitated a moment more, my palm hovering over the man's hand before I touched my fingers to the ice-cold skin.

Frustration, anger, and irritation bubbled up to the surface, cocooned in the dark—a long day with nothing to show for it and an empty belly as the only reward. They were pale in their essence, subsumed in shadow, as weak as poorly brewed tea. As if in spite of strong feelings on any matter, the man had experienced them distantly and left them disregarded on the floor.

And that was it.

I pulled my hand away, parsing through the emotions I had just floated among, the vague and fleeting thoughts and hopes beneath the rage that the next day would be better. There was no terror, no fear, no pain, or evidence of an encounter that would have left this man dead on the floor of a long-moldering building.

"Well?" Morris asked.

"I don't know," I said.

"What?" she said.

"I don't know," I repeated.

"You don't—what do you mean you don't know?" she demanded.

I waved a hand at the body. "There's nothing there to tell me what killed him." I climbed to my feet, pulling my glove back on. "There's his last conscious moments, and then nothing. It's as if he died in his sleep."

"That doesn't make any sense," Morris said.

I shrugged. "You didn't ask me to make sense of it; you asked me to tell you what happened. As far as I can tell, he died while asleep."

"Is it possible his daughter found him dead on the floor and ran rather than report it?"

"It's possible," I said. "There's no evidence of anything else."

"A whole lot of good that does me," Morris said. "How are we supposed to find her?"

I grimaced, turning everything I knew over in my head, but my answer remained the same, and it was that I had none. He had seemingly died of his own volition, and his daughter was in the wind. "I wish I could tell you."

She turned to Victor. "What about you? You getting anything that would be helpful?"

"If I had or was, you would already know," Victor said. "My skills aren't as dependable as Viv's."

Morris clicked her tongue. "So what do we do?"

"Good ol' fashioned legwork?" Victor suggested. "You can always call us back if you come across anything new."

Morris grumbled something that I could not hear.

Victor cleared his throat and spoke before I could ask her to repeat herself. "In that case, I believe we'll take our leave. Morris, always a pleasure. Viv, after you."

I stepped past the body and Victor to head into the cold air outside, not that it had been any warmer inside. If anything, the chill had been deeper. The officer standing guard ignored us as we went by.

"You," Victor said, "are getting dropped off at home, and I will run by the grocers to pick you up some supplies for those cupboards."

"Thank you," I said, leaning back against the seat. I had managed to sit on the self-same spring again, only adding to the bruise already there in my flesh, but it seemed like too much effort to shift to the side to find a spot where the damned thing wasn't poking up against me.

CHAPTER NINE

November 7, 1895:
Case number 1888-11-MP-001436 submitted to Company for review. Warrants requested in packet.

V ictor left me on a couch in my parlor, where I dozed in fits until he returned.

I didn't wake fully when he came back in and slept through him putting groceries away, the sound of cupboard doors opening and closing, and footsteps echoing in my dreams until I couldn't tell what was real and what was only in my mind.

A hand brushed against my forehead—cool, a mild temperament that reminded me of my mother—followed by a pat on my shoulder and words that drifted in the air.

When I finally opened my eyes, it was silent, the stretching shadows and orange light of the setting sun sinking out of view of the front windows, and a cold cup of tea sitting on the table in front of my couch.

I struggled to push myself into a sitting position. One arm had fallen asleep beneath me, pins and needles racing up and down the limb. I could've sworn I heard my back creak and my joints crackle with the movement. I snagged the cup and, despite the bitterness of the liquid within, drank it down, Victor's calm presence rushing past with it.

There was a hint of worry.

I set the cup down once I had drained it and leaned back against the couch cushions. My hair had pulled free of its carefully arranged bun, strands slipping across my face. I puffed out a breath in an effort to shift them from in front of my eyes.

It didn't work.

The click of the lock unbolting startled me; had I still been holding the teacup, I would've dropped it. I turned to face the front door in time to see Victor slip back inside, carefully balancing a canvas bag. I could hear the clink of glass on glass as he shut the door behind him.

"You're up," he said, something of a relieved smile flickering across his face. "You've slept most of the day."

With a grimace, I got to my feet, listening to my joints pop again. "Did you merely sit there and watch me?"

"No," he said. "I sat here and read. You didn't have a fever as far as I could tell, but I didn't want to run off and leave you alone for long if a doctor was going to be necessary."

I motioned at the bag in his hand. "But you did run off."

He lifted it and gave it a gentle waggle, the items inside clacking. "To bring you dinner." He turned toward the hallway. "Come on, I picked up soup. You'll want to eat it while it's still hot. I daresay your tea has gotten cold and won't be worth attempting."

I followed him into the kitchen. "It was cold, and I did attempt it."

He set the bag on the table, reaching inside to pull out a wide-mouthed, stoppered bottle. "Did you? It must have been positively awful. That tea isn't pleasant to drink even when it *is* hot."

"The medicinal stuff rarely is," I said, pulling bowls and spoons out as he took a second bottle from the bag. "How much soup did you bring me?"

"Enough to last you a couple of days," he said. "If you were going to be ill past tonight, I didn't want you to have to think about making meals on top of it."

"You are going to make someone a proper husband someday," I teased, setting the bowls in front of him. He pulled one of the stoppers free, steam following the cork, and poured some of the soup into the first bowl. It smelled of rosemary and roasted chicken. One last piece of carrot followed the liquid out with a plop into the bowl, and he pushed it toward me.

"Eat," he said. "Before you waste away into nothing and I have to explain to our parents how I let this happen."

I picked up the spoon and followed his instructions. I hadn't realized how hungry I was until I had devoured the entirety of the bowl, the metal scraping against the ceramic as I tried to get every last little drop.

"There is more," he said mildly after my third attempt.

I motioned at the empty second bowl. "Are you not eating?"

"I wasn't going to, no," he said. "It would defeat the purpose of leaving you with the lot of it."

"I don't think you'll need to worry about that," I said. "I'm feeling quite a bit better than I was."

"You're looking quite a bit better," he acknowledged. "I suppose I won't need to camp out in your parlor for the night if you're feeling capable of making it up the stairs on your own."

"We could both camp out in the parlor," I suggested. "Roast chestnuts in front of the fire like we used to."

"Drag the blankets and pillows down from the bedroom?" he asked. "At least here we won't have Mother coming in to lecture us that we'll set ourselves aflame sitting so close to it."

"She had a point," I said.

"She did," he said. "Honestly, the number of times we did even riskier things, I'm surprised there's any color left in her hair." He picked the bottle of soup back up and held it half-tipped toward my bowl. "Did you want more before we go prep the parlor for camping?"

I shook my head. He set the bottle down, secured the stopper back in the mouth, and then took both and set them on a shelf in the icebox.

"Right," he said. "You go settle yourself in the parlor, and I'll fetch your extra blankets and pillows."

I started to get up from the table, but he turned and opened one of the cabinets.

"Hold a moment," he said, pulling out a paper bag and handing it off to me. "You'll want these."

I unfolded it enough to peek inside, spotted the glossy brown gleam of chestnuts, and looked up to grin at him.

He shooed me away. "Go get settled."

I headed back into the parlor and settled myself before the fireplace and its low, crackling flames. I took the time to build it back up, carefully layering fresh wood until it was roaring.

I picked the bag of chestnuts up off the hearth where I had set them and shifted, scooting close to the low-slung table and spilling them across the surface. Their husks hadn't been scored through yet, and I made a face. I didn't carry a pocket knife and would have to get back up to secure one.

"Vic," I called. "Can you bring me a knife?"

There was a thump on the stairs, and I stilled, eyes fastened on the doorway. At first, there was only silence. Slowly, I got to my feet, pulling at my skirts where they caught on the leg of the table, and moved toward the parlor door.

"Vic?" I said.

Quick, heavy footsteps shook the ceiling above me, and I looked up, craning my neck back to peer at the plaster.

"Viv, can you move back a step?"

I jerked, startled to find Victor directly in front of me, his arms full of thick blankets and stacked high with pillows. I stepped back out of his way so he could come into the parlor and begin arranging his armload on the couches.

I spared another glance up at the ceiling.

"Did you hear that?" I asked.

"Hear what?"

I motioned up at the ceiling. "The footsteps."

"Viv, how would I hear—how would I *notice* my own footsteps? Technically, I hear them constantly."

I hesitated, hovering by the door, but Victor settled on the floor on the other side of the table and pulled a knife out of his pocket. He picked up a chestnut and dragged the blade down along the top of its shell. "I've got an extra knife," he said, "if you want to come help."

"Yes," I said, with one last glance toward the ceiling. "We'll want to close the parlor door before we go to sleep to keep the heat contained."

The footsteps echoed in my dreams, a landscape of high, gray hedges and reaching branches. They were booming, the thump of hard-soled shoes on wood—not the crack of twigs and rustle of grass I would have expected. Behind me, Lucien's manor loomed in the distance.

A door rattled in its frame. When I turned, it was a mirror, standing in the midst of an otherwise empty field.

I didn't dare look in at its reflection.

When I woke, I found myself staring at the ceiling, dazzling white with the rising sunlight splashed across it through the front windows.

There was a crick in my neck, an ache in the muscle that told me I had slept in an unfortunate position. I levered myself up with a groan, rubbing at my eyes to clear the sleep from them.

We had left the remnants of our feast scattered across the table, the empty, darkened chestnut husks peeled back like shards of broken glass.

Across from me, Victor shifted, rolling so that I could see his face.

He was frowning, an outright scowl etched on his brow.

"Must be an unpleasant dream," I remarked to the air. I glanced at the parlor door. It was still closed. I shoved the blankets back and got off the couch. I headed first for the necessary to take care of urgent bodily needs, and once that was done and my hands washed, I went to the kitchen to prepare breakfast.

I was whisking eggs, sausage already sizzling away in a cast iron pan on the stove, when Victor came wandering in, his hair mussed and lines from the fabric of the pillow etched into his cheek. He yawned, belatedly covering his mouth, and I could've sworn his jaw creaked from how wide it expanded.

"Is there coffee?" he asked.

I tilted my head toward the table. "Have you ever known me not to provide coffee?"

He gave me an attempt at a smile before sitting down and pouring himself a cup. He let the steam rise for a minute before he took a sip and glanced around the kitchen. "You look as though you've completely recovered."

"A quick illness, it would appear," I said, dumping the eggs into their prepared pan and stirring them. "Now we'll just have to hope it didn't pass to you."

"I have the fortitude of an ox," he said, "and even if it had, it won't take hold."

"I suppose if it did pass to you, we'll get to test that theory of yours."

The two of us went silent, Victor sipping his coffee while I finished up the eggs and sausages. I set both down in the middle of the table before claiming my own seat.

"We'll need to head into the Company's office this morning," he said, spooning eggs onto his plate. "As you're well."

"A whole day of paperwork?" I asked.

"For me," he said.

"And me? Am I simply to grace them with my presence?"

"You," he said, with a quick grin at me, "are to deal with getting our paychecks."

I groaned and sat back in my chair, shoulders slumped. "Katherine hates me."

Victor snorted. "She doesn't hate you. She checks over the hours like she does for everyone. She's a penny-pincher."

"We shouldn't have to justify the hours worked," I said. "We worked them."

"If people hadn't been padding their hours, she wouldn't have to," he said calmly, taking a bite of his eggs.

"It's unfair to punish the rest of us because of a couple of bad apples."

Victor's only answer was to shrug.

The Company was located in a nondescript and anti-climactic square brick building. Even its color was unassuming—a drab brown. The front door was up a set of steps, unadorned, flat-faced, without even a knocker. It was unlocked, and Victor and I sailed right through into the lobby.

Like the station back in Lucien's village, there was a singular desk front and center in this area. Unlike the station, there were doors to either side that led into austere waiting rooms. No couches in these; high-backed benches marching along the wall and placed back to back down the middle dominated the spaces.

Victor and the receptionist exchanged brief pleasantries while I slipped past and headed down the hall to Katherine's domain.

Fortunately, there wasn't much of a line. Only one other person stood in front of her window, hands in his pockets as he waited for her to finish. When she slipped a check through to him, he snatched it up and hurried out, nearly knocking my shoulder with his without so much as a by-your-leave.

I approached the window. "Good morning, Katherine," I said, pulling both Victor's and my timesheets from my pocket and smoothing out the wrinkles in the paper as I placed them on the wide sill.

"You're back, I see," she said, picking up the sheets and peering at them with narrowed eyes.

"Was there doubt I would be?" I asked mildly.

"Not on my end," she said, holding the paper up toward the light and examining it, as if she expected some secret would be revealed. She set the sheets on her desk, picked up a pencil, and began making marks as she counted the hours and days listed.

"Oh?" I asked.

"You've been consistently reliable," she sniffed. "Don't take it as an endorsement."

"I won't."

Her eyes flicked briefly from the paper over to me and back again.

We were silent while she added the hours, her pencil scratching across the paper before she set it down and flipped open the heavy tome of a checkbook. In that, she used a pen and ink, notating the hours and the pay before scribbling out two checks and signing them with a flourish.

She handed them off to me. "You may wish to go check your office. There was a rumor someone stopped in to see you—*only* you." With that last cryptic remark, she shuttered her window and left me gaping at the wood.

I folded the two checks in half, slipped them into the interior pocket of my jacket, and headed up to the third floor, where my shared office was located. When I reached the hallway, I hesitated, my steps slowing as I approached the door, weighing whether to glide past with a quick glance or square my shoulders and march inside. I chose to try walking past it, expecting whoever it was to look up briefly enough only to determine if I was entering. Keeping my pace measured and steady, I peeked in through the open door.

He immediately caught sight of me and rose to his feet before I could recover.

"Miss Tailor," Lucien said, a sheepish smile creeping onto his face. He was clutching a hat by the brim. "I'm glad to have caught you."

"I don't know if there is a way you wouldn't have caught me," I said. "You're sitting in my office."

"I—yes, I suppose that would preclude any chance of not conveniently running into you," he said. He gave the hat a turn, running the brim through his fingers. "I was hoping perhaps you could assist me once again."

"With?" I asked cautiously.

"I'm having difficulty acquiring a warrant," he said. "The detective assigned to my mother's case—"

"Brant," I said.

"Excuse me?"

"Detective Brant."

"Oh, yes," he said; his lips and jaw tightened briefly before his face reverted to its pleasant, quite-sorry-to-be-a-bother expression. "Detective Brant seems to be under the impression that a warrant requiring the witnesses to be checked for truthfulness is an unnecessary violation of their rights."

"It's certainly not one issued lightly," I said.

"I was hoping you could help me bypass his—ah, ruling—and plead my case directly to the Company."

I was still standing outside my office, just beyond the frame of the door, and I wasn't sure that I wanted to step over that threshold into that close space.

It felt strangely like it would mean walking willingly into the lion's den.

"I suppose I could try speaking to my superiors and see if there are any steps you could take to—"

"Would you?" he asked; there was that twist of hope in his voice. "I would be eternally grateful."

"Certainly," I promised, knowing full well they would give me the writ and rule, and I could safely send that back to him and wash my hands of the situation. "And if you don't mind..."

He looked about the office, at the two desks shoved in there, the Company's concession to the idea that, while Margaret and I may share an office, we needed separate spaces for the filing and paperwork that followed any case to reduce any chance we would mix up our in-baskets. He focused back on me, eyes wide and curious. "Are you working on a case now?"

"No," I said. "I haven't been assigned to a new one yet."

Renewed interest sparked across his face, and I regretted the words the instant they left my mouth.

"Would you be free for lunch?" he asked.

I hesitated, wondering if I could cite propriety between a client and employee as my excuse to beg off.

"Nothing untoward," he promised. "I merely find myself at a loss and with no one to talk to. The company—" He paused, half a smile flickering across his face at the word, "would be appreciated."

"I'll need to leave a note," I said.

"Certainly." He remained standing by my desk. I realized after a moment that I would have to slip past him to reach the paper and pens sitting on its surface.

Unless I wanted to be standing with him directly at my back.

I gritted my teeth, stepped around him to snatch up a piece of paper and a pen, and bent over the surface to scribble a quick note about who I had left the building with. "Where were you planning on going?"

"There's a little café just down the street," he said. "Looks to be only sandwiches and soup, light fare."

I added that in, signed off at the bottom of it, folded the paper, and straightened. For a beat, we only stared at each other, and I motioned at the door. "After you."

Realization dawned on his face, and he uttered an "Oh" before practically slinking across the threshold, waiting for me to join him in the hall.

"This way," I said as I stepped out after him, turning to the left to head back to the first floor. He followed after me, and my shoulders and back tensed. I wasn't sure I could check behind me to see how close on my heels he was without tripping over my own feet.

On the first floor, I stopped beside the receptionist, slipping the note into her hands. "Please make sure Victor Tailor gets a copy of this," I said, then led Lucien out the front. Once we were on the sidewalk, I stopped. "You'll need to lead from here. I'm not familiar with the café you mentioned."

He moved around me, looked up and down the street, and then chose the direction to the right. I hesitated again, considering going back inside and claiming I had forgotten a report or some other task

I needed to complete; instead, I took the hurried steps needed to catch up and walk side by side with him. At least this way, I could glance at him out of the corner of my eye to catch sight of what he was doing.

Our breath puffed out into the air, compliments of the weather rapidly heading into winter. The sidewalk was nearly empty despite how close to noon it was. It would appear most people had chosen to stay home rather than brave the cold in search of food. Or they were still hoping it would warm up a bit before they had to leave shelter.

"Have you lived here long?" Lucien asked.

"All my life."

"Truly?"

"I have no reason to lie about my upbringing."

There was a flush in his cheeks, but I couldn't be sure if that was a blush or due to the frigid air. "Apologies, it just seems—strange to me. To live an entire life in the city. Surely your parents took you on outings to the countryside?"

"That would require the funds to do so," I said.

He opened his mouth, closed it, and if anything, his blush deepened. "I seem to consistently put my foot in my mouth in your presence."

"I'm sure it is not a phenomenon exclusive to me."

He stopped, and I stopped with him; the two of us turned to face each other.

"You are probably correct," he said. The corners of his mouth tilted upward, the barest hint of a crooked smile. "You do, however, seem to be the one most apt to call me out on it."

"Perhaps you need different friends, in that case," I said. "Rather than any yes men you have."

He huffed out a chuckle, the ghost of a full laugh. He began walking again, and I fell into step with him. "I would not say I have any friends. The only people I see are John and Cook."

"Do you have no one you keep in touch with from your time living in the city?" I asked, surprised.

"No," he said. "It makes people—uncomfortable to be around you when you've suffered a loss such as I have. They want to brush by the subject and leave it as untouched as possible, as if afraid any mention of it will leave you collapsed on the floor like an abandoned puppet. Or maybe your bad luck will rub off on them, and they should end the association before any such similar situation befalls them. So they drift away, leaving you behind as a mere memory."

"Oh," I said quietly. "I didn't mean to intrude on a sore spot."

He shrugged. "I've become used to it."

"Sore spots being trod upon?"

"Yes." He came to another stop. "Here we are."

He pulled open the front door of a small one-story building, crowded in on either side by taller structures. The front of it was all framed windows down to about my knee where flower boxes sat, empty of blooms. Warmth from the interior spilled out, washing over both of us before we stepped inside.

We hovered side by side; it would appear that this café was where the people were. The tables were crowded four to five bodies deep, even the small ones meant to handle two at most. The air was filled with the buzz of their chatter, that roaring murmur of blending words. The waiters glided in and out among the groupings like fish in the sea.

Lucien rose on his toes, peering over the heads, before dropping to his heels. "I see a table toward the back, if I may?"

"Lead away," I said.

He took hold of my upper arm. I flinched—an instinctive reaction—but all that leaked through my sleeve was the warmth of his fingers as he tugged me forward, weaving past tables and chairs.

I was profoundly relieved when he came upon an empty two-seat table and released my arm. I immediately claimed one of the chairs, so he was left with the other. The table itself must only have just recently been cleared of the detritus left by its previous occupants.

He settled into his seat, seemingly unaware of the exuding tension from me, and plucked up the menu left on the table's surface, his eyes flicking down the list as he handed it over to me. "Ladies first."

"You hardly need stand on that propriety," I said, although I took the menu anyway, searching out the sandwiches as the item I would have the least amount of dishes to risk touching.

He shrugged, a smile tugging at the corners of his lips again. "I've already decided on what I would like. I came to this café yesterday and took the time to familiarize myself with their offerings."

I caught his eyes and set the menu down on the table. "Were you planning this?"

He blinked, startled as if I had caught him in a lie he had expected to be able to brush past me. He sat back in his chair. "Not—exactly."

"And what is not exactly supposed to mean?"

He started to answer, paused, and I half-turned to see what had attracted his attention, but it was only a harried waiter, a pad and pencil in his hand, practically looming over us. "What'll it be?" the waiter asked gruffly.

"Tea, please," Lucien said. "For the lady."

"And for you?"

"Nothing yet."

The waiter scoffed, turned away, and disappeared back into the crowd.

"Friendly service today," Lucien said.

"I would like an explanation, please," I said, bristling. My irritation with him was mounting, fueled both by the ruse and the fact that he had placed an order for me without consultation—and anger at myself that I had said nothing while the waiter was at the table.

"I would say," he paused, lips pursed, and he shifted in his chair, "that I find a certain level of fascination with your—abilities."

"So," I said flatly, "morbid curiosity only?"

"I do not know that I would say *morbid*—"

"What other kind could it be?" I said harshly. "When my abilities lend themselves so well to dealing with the macabre?"

He tilted his head to the side, a silent regard, and with the way the light in the café reflected in his eyes, they glittered like broken glass, all sharp edges. His lips drew back in a hint of a smiling snarl. I blinked, and it was merely Lucien, as if the momentary reflection of a predator sitting across from me hadn't existed, his expression only entreating.

"I think perhaps your abilities would have a lighter side to them," he said.

The waiter returned, thumping down a teapot and a teacup onto the table in front of me. "Have you decided?"

"I think we'll need another moment," Lucien said smoothly.

The waiter huffed and once again disappeared.

"A lighter side," I said, bringing Lucien's attention back to the subject at hand.

"Yes," he said, something sparking in the depths of his eyes. He leaned forward, his elbows on the table. "If the Company would send you and your cohorts out sooner, you could do some good in the world instead of being historians pointing the finger at the culprit—"

"And with the volume of cases, how are they to accomplish that?" I asked. "Do you even know the number of people who go missing or are murdered every day?"

"That sounds like a problem with humanity," he said. "If the cases climb that high."

"Anyone who says monsters aren't real hasn't met other people," I said shortly. "So yes, it is a problem with the world at large."

"I feel that we have quite a few opinions in common."

"And I feel that someone should be more upfront with his motives for going to lunch." I pushed the teapot and cup to one side. "I do not appreciate being lied to."

"It wasn't quite—"

"It was," I said bluntly. "An omission of your intentions to get me to follow you out the door is a lie."

He flushed, that reddened blush creeping up the sides of his neck and into his cheeks. If I was being entirely honest, it appeared he was more angry than embarrassed. His fingers had tightened against the surface of the wood, and his jaw clenched, a tick at the back of the muscle. But the expression eased away like water.

"I will admit I should have been more forthcoming," he said, and although he said it smoothly, there was still a clipped quality to his words. "And so now, what would you have me do?"

"Apologize," I said.

"Apologize," he repeated. He said it slowly as if the word left a curious and not entirely agreeable taste on his tongue.

"Yes," I said.

"Alright then," he said. "I'm sorry."

"For?"

He narrowed his eyes. "For?"

"If you don't admit to the wrongdoing as part of the apology, how will I know you're aware of what you did?" I felt as though I was taunting a leopard, poised and ready to pounce, even as the words left my lips.

The grin that tugged at the corners of his lips was wolfish, the beginnings of the baring of his teeth. "I'm sorry," he said, "for misleading you regarding my motives for taking you out for lunch."

"Thank you," I said. "And now, if you don't mind, I find that any appetite I had has fled." I stood, pushing back my chair. "Enjoy your tea."

I swept past the table while he was still staring at me, confusion and surprise in his widened eyes. I was out the front door before he could form any kind of response.

CHAPTER TEN

My dearest Eleanor, it has been three years since you left, and yet I think of you every day. Not a minute goes by where I do not long to hear your voice in my ear, if only for a moment, a brief respite from this hunger. Where have you gone, and why can I not follow?

O nce back in the Company's building, I headed for Victor's office on the second floor. He was down at the end of a long hallway, his door next to the single window in the exterior wall; when I poked my head in, he was seated at the singular desk in the narrow, closet-sized room.

He looked up almost as soon as I looked in, the pen he had been scratching across the paper in front of him stilling. "Ah, Viv, how was your lunch?"

"The tea was bitter, and the conversation more so," I said, perching on the chair in front of the desk.

"How so?" he asked.

"A fascination with my—abilities," I said, mimicking Lucien's tone and turn of phrase.

"So, not a friendly offer to a peer."

"No," I said sourly. "And peer, what peer?"

He shrugged. "To an employee, then."

"That would be closer," I said. "We're eons away from each other in terms of social standing."

"In terms of manners as well, it would appear," Victor said, his eyes flicking back down to the paper. He scribbled out another sentence. "And what is his reasoning for being in town?"

"Detective Brant will not agree to seek out the warrant we suggested, so he is here to appeal to the Company directly and asked that I make a statement in his favor."

"And his approach to that is to invite you to lunch so he can ask nosey questions?"

"Yes."

"Poor way to go about it."

"Indeed."

The two of us were silent for a time. I sat, half-pouting, across from Victor, watching the pen glide across the paper. "What do you plan on doing now that he's revealed his cards?" he asked.

"With regards to what?"

"Putting a good word in."

I hesitated, weighing my options against the unsettled feeling in my chest, like a hand that reached in to squeeze my lungs shut. "Yes," I said.

"That," Victor said, looking back up from the paper, "is not an answer."

I blinked and shook my head. "I meant, I'll still put the 'good' word in, with the caveat that we not be the ones who assist with it."

Victor set the pen down. "Do you want me to help you compose it?"

"No," I said. "I believe I can string together those sentences on my own."

"How long do you intend to let him sweat on whether he's ruined his chances?"

I stared down at the paper and the curling words etched onto it. "It's his mother."

"So not at all."

"No," I said. "Not at all."

The drawers of his desk squeaked, a grinding kind of protest as he pulled them open, plucked out another piece of paper and a pen, and set them in front of me. "The work always goes more quickly with company," he said. He picked up his own pen and went back to whatever task I had interrupted.

With a sigh, I picked up the pen, the tip hovering over the page.

When Victor and I went home for the evening, I left my letter with the receptionist for delivery to the relevant office. I wasn't sure Lucien would be grateful for the composed words it held, the offering and reasoning with my caveat laid out so clearly on the page. It could very well result in a denial. Truthfully, I was unconcerned about the results, provided I wasn't the one bringing the resolution to him.

The sun was setting by the time Victor dropped me off at my front steps—long shadows crept up the streets and between the buildings—and I hurried inside and locked the door behind me before removing my gloves. My stomach complained loudly all the while.

I chose to satisfy its demands with the leftover soup sitting in my icebox, the light in the kitchen dimming, darkness bleeding in at the edges. I was scraping the last remnants out of the bowl when there was a thump above me.

I paused, my spoon set against the ceramic, and peered up at the ceiling. The seconds stretched as I waited, and I had begun to think I had imagined it when the sound repeated.

I let go of my spoon, the metal clinking as it slid down the side of the bowl and rattling when it hit the bottom. I pushed my chair back from the table and rose, eyes still on the ceiling.

Silence again.

I held still, listening and checking back through the moments since I had returned home. The door had been locked, and the windows at the front were intact. As far as I knew, my house was empty of anyone but me.

The minutes were ticking past, and the quiet itself began to grow, its own form of living. I wasn't sure how long I stood there before I released my hold on the chair, half an eye still on the ceiling, as I picked up my bowl and spoon and washed them off in the kitchen sink, setting them in the rack to dry.

By the time I was done, I had to admit to myself that I was being silly, and the noise had been nothing more than the house settling, those odd creaks and groans as the wood expanded and contracted. Still, I considered taking the fireplace poker upstairs with me, if only as a reassurance that I was armed. Maybe that knowledge would be all I needed to help keep those odd dreams at bay.

I finished cleaning up the kitchen—wiping down the table, counter, and stove—and headed for the parlor, where I plucked up the poker. Its heavy weight dragged my arm down, its metal cold and rough against my palms. I adjusted my grip, hefting it so I could swing it easily, before heading up the stairs to my bedroom.

I had left the little lamp on my bedside table on, its blue glow a pallor cast over the room. Or maybe Victor had unintentionally left it lit the night before when he had retrieved bedding for us. The how didn't matter. For now, I was grateful for its light and that I wasn't left fumbling in the dark.

I shut the door behind me and left it unlocked as I checked through the room, including under the bed and inside the wardrobe. I was the only one here. I turned around to lock the bedroom door, caught movement and a figure out of the corner of my eye, and jumped back into the wardrobe doors.

It was only my reflection in the mirror above the dresser. We stared at each other—or rather, I stared at her—eyes wide, poker clutched to my chest.

There was a ripple across the glass.

I blinked, narrowed my eyes, and stepped toward the mirror, but the surface was still. The only motion there was the movement of my reflection as it repeated my shifting. I walked right up to it, hesitated as I watched myself, and then reached out and touched my hand to the glass.

I blinked, narrowed my eyes, and stepped toward the mirror, but the surface was still, the only motion being my reflection as it repeated my shifting. I walked right up to it, hesitating before I reached out and touched my hand to the glass. It was cool, and I stood there, palm to palm with my own image, and sensed absolutely nothing. I laughed a nervous giggle and pulled my hand away. I was jumping at shadows again; I would have said it wasn't like me, but that would have been a lie.

I locked my bedroom door and debated the most advantageous position for the poker, deciding to place it beneath the pillows of the bed. The ash it left on the sheets would be a pain to clean, but the poker itself wouldn't be visible to anyone who entered the room. That done, I changed into my nightgown, ignoring the gestures and movements of my reflection as they mirrored me, although they caught my eye more than once. I considered digging out one of my shawls and throwing it over the glass to cover it.

But that would be giving in to my silly superstitions. Instead, as a concession to soothe my anxiety, I left the lamp burning when I climbed into bed and pulled the blankets up to my chin.

The room was dark. Either someone had switched my lamp off, or it had burnt out, whatever magic inside it that made it glow used up entirely—something I'd heard occurred only rarely. It was possible I had reached out in my half-asleep state and turned it off myself. Or I was wandering that nightmare dream-scape—the only thing that would explain the presence hovering next to me.

The weight at my back shifted, the soft lilt of some-one's voice as they hummed a song I wasn't familiar with. Their hand brushed down the length of my arm, cool as their fingers slid along my skin and traveled back up, circling the edge of my shoulder before re-peating their path.

They shifted again, their full length pressed against my back, their nose and mouth at the nape of my neck, their breath stirring the strands of hair and raising goosebumps in my flesh.

Their hand came to a stop atop my own, the weight of their arm resting on my body. Their fingers curled, wiggling their way in next to mine so the tips touched the skin of my palm, some mad parody of a grasp-ing hug as their grip tightened. The timbre of their voice deepened, from that humming lilt to a satisfied chuckle as their face lifted; I could track where they moved by their breath as it gusted along my throat, the curve where my neck met my shoulder.

"Vivian," the voice whispered.

It was the first time I had heard them speak in one of these dreams, and I jerked at the same time they bit down.

I lurched, a desperate scramble to drag myself away and free of them, but there was a leg thrust over the top of mine, and it clamped down, their fingers con-stricting, their arm pulling as I kicked and bucked. The bite at my shoulder burned, a venom that ate

its way in along the muscle. It wasn't long before my
movements slowed, limbs too heavy to lift. I was left
gasping and helpless, a whimper lodged in my throat.
The sensation at my shoulder was one I could barely begin to describe—a drawing out like they were
drinking, but I was no cup.

The mouth adjusted its grip, nipping at my flesh as
its lips worked their way up my neck with the light
press of a tongue as if they were savoring the taste of
my skin. It was a strange sense of relief when their
touch retreated, a moment of respite before the nerves
started screaming. The leg and arm released me, but I
was still stuck fast: no amount of demands or attempts
to thrash seemed to rouse my body.

Their fingers began their path up and down my arm
again.

Light streamed directly across my face, and I raised
a hand to block it as I blinked blearily at the room.
My bedroom lamp was still on, its blue glow waning
against the competing luminescence of the sun.

I shoved myself up, fighting against the blankets
tangled about my arms and legs. Once I had freed
myself, I staggered over to the mirror, tugging at the
neckline of my nightgown to expose the curve where
my neck met my shoulder.

There wasn't a single mark in the flesh: no cuts, no
bruises, not even the slightest hint of a scratch. I stood

there, staring at it and my own face, my eyes flicking back and forth, but nothing changed.

I found myself grinning foolishly into the mirror and shook my head, the smile fading away. The last assignments must have gotten to me. It was only my brain trying to make heads or tails of the latest events, and it had combined them into some sort of fever dream that piggy-backed off my recent nightmares into an even more horrific amalgamation. Ghosts, wraiths, whatever name was assigned to it, didn't exist.

Still, I shot a look back at the bed and the side near the window, but what evidence I expected to find, I wasn't sure. Footprints seared into the wood? A handprint on the sheets?

Those kinds of monsters weren't real.

Hopefully, whatever cobwebs had remained would clear, and the nightmares would stop. With a sigh, I stepped back over to the bed, straightened out the bedding, pulled the sheets and blankets tight, and fluffed up the pillows. I chuckled at the poker as I removed it and set it by the door to return to the parlor. I finished making the bed and got dressed for the day.

That done, I hefted the poker, moving out my bedroom door and down the stairs. With a quick stop to place the poker back in its rack, I went into the kitchen for an apple and some cheese.

Another peek out the window showed quickly gathering clouds on the horizon, dark gray and heavy. It seemed winter had decided to put in an early appearance. I grabbed my thick woolen jacket, scarf, and

hat off the stand in the entryway and, now appropriately fed, watered, and bundled up, went out my front
door.

To be entirely honest, I wasn't sure I had ever hurried out of my own home quite that quickly before,
but there was something lingering, a presence that
hovered at my shoulder and managed to stay just out
of sight every time I turned to catch a glimpse of it.

I could keep putting it down as a combination
of things—Lucien's manor, the nightmares that had
started there, a single strange body, a missing woman,
and Lucien's entry into the city—but it felt like something more, and that sense stayed with me the farther
from my house I went.

There were no notes for me at the front desk when I
arrived at the Company's building, and nothing waiting for me in my office when I checked. It left me with
little to do, as Victor hadn't arrived yet. I didn't often
associate with the others that the Company employed.
If anything, I avoided them, and they, in turn, avoided
me, an arrangement we were all satisfied with. I ended
up waiting in Victor's office, staring out the window
as fat snowflakes began drifting downward to gather
on the sill.

It made me hope we wouldn't be called out for any
assignments farther than walking distance. The snow
would make the streets slick if it didn't stick—a hazard
for the carriage and anyone else foolish enough to be

out in this weather—or a challenge for the conveyance to negotiate as the snow began to pile up if the roads were cold enough.

It was too bad no one had yet figured out how to get sleighs to move on their own.

"You're in early," Victor said as he brushed past me, shedding his jacket and scarf to hang them on the coat rack in the corner behind his desk.

"I would hardly say nine o'clock in the morning is early," I said.

He pulled out his chair and settled in, leaning back as he looked at me. "You're looking better." He shifted, pushing aside papers, picking some up and examining their contents, and rooted around in the drawers for a writing instrument.

"I would not say I am," I said.

He paused, looked up to catch my gaze, and set down the papers he had gathered together. "Are you still unwell?"

"No," I said, "not a—sickness."

He waited, eyebrows raised, and the fingers on his desk twitched.

"I keep having these dreams." I halted, the words coming in fits and starts. "They started at Lord LeVerre's manor, and I assumed they would stop once I was no longer sleeping in someone else's bed."

He scratched at his chin, but his gaze didn't waver as he waited for me to continue.

"In them, there's always a—presence at my back, and I can't move. I can feel their hands, their breath, and last night they..." I faltered; the dream was ragged, torn through the middle, and I couldn't be sure what part I was forgetting. "I think they bit me?" The words sounded weak even to my ears, that uncertainty hanging in the air between us.

"They sound like nightmares, to be sure," Victor said slowly. "Are—were there any marks left on you?"

"No."

"Lingering emotions that don't belong to you?"

"No," I repeated. I hesitated before diving forward. "There's no sense of emotion coming from them in the dreams, either. It's completely absent, like they're made of glass."

"Have you ever touched anyone in any of your dreams before?" Victor asked curiously. "When you dream, do you sense emotions from items and people?"

"I—" I blinked, considering his question. "I'm not entirely sure," I admitted. "I think I have, but I can't be certain."

"They sound like mere dreams," Victor said. "I don't want to dismiss any concerns you have, but we've only been home a few days, and he and his house were—odd, to put it politely. Certainly, those might be the kinds of things to roost in someone's mind for a week or so afterward?" He drummed his fingers on the desk. "And with him showing up in town, perhaps that reinforced the association in your mind?"

"Perhaps."

The matter didn't feel entirely settled, even as Victor leaned back in his chair. "Are they nightly?"

"Yes—" I started and then stopped. "No."

"No?" he asked. "Which is it?"

"No," I said. "They didn't happen when we camped out in the parlor."

"Maybe you just need a change of scenery?" Victor suggested. "Switch bedrooms for a few nights; see if they leave."

I wrinkled my nose and stared at him. "Are you seriously suggesting I move back and forth between rooms to try to 'cure' myself of nightmares?"

"If it works," he said. "Or maybe strip your mattress and pillows and take everything over to the laundress to be cleaned? Maybe something from the house followed you home and is infecting everything."

"Emotions don't jump from item to item," I said with a sniff.

"But maybe your exposure to whatever it is has infected you," he said, half-teasing. "Maybe you accidentally packed up a handkerchief or some other item that belonged to the previous occupant of the bedroom you stayed in, and now you keep managing to brush up against it."

"Oh," I said.

"Oh?" he said. "Have I hit upon something with my wild theories?"

"There was a hand mirror; it's sitting on my dresser. It didn't look familiar, even though it matched the interior wood of the trunk." I paused, thinking back. "But it didn't have any emotions attached to it."

"You said the same about his mother's desk." He leaned forward, one elbow up on the desk. "Maybe you had already taken ill, and it affected your abilities?"

I sat back, rubbing one finger back and forth on the worn seam of my glove. "I can't say that's not a possibility," I grumbled. "The only other times I've been ill, I was a child; I would have been surrounded by familiar people and emotions. I don't know that I would have noticed if something was blank."

"The mirror was fully blank?"

"No," I said. "The sense of whoever made it was still there. The same with her desk."

"Like your power skipped past the more recent emotions?"

"Yes."

"You could try picking up the mirror tonight," he suggested. "After you return home and see if anything has changed." He paused, brows knitted. "Not changed; I don't think that's the word I meant."

"Returned?" I suggested.

"Closer," he said. "We can go with that, although I doubt the emotions would have been absent to start with."

There were footsteps hurrying their way down the hall, the clacking of hard-soled shoes. We shifted so we could watch the door, and the messenger who popped his head in—his hair disheveled, a cheerful grin on his face—had an envelope in his hand. He held it out toward me. "Assignment for the Tailors."

I took the envelope from him, the paper sliding across my palm, a corner sticking in the threads of my glove. The messenger disappeared back out the door while I pulled out the folded paper it contained.

"Well?" Victor asked. "Where are we being summoned?"

"Berkley Street," I said, scanning the page.
"For?"
I sighed. "A murder."
Victor groaned as he rose from his chair and pulled his jacket and scarf free of the rack they were hanging on. "Those seem to be uncommonly common recently."

My hopes for a nearby assignment were dashed with the street name emblazoned in black ink across white paper. The location necessitated that we huddle on the seats of Victor's carriage and let it lumber its way across the city, down toward the river.

Mud River was what the people situated along this section called it, in complete disregard for its given name. Despite the pristine snow gathering on the roofs, the sidewalks, streets, and down at the banks and the water itself, it was stained a rusty brown, the color of the earth leaching into the wintry blanket created by the swiftly falling flurries. The building—for lack of a better word to call the sagging, drunkenly-leaning structure I found myself peering out the carriage window at—was as gray as the clouds hovering above us.

Victor joined me at the window, his shoulder bumping against mine, our breath frosting the glass as we examined what I assumed was the front door. A single policeman slouched beside the gaping hole in the wall, jiggling his legs one at a time as he glanced down the street at our carriage.

"Come on, then," Victor said. "We'll hardly get this done and over with by sitting here." He shoved the carriage door open and practically slithered out to land on the snowy sidewalk. He grabbed at the frame, paused, and then gingerly stepped back and held his hand out toward me. "You'll want to be careful; it's already icing the streets."

I slipped my hand into his and braced myself on the frame as I set my feet on the pavement. The ground beneath my soles was slick despite the gathering snow, and Victor and I had to watch each step as we headed for the entrance.

The officer didn't pause his shifting, but gave a quick nod in our direction. "Tailors."

"Ben," Victor said. "I don't think we need to stand on formality."

Ben gave us a grin that was more of a grimace. "Unlike you, I'm on the clock; formality is par for the course."

"Who are we dealing with today?" Victor asked.

"Flannegan," Ben said. "You'd best hurry. He doesn't like waiting, and he's already irritated."

"I don't see how that's our problem," I muttered but followed Victor through the front door and past its crumbling frame.

"Be nice if we could get murders done in a building with heat," Victor said.

"It would be far more pleasant," I agreed.

There was a small grouping of officers inside, hovering outside of a room just off the foyer. With how quickly they moved out of our way, I began to suspect Flannegan had quite the reputation.

I stepped past Victor and was the first through the door to find the man in question.

He was tall—long and lean—and I imagined that his stride when he walked would be loping, like that of a greyhound. The room itself was dim enough—even with no curtains on the windows—that his hair and eyes could only be described as brown; without the light required, I couldn't pull out any of the shades or tones. I cast a glance at the rest of the room and pulled my eyes away from the wall and the cracked, pitted mirror that hung there and reflected back our dark shapes as if we were wraiths and not living beings.

"You the Tailors?" he barked before I could get more than two steps into what I assumed was the parlor.

"Yes," Victor said.

"Good." Flannegan moved to the side, exposing the body sprawled across the empty floor behind him. He motioned a hand at it. "Tell me what killed him."

"It doesn't quite work like that," Victor said slowly.

"Then how does it work?" The impatient bite to Flannegan's voice increased; something buried beneath it sounded like the longer this took, the closer the man was to breaking. Whether that crack would be tears of grief or a tantrum over being denied, I wasn't entirely sure.

"I might be able to tell you the murder weapon or even the murderer," I said, moving forward, the hem of my skirts whispering over the wood floor, which creaked with every step. "But like all things in life, there are no guarantees." I knelt by the corpse, fabric puddling around me, and pulled off one of my gloves.

My breath was ice in the air, achingly sharp, and I hesitated, my hand hovering over the torso, and I shot a glance at their face. Their eyes were closed, strands of hair swept across their brow; I was tempted to smooth them back, away from the waxy pale skin, until I spotted the dark purple mottling of their flesh that had settled in the skin along the back of the jaw and sides of their throat.

I set my palm flat against their chest.

It was a roar in my ears, a scream that left me blinded as much as I was deafened, a shock to my system. I jerked my hand back, blinking as I waited for my sight to clear from the red that had washed its way through it.

"Well?" Flannegan said before I had a chance to recover.

"He was—aware at the time that he died," I said slowly. I was still waiting for the rage to subside, surprised by the lack of cushioning distance the emotions of the dead usually held.

Perhaps his death had been too recent for that to take effect.

"And?" Flannegan demanded. "Who killed him?"

I swallowed back against the stuttering breath in my lungs, the knowledge that I would have to endure the man's experience with death once again. "I don't know yet," I said, and this time, reached for the exposed skin of the corpse's throat, just beneath his chin.

The rage slammed back into me and left me reeling, drowning as it tossed me amongst its waves. I tried to swim down past it, to sink ever deeper to try to make sense of why this anger so consumed him that it swept away everything else. I could feel the edge of it, a yawning void, and when I touched it—

There was nothing.

He was drained of everything, of a life lived, of the emotions and moments that made up a person and all that they were. All that was left was that unending rage frozen in time.

I pulled my hand back and sat there with bile rising in my throat.

"Viv?" Victor's voice broke through the fog that had gathered across my mind.

"Who killed him?" Flannegan repeated.

"I don't know," I said.

"How can you not know?" he snapped. "The body is right there, and you're a soul reader. Read the thrice-damned thing!"

"I did," I said. Victor shifted to step between Flannegan and me. My voice sounded reedy and unsure, my balance still unsteady.

"Detective," Victor said calmly. "I urge you to remember yourself. You were informed at the start that my sister's abilities are not infallible."

I had to peer around Victor's legs to catch a glimpse of Flannegan's face. His expression seemed to struggle between a serene countenance and the distinct irritation that kept flickering to the surface.

"Explain, please," he said. I could hear the bite in his tone that told me he was fighting to keep his voice

pleasant. In truth, he sounded as if he would've preferred to grab me by the arms and shake the answers
out of me.

I motioned at the body. "The only thing left for me
to find is his anger. Everything else is—gone."

"Gone?" he said dumbly.

"Gone?" Victor asked sharply as he turned to face
me.

"Gone," I repeated.

He shot a quick glance at Flannegan, who was far
more eagle-eyed than we had realized.

"What does that mean?" Flannegan asked. "What is
everything?" He was looking back and forth between
Victor and me with narrowed eyes.

I sat back on my heels, reluctant to rise, as if it would
further raise the man's ire. "It means there's nothing
there to find. His rage—" I paused, still tasting it on
my tongue: salt, iron, and blood. "It's as if his anger
at the time he died burned out all other thoughts, all
other emotions and memories..."

It was Flannegan's turn to hesitate as he took in precisely what I was saying. "Is this a common occurrence
in these cases?"

"No," I said, and because it would hold no value
for me to keep it back and could in fact impede the
investigation, such as it was, into this man's death,
"I've never seen anyone's—existence—subsumed in
this way before."

"So what—what do we do?" Flannegan's voice
had diminished—the tone, the force, gone out like
a candle. "He has a daughter; she's missing. I

thought—you can't tell me if she was the one who did it?"

Victor picked up on the undercurrent of his words before I could. "Who is she to you?" he asked sharply.

"My fiancée," Flannegan whispered. "She works the desk at the station and didn't report in this morning. Her father has—has had some trouble recently, and had only just relocated to this...house. It was the first place I thought to check after her own home." His voice strengthened with each word, the panic, and bluster from before heightening as he spoke. "There has to be something here you can read!"

I hadn't realized there was anyone on the force who had come to view those of us who worked at the Company as somehow holding all the answers, the one guarantee in cases like these with a room void of any and all other evidence.

I looked around at the nearly empty space, the moldering furniture, and the walls. "Take him to the morgue," was all I said.

CHAPTER ELEVEN

Policy 00589641LFSO Claim Number 1659-DE
Client has been advised in writing that the investigation is a closed matter and will not be re-
opened.

The ride back to our offices had been quiet, both
Victor and I engrossed in whatever thoughts we
had, and by the time we reached the building, the
snow was thickening on the ground and crept up over
our toes when we alighted from the carriage.

It was a relief to enter through the Company's front
door and into the enveloping warmth, although the
silence wasn't any less stifling. The receptionist at the
desk barely glanced at us, and we said nothing to her
as we slipped past and up to Victor's office.

We both settled in our seats, and Victor pulled out
one of the creaking drawers at the bottom of his desk,
retrieving both two empty glasses and a decanter nearly full to the stopper with whiskey.

He set them on the surface with a thumping clink,
pulled the stopper free, and poured us both a serving
without saying a single word before pushing one of
the cups toward me.

"Why do you even have that?" I asked.

"It was a gift from Morris," he said. "And it was one of those things I intended to give away myself and just never got around to doing so."

"We never drink," I said.

"This feels distinctly like the time to bend, or even break, such a rule."

I stared at the amber liquid, and in it all I could see were Lucien's eyes.

"Any visions?" I asked. I needed something to break the almost soundless existence we seemed to have found ourselves in.

"No," he said. "And I find myself in the odd position of fearing what kind of information one would impart."

"It couldn't be any worse than what I've come upon so far today, could it?" I said. I tried to keep the words light, but they fell flat. I could almost see them, splayed out across the wood like the bodies from the past two days, and Lucien between them.

The chuckle he gave me was wan. "I would certainly hope not."

I picked up the whiskey and took a sip: smoke and oak. It was too smooth and didn't impart the burn down my throat that I had been hoping for. Perhaps I would need gin for that.

Victor picked up his own glass, cradling it in his palm as he stared at the swirling liquid. "I think that we have a problem."

I took another sip. If anything, I wasn't going to let quality liquor go to waste, although perhaps Victor would finish my glass as well as his. "And what problem would that be?" I asked. The whiskey was already warming my stomach, and if I kept drinking, it would spread through my head and limbs as well.

"Either we have something strange and unprecedented going on, or your recent illness has had a more lingering and possibly permanent effect on your abilities."

I gave him a half-smile; it felt pasted on. "Which of those is the simplest explanation?"

"It doesn't feel like either of them would be the simplest," he said and took a sip of his whiskey. He set the glass back down, leaning forward. "There was nothing else there?"

"Nothing," I said.

"I don't understand how that's possible," he muttered.

"I believe that's where we're both floundering."

He sighed and rubbed at his forehead. "We'll have to write it up in the report."

There was an unsettled chill at the base of my spine, something that worked its way up my back and surprised me with its strength. "Will they retire me?"

"For one instance?" Victor said and shifted, searching his drawers for the correct form before setting it on the desk and pulling out a pen as well. "Unlikely. They'll want to wait and see if the trend continues before they present you with a severance." He stared down at the page as if the words already printed there were a mystery to him. "I'll be at this report all night, certainly. How much have you saved up?"

"Enough that this would be a stumbling block," I said. "I've already got my eye on a little storefront. The hard part would be finding providers and an employee. And customers."

"And the first year," Victor said.

"And the first year," I conceded.

"We can't know that no one else has encountered something like this before," he cautioned. "So we could be bracing ourselves for the wrong outcome."

"The other outcome seems to be I stay employed for quite a bit longer," I said. I set my glass down and got to my feet. "Write up your report and what will be will be."

The bravado I displayed for Victor didn't take long to slip away, already melting by the time I reached the first floor and headed out the front.

It didn't help my mood when I pulled the heavy wood door open to be confronted by Lucien standing on the steps, his hand still extended toward the knob, blinking owlishly up at me, snow sitting on his shoulders and melting against his hair.

"Why on earth aren't you wearing a hat in this weather?" were the words that popped out of my mouth.

Confusion rippled across his face, then realization and a timid smile pulled at the corners of his lips. "You don't appear to be in possession of a hat yourself, so I could ask you the same question."

I snorted and shoved past him, shutting the door behind me with a bang. He was forced to skip to the side and down a step to keep from being pushed. "*I*," I said, "at least arrived at work this morning *before* the weather took a turn. What's your excuse?" I had left my hat hanging in Victor's office, a causality of my own distraction.

"I believe I owe you thanks," he said. "As the Company contacted me this morning to let me know my plea and case were under review."

I paused and half-turned to face him, irritation bubbling under my skin. "That was unusually swift of them."

"Do they not often act quickly on these kinds of requests?" he asked. The words sounded innocent enough, but beneath them was something knowing.

"Not within a day," I said. "I expected there to be at least a week before they said anything about the submission in the first place." I turned away from him and started down the sidewalk. The snow had continued to thicken its blanket while I had been inside, and while I would not say it was much, it was still higher than the toe-deep carpet that had already existed. The walk home was going to be a slog.

Lucien fell into step beside me. "Where are you headed?"

"To dinner," I lied. I would not chance leading this man to my home.

"Alone?"

"I find I prefer it that way," I said.

"Do you truly?" he asked, and it had the air of honest curiosity to it.

"Yes," I said. "Why?"

He slipped his hands into his pockets, shoulders hunched up, and he blew out a puff of air; a small white cloud quickly dispersed. "I just rarely see you without your brother and thought perhaps it would continue to be the same here."

"We were at your home for an assignment," I reminded him. "What other company would I seek out?"

There was snow still catching in his hair, glittering as it stuck to the strands. Flakes of it were brushing past my own cheeks, and I was sure it was settling on my shoulders.

He glanced upward, eyeing the sky. "This storm is only going to get worse."

I started walking. "Then perhaps we should both head to our respective homes before it does."

He fell into step beside me. "At least let me escort you to your house to make sure you've arrived safely."

"I'm quite capable of handling a walk," I said.

"I'm sure you are," he said. "But I can't in good conscience just let you walk away into a snowstorm and risk losing your way."

"And if we both lose our way?"

"Then I shall have died gallantly."

I shot him a look through narrowed eyes, but in the dimming light and the strengthening flurries, I couldn't be sure if he was mocking me.

"Fine," I said, packing as much of my misgivings into that single word as I could. "But who exactly will escort you to your place of residence to ensure you don't lose your own way once you no longer have me to guide you?"

"I've retained a carriage," he said.

I stopped, turning to face him. "You have a carriage."

"I do."

"Then why are you walking?"

"You insisted on doing so."

"You are mocking me," I said flatly.

"I would have thought that perhaps more, I am indulging you," he said. He stepped in toward me, and had I been sure of my footing, I would have taken a step back to reopen the space between us. "You do not—trust me."

"No."

"I can't blame you for that."

"I certainly hope you wouldn't since it would only strengthen the reasoning for it."

The words caused the flicker of a smile, something amused without the predatory baring of his teeth. "I've been told by some that I tend to be—intense once I've become comfortable around certain people. That I stop toeing the line of holding back in polite society."

"I wouldn't say they're wrong."

"Is that the impression you get of me, Miss Tailor?"

"Yes," I said.

He was standing barely a hair's breadth from me, and it forced me to tilt my head back to keep my gaze fastened on his eyes.

They were the only thing of color in this gray and white landscape.

A door slammed shut somewhere, the bang echoing, a sound without source. Lucien looked away from me, head turning as he searched both sides of the street.

I eased away from him and started on my path down the sidewalk.

He caught up to me shortly, kicking sprays of snow up as he fell into step beside me.

"I can make it on my own, truly," I said. "It's a straight shot down the block for me, and I'll be home before your conveyance can trundle its way halfway up the road."

I had lied about the general location and now looked for anything to convince him to leave and let me continue unaccompanied. Especially as the streets were beginning to empty of any of the last stragglers. Victor would likely be spending the night within the Company's walls rather than brave the cold when he finally finished his report, and I had already begun to seriously consider turning around and heading back inside those hallowed halls.

"I would be remiss," Lucien said, "if I let someone who has already done so much for me walk home alone in a snowstorm. At least let me escort you halfway."

I scowled, picking through his words, wary that this was only another attempt to ask me questions to assuage his curiosity. Still, the expression on his face was contrite geniality, and I could not bring myself to argue with him on the subject any further. In truth, I was not entirely sure I wanted to dismiss him.

"Alright then," I said. "Halfway only."

He smiled at me with a gleam to his eyes that had me considering if I should take back my words, but he cocked his elbow up and out, the very picture of a perfect gentleman despite the coy upward turn of his lips. A sly grin that seemed to say I had given him exactly what he wanted before it slipped away, and it was merely Lucien again.

I hesitated before I hooked my arm around his, and he gently tugged me forward. I had never walked arm-in-arm like this before, my steps unsure until I realized he was matching his gait to mine and my own pace smoothed out.

"Where is halfway to your home?" he asked after several minutes. Our breath puffed out white smoke into the air.

I glanced up the street and found a spot that seemed a reasonable distance away, short enough that I would only have to endure his close presence for mere moments more, although I found a part of me loath to relinquish my grip on his arm. The limb was steady, strong beneath my fingers where the brown leather of my glove rested against the dark wool of his coat. I wasn't quite sure what I had been expecting, as if I was shocked to find other people just as solid as I was.

"The end of the block there," I said.

"Truly, you don't live far from where you work," he said.

I had no response that wouldn't result in further lies, so I chose not to comment.

It didn't take us long to reach the corner I had indicated, and here we paused, our arms still entwined, before I released my hold.

He caught my hand with his.

The press of his fingers to mine was surprisingly tight, the implication of a vise, a contrast to the
warmth of his palm leaking through the fabric of our
gloves. "Miss Tailor—"

"I can make my own way from here," I said.

He dropped his hand, and I had to resist the urge
to rub at my fingers to remove the lingering heat he
had left behind. He hesitated a moment longer, his
russet eyes a deeper shade in the gathering dark. "Are
you certain?" he asked.

"Quite. It isn't far."

He nodded. "If you're sure." He reached up as if to
tip his hat to me, his hand stalling on the way, and this
time, the smile on his face was sheepish. "Miss Tailor, always a pleasure." He turned and walked away,
quickly swallowed up by the falling snow.

I started back in the direction of my house, the snow
crunching beneath my boots. At this point, the streets
might as well have been deserted for all the people I
spotted through the thickening gloom. Once I had
gone up the sidewalk, I paused long enough to glance
around and listen, but there was no creak of rumbling
wheels or shadowy shapes, so I turned the corner instead of continuing straight. I huddled in on myself as
I walked, my shoulders up by my ears, peering about
as if I expected Lucien to pop out of a snow bank or
from behind a set of stairs.

No such thing happened, and I reached the steps
leading up to my front door without incident.

Perhaps Lucien and I were a pair, the only two mad
enough to go out into the snow without adequate

protection from the cold. Anyone else I had seen had been so bundled up that only their eyes were exposed.

It took me a moment to unlock the door, brushing snow away from my face and the lock, the flakes sticking to the metal and wood, and I slipped inside into warmth and darkness. I took the time to light the lamps, the blue glow that accompanied them adding a chill to the rooms. By the time I was done with a hurried supper and peered back out the window, I guessed we would have a foot of snow by morning. I moved to my parlor and poked around at the books I had on the shelves but could not find one to select and read. A restless kind of energy crawled along my spine and through my limbs, the need to be moving when I had nowhere to go. It seemed I would be best served by going to bed rather than fretting away.

When I reached my room, I found the bedside lamp already on.

I frowned, hesitating in the doorway, sure I had turned it off that morning. I stepped forward and headed for the light, intent on clicking it on and off to see if anything was wrong with its operation.

I caught movement in the corner of my eye, and I turned.

But the only thing I saw was the mirror and the edge of my reflection. I had expected to see something over by the wall and the window with the way I was facing, but there was nothing there.

I changed course, edging along the bottom of my bed, intending to check down the side closest to the curtains. Maybe a bird had come down one of the

chimneys in search of shelter from the storm and gotten stuck in the house.

Another flash of movement caught my attention,
and I looked up, expecting to see only my reflection
staring back at me.

The woman in the mirror was someone else entirely.

I squeaked and stepped back, my legs hit the corner
of the bed, and my balance tipped.

I didn't fall; rather, I gracelessly collapsed into a sitting position, caught by the bed. By the time I looked
back at the mirror—less than a minute in full—the
other woman was gone, and all I could see was my
wide-eyed image, poised for flight.

I spent the night in the parlor, too unsettled to return
upstairs and chance more dreams. Not only had I
thrown a shawl up over the mirror to cover the glass,
but I had locked my bedroom door behind me, gathered pillows and blankets from another room, taken
those downstairs to the couch, and locked the parlor
door as well. I left the lamps and the fire burning all
night, so any time I woke, I was surrounded by light.

By the time morning dawned, I was bleary-eyed and
exhausted from constantly jerking awake, expecting
to hear footsteps above me. That I had slept in my
clothes from the previous day had not helped; with
every shift, the fabric seemed to rub and strain in ways
entirely unexpected.

Nothing else had occurred, and with the sun peeking over the horizon, casting a dazzling light that bounced off the white world outside, I had to admit I was letting the nightmares and my own fears get to me.

With a groan, I shoved the blankets off my legs and got to my feet, staggering over to the window to peer out. It certainly looked as though I had been correct: the snow was piled up at least a foot deep. The world outside my house was still—buildings frosted in silver, little tendrils of smoke curling upwards from the chimneys. Likely, no one would brave the streets until noon, when the day was already as warm and bright as it was going to get.

I still needed to dress for the day, as there was always the chance that the Company would send a messenger. Their doors were never closed—the desk at the front was always manned—and I wouldn't be surprised if they did, in fact, have at least one employee who never left but haunted those halls day and night.

I bet it was Katherine.

I moved away from the window, unlocked the parlor door, and peeked into my foyer. It was empty, as were the stairs leading up to the second floor, both brilliantly lit by the light streaming in from the outside world. I eased out of the parlor, leaving the door gaping as I headed to my bedroom. It was dimmer up there; the windows were only in the two bedrooms and the bathroom, with none in the hall. But the doors to the second bedroom and the bathroom were open, letting the sun from their space creep into this one.

I unlocked my bedroom door, and my hand lingered on the knob, the metal cold under my fingers—almost icy as if it was instead made of glass, empty and devoid of feeling, even my own. I shook my head at the fancy—I was letting strange cases affect even my waking moments—and I shoved the door open.

My bedroom was as brightly lit as the rooms downstairs were, the lamp left burning on the bedside table a flicker in comparison to the sunlight. Nothing had been moved; the bed was neatly made up, and the nightgown laid across the blanket was still wrinkled from where I had sat on it. I lingered at the threshold, studying the room until I was certain I wasn't stepping into some form of trap, although the logical side of my mind seemed to huff and puff, demanding to know what kind of trap a trick of the light with my mirror could possibly set.

It was a reflection and nothing more.

Still, my room now felt strangely akin to Lucien and his lion's den, and if I broke that invisible line and stepped inside, there would be no going back from whatever it was that we had unwittingly unleashed.

"Humbug," I said—more a whisper than a statement—as if the words would banish the sensation of a yawning pit before me. I stepped through the door and froze just inside the room, waiting with drawn breath, and when nothing occurred, I let it out, a long sigh that sagged with my shoulders. I moved over to the wardrobe and selected clothing for the day: a shirt and skirt in bright colors that would stand out amidst the snow, a scarlet hue against the white.

I snuck a glance at the mirror.

The shawl had slipped at some point in the night, and while not unexpected, was why my hands stuttered to a stop. My fingers fiddled with the fabric of my shirt and jacket as I tried to watch the glass. The majority of the mirror was still covered by the woven garment, but what portion was exposed reflected only the room, nothing more.

I yanked the remainder of my jacket free and hustled from the room, pulling the door shut behind me. I didn't hear the latch catch but continued toward the front bedroom. I laid my clothes out on the bed, then went to the bathroom to freshen up before I dressed for the day.

The first floor felt safer—an oasis in a desert—as I stepped into the kitchen. The light here was brighter, and the space felt wider, less stifling, without the looming sensation of something gathering. Still, I glanced at the ceiling and waited silently, half-expecting to hear footsteps. When I didn't, I went back to cooking breakfast. The longer the day went with no events, the more sure I was that I had to have been imagining the whole thing. Apparitions and hauntings aren't real, and the only monsters that exist are people.

When finally the sun began to set, bleeding orange into the snow and creating streaks of pink in the sky that shot through the gray clouds, I was certain I would sleep in my own room for the night. I wasn't going to let nightmares and an overactive imagination rule what I did in my own home.

I gathered the blankets and pillows left on the couch and returned them to my extra bedroom. I spent additional time fussing over their placement in the wardrobe, then lingered in the hallway once I was done, a reluctance to head into my room that was at odds with my thoughts.

I pushed past the still-open door. I would not have had the fortitude to do so had it not been for the glow of the bedside lamp; its light was the one thing that convinced me nothing in the room had changed.

The first thing I did was check the mirror: the shawl was still in the same position. I stepped up to it to pull the fabric farther over the glass, and the flash of movement I saw reflected back at me was lower than my arm.

I froze in place, torn between my desire to re-move the shawl entirely and to hastily finish covering the mirror before beating a healthy retreat down the stairs. My heartbeat was in my ears, the blood rushing in my veins equally as loud, and my breath rasped and caught in my throat as I hesitated, vacillating between the two.

I yanked the fabric free. It slithered off the glass and wood frame to land in a heap atop the dresser.

The mirror was empty, but for me.

I laughed, light-headed at first before it felt as though all sensation spilled out of me and left only cold exhaustion in its wake.

I took the time to cover the mirror again and then went to bed.

There was a burning in my wrist, a draw from my flesh, a sense of relief as something sharp slid free of the limb, then the feel of lips pressed gently to the skin. Above me, a voice hummed the melody of a song I didn't know.

I could see our shapes reflected back at us, dark smears in shadowed glass, and a pair of russet eyes.

Morning saw me fighting my way down the somewhat passable sidewalks. The workers in the city had been busy, creating trough-like pathways through the snow, and in the larger fairways, they had cleared the pavement entirely.

Once out my front door, the chill bit at my nose, cheeks, and ears, in spite of the scarf and hat I had with me. I headed for the Company, my skirts brushing against the snow and leaving a trail of dustings that tumbled down beneath my feet. When I reached our employer's street, the sidewalks were even emptier—barely any flurries were left trapped between the cracks in the pavement, the whole surface swept as clean as one could hope for.

I shook off my skirts once I reached the front steps, a vague attempt to brush off the gathered snow so it wouldn't leave the wet spots on the cloth. All I really succeeded in doing was getting snow stuck to my gloves.

The receptionist was not at her usual post. Instead, it appeared I'd arrived early enough to have come upon the changing of the guard, with one receptionist gathering up her jacket and scarf and the other hanging her items up on the coat rack placed discreetly in the corner beyond the desk. There was a chorus of good mornings before the first disappeared out the door into the cold, and the second took her seat at the desk. I moved past her into the hallway, and up to Victor's office.

His desk was littered with crumpled pieces of paper, but the whiskey decanter and glasses from the other night were gone. My hat from the previous day was still hanging forlornly on the coat rack.

The man himself was absent.

I hovered in the doorway, wondering if I should try searching for him throughout the building or if I should leave him a note for when he returned. The thought that there may be an official letter of release from employment waiting for me on my desk stayed my hand.

"Did you enjoy your snow day?"

I jumped, my heart tripping over itself even when I found myself face to face with my brother. There were dark circles under his eyes, and the lines on his face looked as though he had fallen asleep at his desk, and the paper had left impressions in the skin. But he had a smile for me.

"As much as one can when one doesn't leave the house for its entirety," I said.

He motioned at the doorway. "Were you coming to see me?"

Belatedly, I slipped inside and he followed, the two of us taking seats before either one of us spoke again.

"Did you turn in your report?"

"Yes," he said, leaning forward and poking through the balls of paper on his desk before gathering them together and sweeping them off the surface into a nearby trash can. "They are in fact, taking it as a serious matter and are assigning a second soul reader to examine the body and verify what you sensed."

I sagged back against my seat, a puppet whose strings had been cut. "So I still remain an employee?"

"Yes," he said. "They did ask that we take a trip to the morgue for you to perform your own second reading as well, with the hope that continued exposure to the body would trigger a vision for me."

"Do you think it will?"

He shook his head. "Your guess is as good as mine. They come and go as they please, when they please, how they please."

"If they please."

"That too."

We were quiet as Victor continued fussing with his desk, straightening any papers he had not used and lining his pens up neatly in a row.

"Have you been home yet?" I asked, studying the wrinkles in his shirt and vest.

"No," he said. "I did, rather embarrassingly, spend the last two nights here. The first was to complete my report, and the second was because the snow was piled rather high, and I preferred not to face the cold."

He shifted one of the pens, rolling it back and forth. "Have you had any more nightmares?"

"Maybe the vague sensation of one last night," I said. My wrist itched, and I pushed a finger under the edge of my glove to rub at the spot. "I spent the night previous to last sleeping in the parlor, and that seems to have broken whatever hold they had on me." I laughed, a wan sort of chuckle. "I thought I saw someone in my mirror, and that was what drove me to change rooms. So paranoid and affected I couldn't recognize my own reflection."

Victor's own laugh was just as pale as mine. "So those are back, are they?"

"What are back?"

He made a vague motion toward the wall behind me. "You used to have those kinds of nightmares when we were young. You would wake me and Mother in tears, claiming there was someone watching you from the mirror in your room."

"Oh," I said. "I don't recall those."

"I'm not surprised," he said. "You were always still half-asleep, stumbling over your own two feet when you would come climbing into my bed. I only remember your words because your fear would wake me fully."

"You've always been a light sleeper."

"And it didn't happen often enough that it seemed like anything at all." He drummed his fingers on the desk. "There must have been something about Lord LeVerre's manor that brought them back."

"Perhaps it was all the dust," I said, aiming for humor, but it felt flat.

"Perhaps," he said. "I think it was more his aversion to light." He sighed, groaning as he climbed to his feet. "Come on, then. We should head to the morgue while we know it won't be busy."

"Is there ever a rush there?" I asked, but followed his example. "Did you want to stop at your apartment first for a change of clothes and a chance to freshen up?"

He grimaced, brow furrowed. "To be honest, I'd rather not take the time for that until after we've fulfilled our duties. I'll want a change immediately following our exiting the morgue, so it makes no sense to do it before."

CHAPTER TWELVE

File V-2338
Item C: Recovered from scene: one nickel-plated
pocket watch and chain. Metal is unadorned.

Our ride over to the morgue was spent in relative discomfort, with that ever-present spring pressing up against me no matter how much I adjusted my seat. Eventually, Victor begged me to sit still as my constant shifting was driving him mad.

The morgue itself was a massive building, built more like a warehouse. As it housed dead bodies both for investigations—criminal or otherwise—and for those without the funds for their departed's final arrangements, a large footprint was required.

The morgue's façade was an intimidating sight—heavy columns, copper-green with age and exposure, and similarly solid and patinated door, although Victor seemed to have no trouble pulling it open. We entered the cavernous lobby, our footsteps echoing along marble floors and walls, a tan shot through with streaks of white.

Shouting voices bounced off the surfaces, growing louder as they drew nearer.

"I don't care if you throw the tools in a fire until they glow red; find a way to sterilize them! Drown them in gin for all I care. Just do it!"

The voice's owner rounded the corner looking, in the purest meaning of the word, frazzled—hair sticking on end as if he had run his fingers through it repeatedly. He spouted rapid-fire instructions to the aide trotting along behind him. "This will spread; it will spread to every corpse it can. Burn the body in question, *but don't touch it with bare hands*. Anything it touches needs to go in the fire too—yes, even your clothes. Don't give me that look, young man. We could *lose* any and all evidence, and the smell, gods above help me, the smell. Open the windows, turn on the fans, and tell anyone who complains about the cold to see me." He paused in his tirade when he spotted us, and his assistant took the opportunity to turn tail and run. "John! John, I wasn't—for shit's sake," the man swore, turning back to us. "Can I *help* you?" he demanded, each word sounding more and more aggrieved.

"Vivian and Victor Tailor, from the Company," Victor said. "We've been sent to examine a body that was brought in yesterday?"

"Oh, oh, yes, yes, right this way." The man turned and headed back down the hall, and Victor and I were forced to hurry after him to keep up. "I apologize for the lack of greeting. We have a case of tissue gas, and if we don't resolve it immediately, it will spread to the other bodies." He hesitated, his pace slowing as he checked the doors we passed. "I do hope—ah, here we are, no, the one they sent you for isn't infected.

If it was..." he laughed—an uncomfortable, tight and short chuckle. "Well, fortunately we don't have to worry about the *was*."

He ducked in through the doorframe to Exam Room 17, according to the plaque on the door.

The back wall of the room looked similar to a librarian's card catalog. Large, square doors of gleaming, white-coated metal that looked more like porcelain took up the majority of the space: two drawers high and six across. Rectangular sea-green glass tiles covered the walls, and the floor was more of the tan and white marble from the entrance. With no windows to let in natural light, the blue glow of the lamps on the walls and in the ceiling gave the whole affair the feeling of being underwater.

We swept past the white-coated embalming tables. Their edges were lipped with a channel that led to a hole, directing whatever various liquids they encountered to flow toward drains in the floor.

The man counted down the rows, checking the numbers affixed to the front of each cabinet and muttering under his breath before he found the one he wanted. He pulled at the handle, backing up as the drawer opened with the click-clack of wheels on rails to reveal the victim from the previous day. I did not yet see any further bloating or discoloration from my position, although I was reluctant to step any closer.

"Well?" our guide said. "Come examine him; I don't want the drawer open too long." He tapped the tiled wall above the corpse. "The compartments are chilled to keep the bodies from decomposing before we can examine them. So the sooner I can shut the door, the better."

I edged past the tables and up to the drawer. Victor followed silently at first, but his steps behind me faltered. I twisted to face him—his hand was pressed to his chest, his jaw clenched as he scowled at the floor. He waved me off before I could speak.

"It's just the dust," he said.

"Dust?" our guide asked. "Unlikely. We pride ourselves on the cleanliness of our facilities."

The glare on Victor's face faded away as he straightened. Only the relief in his expression kept me from snapping at the other man for breaking the tenuous hold Victor's visions held on him.

"Check the victim please, Viv," Victor said. I turned toward the drawer as I tugged my glove off and stared down at the body, trying to decide where best to place my hand.

Other than a sheet covering his modesty, the body was nude, and looked as close to alive as one could get. I saw no additional mottling of the flesh beyond *livor mortis*—no other signs of further damage.

I pressed my palm to his bare chest.

I was swamped with his rage. It coated my tongue and spilled its way down my throat until it choked off my breath, painting my own vision scarlet. There was a hand on my own shoulder, the tips of something as sharp as knives sliding up towards my neck.

I gasped and yanked my hand back, staggered away from the body, and would have fallen if not for Victor. My hand was curled at my chest, as if I could press down on my heart and still its frantic beating.

"Is it still the rage?" he asked.

"Yes," I said. "The rage and something else."

Victor shifted. I faltered, and he paused long enough to steady me before he released his grip.

The clacking of wheels distracted me from my thoughts, and the way they chased each other around in my head. Our guide had shut the drawer. "I take it you two can find your way to the exit?" he asked. "I have to be sure my aide is handling our situation the way I ordered him to."

"Yes," Victor said, and the man didn't wait a second longer. He left the exam room with us still standing there.

Victor waited a long beat, his eyes on the door, before he leaned in toward me. "What's the something else?"

"I think he—" I couldn't shake the feel of steel on my throat, pinpricks that reminded me of teeth. What could I tell Victor that would come out sounding sane? That my nightmares had threaded their way into my every waking moment and now even into my readings? If anything, I would end up—at a minimum—suspended until either the issue resolved itself or the Company determined I was no longer fit for duty. Deemed incompetent by the repeated exposure to the worst of what humanity could wreak on each other. I almost laughed, but it came out instead as something of a wheeze, reedy and thin. "I think my dreams might be having a bit of a residual effect on me during the day," I admitted.

"So there was nothing else there to find?"

"No."

Victor hesitated, shuffling his feet. "I think I'll leave this off the report for now," he said.

I did not find the words brought me any sort of relief.

Victor's reluctance to inform the Company of anything going on in my private life did not mean that there was no paperwork to fill out at all. But it did mean I and my skills were currently irrelevant, and my time would be best spent not loitering about on the Company's dime.

I found myself alone, on my way to the café just down the street to pick up sandwiches while Victor remained behind and managed the dull work of filling out each and every line with flowery prose of what we had, or in this case, *hadn't* managed to unveil.

The windows of the café—the very one Lucien had escorted me to the other day—were fogged up from the warmth inside, making it impossible to see more than vague blurs of color through the glass. The waiters were flashes of bleeding shapes moving among the crowd until I pulled open the door. With the blast of heat also came the noise: dozens of voices all clamoring at once, along with the clatter of cutlery.

I joined the line of people to the side waiting to give their carry-out orders to the lone server at a wooden stand. It moved achingly slowly, and those with food exited back out the door with no regard to how closely they brushed up against others.

More than one of them trod on my skirt.

"Miss Tailor?" The voice that said my name contained a hint of delighted surprise.

I sighed, half-twisting so I could flick my eyes upwards to meet his gaze before turning my attention back to the front. "Lord LeVerre."

"I think we know each other well enough that you could call me Lucien."

"I don't," I said.

I couldn't see his expression with my back to him, but the skin along my arms, shoulders, and the nape of my neck prickled as if my very flesh could detect his displeasure at my dismissal. I had to fight the instinct to either turn and check or crowd forward into the back of another person to try and open space up between Lucien and me.

"Do you come here more often than I suspected?" he asked, a bite in his tone—a warning that I should not ignore his question.

"No," I said cautiously, and I shifted, turning my head to glance at him. He looked idly curious, as if he truly, simply, wanted to know. "Victor and I thought perhaps we should give this café a try based on your own recommendation."

The smile that bloomed on his lips looked genuinely pleased, in spite of the fact that it exposed the tips of his teeth—a grinning predator. "Then I suppose I should take it as a compliment that my opinion resulted in you trying somewhere new."

The line shuffled forward, and Lucien and I moved with it. We could not stall when there were others queuing up behind him.

"I suppose I would also take such actions as a compliment," I said, which made the smile on his face tighten and the look in his eyes harden, bordering on stone. Their shade in the shifting light of the café edged nearer to garnet than the russet they were in the full sun, or even in the flickering flames of a lantern.

He stepped closer, the innocuous actions of a man attempting to make space in the line, but the feeling of an eel twisting in my guts made me wish I could also move forward. I was already crowded in too near to the back of the man in front of me. "I find you tend to knock me off balance," Lucien said. "I'm never entirely sure where it is I stand with you."

"I would say the best thing you could do is to assume we stand as employer and employee on either side of a line that cannot be crossed."

He paused, his head tilted to one side, for all the world looking like a cat with a bird caught between its paws. "And so we cannot come to know one another?"

"I would say," I repeated, "that the knowing should only ever be on the surface."

"I find that disappointing," he said, and it came with a tone of admission. "As you are someone I would like to know further."

My mouth was dry, my throat thick, and I was treading the knife's edge between polite rejection, and tumbling down into something I was sure I did not want to discover. I turned my face away from him, counting how many more patrons before I would reach the front of the line and could place my order and flee. "My very...position...with my employer means that is a path neither of us should be wandering down." A half-truth—perhaps something that would encourage him to reconsider whatever pursuit he had in mind.

"And if you did not have that position?" he asked. "If you instead had that flower shop you would prefer?"

I opened my mouth and closed it, trapped now by my own careful treading. I looked down at my gloves, rubbing a finger on the seam. "I do not think my position in life will ever much matter. Something beyond what I am is not something I can ever have."

A full truth at least.

"I see," he said, and with that we fell silent in the surrounding din.

I returned, fortunately, alone to the Company with sandwiches for Victor and me. Without tea, however, we would have to make do with whatever offerings Victor had in his drawer or the Company provided in the building's small kitchen.

My steps echoed as I hurried up the stairs and down the hallway, a *staccato* drumbeat in my ears. I was heavily relieved to reach Victor's office, to find him seated at his desk, pen scratching against paper.

I set the bag of sandwiches down before struggling out of my scarf, hat, and coat, and then plopped gracelessly into a chair.

Victor didn't look up from the section he was marking. "You seem out of sorts."

"I ran into our Lord LeVerre in the café."

He set the pen down, looking up to meet my eyes with his. "And?"

"He expressed an interest in knowing me further. And, I suppose technically, although he may now wish to rescind it, gave me permission to call him by his given name."

"Well that's a development," Victor said, leaning back in his chair. "Congratulations, you have a suitor."

I rolled my eyes. "Don't."

He grinned and leaned forward to pick up his pen. "Not all suitors are desirable ones."

"I don't want any suitors at all," I said, wiggling a hand at him. "How could I possibly live a married life?"

He sighed and set his pen back down placing an elbow on the desk and resting his chin in his palm. "Do you not think that perhaps your abilities may be a help when it comes to understanding someone you deeply love, rather than a hindrance?"

"I do not love Lucien."

He blinked. "I'm not saying you do. You barely know the man, same as me. Certainly a weekend spent at his manor isn't enough time to agree to marriage." He held up a hand to forestall any protests I had. "I'm not even saying you would learn to love him specifically. I speak nebulously that perhaps in the future, there will be someone who holds your whole heart in their hands."

"I don't believe that will be a future for me," I said stubbornly, reaching for the bag on the desk, the paper crinkling. I pulled out the sandwiches, setting one directly in front of Victor, who grimaced and rubbed at the space between his eyes, brow furrowed.

I paused. "Are you well?"

"It follows him," he said.

I dropped the sandwich clutched in my hands, and snatched the pen and paper. "What follows him?"

"The dust. He's lost his air again."

I scribbled down the words. "Who has?"

"Who has what?" Victor asked.

"Lost his air," I said patiently. "Who's being followed?"

He stared down at the desk, rubbing his finger over a water stain. "I would assume our Lord LeVerre." He tapped his finger, a single digit compared to his usual drumming. "It would make no sense that you're the dust."

"I'm the dust," I said dubiously. "I can't possibly have become his dust the moment we stepped inside his house."

"I said it would make no sense," he said irritably. "It would have to be that the house is the dust."

"Do you think he's going to return home?" I asked.

Victor leaned back. He looked wan, the shadows under his eyes and cheeks deeper. "Maybe the Company looked into his case and refused his request to assist in obtaining a warrant."

"Well that's an easy enough question for us to answer," I said, as I climbed to my feet.

"Viv, what do you intend to do if they did?"

I hesitated, and then sat back down. "Nothing."

"So what good will the information do us?"

"None," I sighed.

He snagged up the form I had used for my notes, turned it over and retrieved his pen. "None," he agreed. "There are some rocks best left unturned."

We ate our sandwiches in silence once Victor finished his paperwork. I then returned to the third floor to haunt the halls and my office while we waited for some manager or other to either request we delve further into these investigations or assign us to yet another case. I found that I could not sit still, with this need to be doing something crawling its way through my veins and limbs.

It seemed that much of my life hinged upon waiting. Waiting for something to happen, waiting for approval, waiting for results. And once we had a case or a request for further assistance, it could easily take them a week or more to process the paperwork, letting it languish on a desk somewhere while they attended to more "urgent" matters.

Perhaps that was why I longed for something else: this constant delay when my own abilities meant we could simply move forward and find answers the very same day. I was tired of being hindered by protocol and procedure, and I had a potential pathway out of it and into a life where I set my schedule.

I paused in my pacing, standing just outside my office door, although I could not say what brought the thought about. I could, without the Company's blessing, seek out Lucien with the excuse that it had nothing to do with his case.

He was interested in knowing me further, after all. And they could not make demands on who I chose to socialize with beyond severing my employment for involving myself with a client.

But Lucien was no longer a client if they had refused to assist any further with his case.

I would need to be sure of that, so I climbed the additional two flights of stairs up to where management sat—higher than the rest of us with the supposed view to match. A landscape of rooftops and chimneys hardly seemed the perk they presented it as.

I first needed to ascertain if his case still sat on someone's desk. If it did, there would be nothing I could do until it finished passing through their examination.

When I poked my head around the door to peer into the managers' hallway, I discovered that it was empty. I stood on the threshold, vacillating between satisfying my own curiosity or going back to my office and continuing on as expected.

I stepped onto the wood floor of the hall. One would perhaps expect some sort of grandiose moment—a realization, a stroke of genius when stepping through the doorway. There was none of that. It was only another dreary hall in a relatively dreary building meant only for efficiency.

I had to admit, as I lingered near the stairs, that I had expected there to at least be a receptionist here, someone who would dole out the various piles of paperwork and guard the doors lest the managers be disturbed. There wasn't even a desk in the hall to block anyone's passage forward. I wandered until I reached the nearest office and could examine the plaque fashioned to the door.

"Reception," it read.

"Can I help you?" said a voice from within the room, and I started. I had been so intent on poking around under the impression no one was here that I hadn't done the logical thing and checked for a person in the room itself.

I turned to find myself facing a woman seated ramrod straight at her desk, hands neatly clasped together on the surface, and a welcoming smile on her lips.

Well, I was already out of the pan and into the fire. "I'm trying to inquire into the status of a case for review."

She plucked up a pen and paper that had been waiting beside her elbow, set the tip of the pen to the page, and looked expectantly back at me.

"A Lord Lucien LeVerre asked for assistance in obtaining warrants regarding the interview of witnesses."

She scribbled down some notes on what I said, set the pen on top of the paper, and leaned to the side. The squeak of an opening drawer precluded the rustling, rifling noise of files being pushed around, and she pulled one up and out with a flourish before settling it on the desk next to her note. She flipped it open, and I waited, watching as she scanned down the page, the print on it too small for me to make out the words from my position beside the door.

She closed it, and then settled back into the position I had initially found her in. "Under review."

"Still?" I asked.

"These reviews can take time," she said, her tone saccharine sweet. "Once the review has been finished and a determination made, the client will be contacted with our ruling."

She said nothing else, and after a moment I realized I was staring, half-expecting her to be revealed as some sort of automaton, and not a human.

"Thank you," I said belatedly, and barely waited the time needed for her to respond with the customary *you're welcome* before I had turned tail and headed back to my own floor.

The information shattered any sort of half-formed and poorly-planned ideas I had, that perhaps Lucien would show his gratitude by funding that flower shop I longed for.

CHAPTER THIRTEEN

File C-1851
Item G: Advertising pamphlet emblazoned with the
words "The Crown Theater Presents."
Listed shows have been struck through, and the ink
has spread, obscuring the names entirely.

I was in my office, examining the seam in my glove, which I still hadn't repaired, when Victor came in bearing a fluttering piece of paper and my coat and scarf.

"We've got a new case," he said. "And for this one, they want us to hurry."

"What happened?" I asked as I rose and scurried around my desk to pluck my items from his hands and follow him out into the hall.

"A third woman has gone missing," he said as we descended the stairs, the sound of our footsteps echoing off the walls in this narrow space. "And the circumstances are eerily similar to the first two."

"You mean they've actually read the details of your reports?"

"What would be the point in making us fill out those blasted forms if they didn't at least skim them?"

We swept through the entrance and climbed into the carriage. "There's another body on the floor as well."

"Crude way to put it," I said.

"How else would you have stated it?" he asked once we were settled and our conveyance trundled forward.

"I don't know."

"Merely not that way."

"That would be the gist of it, yes."

The two of us went silent, the only noise being the rumble of the wheels on the stone streets and the creaking of the carriage itself.

"I was thinking," I said slowly.

"You're often thinking," Victor said. "What makes this time different from the others?"

"Lord LeVerre," I said. "If he's so...concerned with me, perhaps he would make a good patron to fund my flower shop?" His initial silence in response made me itch with the need to fill the quiet. "I have enough to get started with a modest storefront, but the initial offerings would be sparse. And if I had someone to add the money needed to ensure a healthy supply of product..."

Victor caught my eye, a frown on his face. "I don't know that I would recommend that, Viv."

"Why not?" I asked tersely. "Because of your visions?"

"Those and the man himself."

"You seemed rather impressed that he was interested in me in the first place."

"I made the comment lightly because I knew nothing would come of it," he said, and his tone had sharpened. "The man's already made you uncomfortable with his questions over your abilities, and now you want to financially tie yourself to him?"

I opened my mouth, shut it, and then flopped back against the cushions, glaring at Victor.

"I know what you see in him is an escape from the Company and one that you think would be on your terms, but I worry you would just be tying yourself to a worse situation." He shifted, jiggling his knee. "You think you would be free to stop using what you can do at someone else's beck and call, but the Company has strict protocols in place because we are tools they *care* for."

"I think they care for their profits," I said stubbornly.

"No business can operate without some form of profit. Otherwise, it stifles growth and the company's ability to flourish. Profit means they can put money back into the business to expand their offerings while giving better compensation to the employees, who are the backbone of why they had a profit to begin with. *We* are the Company. Without our skills, they cease to exist, and so do their profits." He leaned forward, hands clasped between his knees. "Lord LeVerre will have no such compunction to make sure that you yourself are kept healthy and well. And you do not know that he won't hold his patronage over your head."

I snorted. "You think he intends to romance me in an attempt to turn my head so I'll do his bidding rather than being forced to wait for a response regarding his warrants?"

Victor shrugged. "You said it." He clasped my hands and gave my fingers a squeeze. "I ask that you tread carefully around him. Maybe his interest is innocent, and he truly wants to know you better, but I do not trust him."

I could see my flower shop slipping away as if my choices in gaining it had narrowed down to only one man, one path, little hooks that dug into my skin and left me impatient and reckless with the way they itched and scratched at my flesh.

"There are other ways, Viv," Victor said.

I held my tongue on the question I wanted to ask—which was what other paths, which ways—and merely nodded. Victor gave me a small smile and released my hands, leaned back in his seat, and shifted the curtains so he could peer out the window. "We're almost there," he said conversationally. "Hopefully, the reading required is a short one."

"And where exactly are we going?" I asked.

Victor reached into his vest pocket and pulled out the Company's assignment. "It appears that we're being sent to the asylum. The letter lists a dead orderly and a missing nurse."

I grimaced. "It seems odd, doesn't it, that they're always in these pairs?"

Victor looked back at the paper, his brow furrowed. "It is indeed. And that is something I think we will want to include in our reports—a suggestion that they alert the detectives assigned to these cases that there must be a connection."

The carriage came to a rocking halt, and with a groan, Victor threw the door open and maneuvered his way onto the trampled snow of the sidewalk. He waited until I had managed to alight, and we went up to the front of the asylum—a towering, square building whose entrance was flush with the sidewalk. A heavy iron door guarded the way in.

"It looks like a prison," I said.

"I think it used to be one," Victor remarked mildly.

"And people choose to leave their family members here?" I asked, still studying the looming stone walls.

"So I've been told," Victor said. He shifted, tilting his head back so he could examine the building as well, while my own eyes roved over the shape of its roof, more green-toned copper. It must have been quite impressive when it was new.

We paused, hesitating at the door with no officer standing outside to greet us. After a minute, Victor stepped forward and knocked on the metal. A slit at eye level slid open, and a pair of blue eyes peered out at us.

"State your business."

For all the world, it seemed like the eyes were speaking to us, although logically, I knew they were attached to a person.

"Victor and Vivian Tailor from the Company," Victor recited. "We're here concerning a detective's request for assistance."

The eyes narrowed and the slit of metal slid shut with a screech. A moment later, the door groaned as it swung halfway open. The man standing inside stepped forward, both he and the bulky door barring us from entry. He held out a hand. "Assignments, please."

Victor pulled out the envelope with its folded paper and handed it over.

The man snatched it and took his time pulling the letter free. He unfolded it, studied it, and then reached into his vest pocket to retrieve a pair of spectacles and put them on before reading the letter again. Finally, he huffed, stuck the paper none-to-gently back into its envelope, and handed it to Victor. He took the time to remove his glasses and place them with much more consideration into his pocket. "Everything seems to be in order."

"Yes, sir," Victor said.

The man tapped his foot, a frown on his face. "I'll not have you disturbing the patients," he said severely. "They're upset enough as it is."

"Of course," Victor said. "We aim to be discreet and should only need access to the body and the location where it was found."

The man's frown seemed to tighten, lips pursing. "The detectives have not yet allowed us to remove it," he complained, "which is most *distressing*."

"Understandably so," Victor said, but I could hear the undertone to his voice that signaled he was shortly going to lose what patience he had. "If you wouldn't mind...?" He paused, letting the sentence hang in the air while he and the man stared at each other before trying a different tactic. "If you could let us through to see the detectives, Doctor...?"

"Malady," the man said stiffly.

"Bit on the nose for a name," Victor said.

"I did not choose it, although I find it led me to the correct position in life."

"If we could—"

"No, we could not," Malady said, and he shut the door in our faces.

Victor sighed and knocked on the door. "Doctor Malady, we have our assignment. If you could please not make this affair more difficult than it needs to be—"

The door jerked back open.

The man who opened it this time was broad across the chest and shoulder, with salt and pepper hair and beard trimmed close to his face. "Can I help you?"

"Where's Doctor Malady?" Victor asked warily.

"Returning to his office." The man shot a look over his shoulder and then refocused on us. "Can I assist you?"

Victor's voice held notes of one aggrieved while attempting to keep some manner of cheer to it. "We're Victor and Vivian Tailor from the Company. We were informed that a murder has occurred on the premises, and the detective in charge has requested our assistance."

The man crossed his arms and leaned against the doorframe. "Assignments, please."

Victor pulled the envelope back out, which was beginning to look quite the bit worse for the wear, and handed it over to our current gatekeeper. He was much less ruffled in his movements than Malady was, unhurried and calm, even taking the time to smooth out the wrinkles in the paper. He scratched his head, running his palm along the short bristles. "Everything seems to be in order." He shifted, tucking his arms in tighter. "Would you prefer to finish this discussion inside? I admit my bones don't like the cold."

"We would, yes," Victor said.

The man stepped out of the way, and Victor and I slipped past him before he could change his mind and bar the way in again.

The entry of the facility was far more pleasing in color than I expected. Most hospitals had a chilly, sterile demeanor to them, something that translated to the walls and tile. Here, the plaster had been painted over with a soothing gray blue. Golden-stained wood floors with wide planks ran the breadth of this hall and, I assumed, farther in and throughout the building.

"We did quite a bit of renovation work when we acquired the building," our current guide said, motioning a hand at the entryway.

"The atmosphere is friendlier than one would think to find from the exterior," Victor said.

"We thought it best if our patients could view this place as home."

"In the interest of efficiency," Victor said, "could you please lead us to the body?"

The man blinked, briefly opened his mouth as if he intended to say something, and then shook his head. "This way, then. We'll have to cross through the first-floor ward."

Victor and I trotted after him as the man had long legs and an equally long stride. It wasn't far to an open door, and through it, a room filled with couches and chairs carefully arranged into seating areas. Another area was set up with tables and chairs on which rested chess boards and packs of cards.

Our guide pointed briefly at the tables. "We try to give the patients plenty of ways to keep themselves entertained. A couple of them have become quite skilled at chess…" His words faltered, and he headed over toward the seating. He stopped by a couch where a woman sat with her head bent, a book open in her lap.

"Eleanor," he said, his voice holding a note of tired patience. "Everyone should be in their rooms right now. What are you doing sitting here?"

"There was a woman in my mirror," she said.

I started, a chill creeping up my spine and settling in my chest, and were it not for Victor standing with me, I would have turned around and left.

"Do you mean your reflection, Eleanor?" the doctor suggested. "I find I am startled by my own, especially at night when the lights are low."

She looked up from her book, eyes wide, tilted her head, and watched the three of us for long enough that I was beginning to feel rather trapped by her gaze. There was more of an aura of that of an oracle than of madness about her.

She turned her attention back to the book in her lap. "No," she said. "I know my own features. These were not them."

"How strange," our guide said agreeably. "Perhaps it would help to remove the mirror from your room until the woman no longer appears in it?"

"Yes," Eleanor said. "I do not like her. Her movements are strange. She presses her palm to the glass as though it's a door. I don't want her in my room again."

"I'll get our orderlies right on it," he said. "In the meantime, will you promise to wait right here until I return?"

She tilted her head to the side again, eyes bright, for all the world like a bird perched on a branch, poised and ready to take flight. "Yes."

Our guide nodded and headed farther into the building, leaving it up to Victor and me whether we would follow. We did, although I cast one last glance over my shoulder at Eleanor, whose eyes had returned to the pages of her book.

We went trotting down another hallway, and here we stopped outside an open door, pausing long enough that I recognized the cadence of one of the murmuring voices within. I didn't wait for any confirmation. I swept into the room with Victor close behind.

"Morris."

"Miss Tailor," she responded and motioned at the man beside her. "We were just discussing you and your brother. I believe you've met Detective Brant?"

"I—yes," I said after a confused moment.

Behind me, Victor shifted and coughed.

"Miss Tailor. Mr. Tailor, how do you do?" Brant asked pleasantly.

"Well enough," I said. "Although I admit to some surprise at seeing you here. I thought your jurisdiction was in the country."

"Yes, well, that is a long story involving an acquaintance of ours, which I believe can wait a moment?"

There was a long, awkward pause before Victor stepped forward. "Morris, if you could give us the facts of the case before Vivian reads the room and, if possible, the body?"

"If possible?" Brant asked.

"The fresher they are, the less Vivian seems to be able to pull information from the victim," Victor said bluntly, with the air of the issue not being one that was recently discovered. Morris frowned at him but let the statement lie, although her eyes flicked in Brant's direction and back again.

I turned to study the room. The white-painted brass bed was unmade, with folded blankets and sheets resting at its foot. A wardrobe stood against the wall closest to the door, and nearby rested a small table with a pitcher and basin, a modest, wooden-framed mirror hanging above. The body was splayed on the floor between the end of the bed and the table, collapsed in a most uncomfortable-looking position. His legs were folded beneath him, his back half-arched, arms spread out to either side, and his head twisted so that his blank eyes stared out at the underside of the bed.

As I examined the space, Morris pulled out her notepad, the pages rustling as she turned them. "James Black, thirty-three, was found this morning on the floor by an orderly, a Mr. Alan Flanders. Mr. Black and a nurse, Judith Harper, presumed missing, were assigned to preparing the room for a new patient set to arrive today."

"No one's confirmed Miss Harper's disappearance?" Victor asked.

"We have officers checking her place of residence and anywhere she frequented, but at this time, we felt it best to assume a similarity to the other two."

"How is Detective Flannegan?" Victor asked.

"As well as can be expected, given the circumstances," Morris said.

"Has there been no movement on the case?"

"None, and the paperwork to have his fiancé's rooms read has been submitted, but I suspect it's still sitting on a pencil pusher's desk somewhere."

Victor sighed. "I'll inquire as to its status. In the meantime, Viv, do you want to start with the room or the body?"

It is always a disconcerting thing to have the eyes of everyone in the room focused on you, and this time was no different. "The room," I said. I tried not to make a show of tugging off my glove, as the movement felt all too often like a dramatic flourish.

I hesitated, contemplating where to start, and curled my fingers around the metal of the foot of the bed frame. It was cool to the touch—the emotions that filtered up to me just as clinical and brusque, the long swipes of a cleaning rag run over it as part and parcel of their preparation. I moved from there to the blankets, their fabric soft and worn. There was the hum of a song, a tune I felt I should know but couldn't quite place. I stepped around the corpse as widely as I could in such a close space, but still, my skirts brushed up against his legs and torso as I moved past him and ran my fingers down the table and along the handle of the ewer. There was nothing there that stood out beyond the tune. Whoever had done the cleaning in the room must have been fond of it, with how warm the notes were.

I was floating in infinite, endless patience, buoyed by calm seas, water as still and deep as glass with no wind to ruffle the surface.

I placed my hand on the wall, but it was more of the same, with nothing I could point to as untoward events. I sighed and turned away, considering the body on the floor. I moved toward it and caught my reflection out of the corner of my eye before I knelt and pressed my fingers to the corpse's cheek. His was not the calm presence I felt in this room. He was instead tightly wound, a vibrating string, all nerves and tangled intentions, with a longing that remained just out of reach. He felt half-finished—these threads of who he was snapped off as if whatever had begun weaving them together or pulling them apart had been interrupted.

And that was as far as I could go.

I pulled my hand away.

"Anything?" Morris asked, but her voice sounded resigned.

"Nothing," I said, and even to myself, I sounded vaguely disappointed. "It's as if whoever is coming in leaves nothing of themselves behind, and I don't see how that's possible."

"Maybe they're not coming into the room itself?" Brant asked. "What if instead they're luring the woman out?"

I waved a hand at the body. "Then how are they accomplishing this? No marks left—it's as if they've merely dropped dead."

Brant shrugged. "That's for the coroner to determine, isn't it?"

From where I was crouched, I could easily see the sideways glance Morris shot toward him before she focused back on me.

"I begin to suspect that our perpetrator isn't an opportunist," she said. "I think they're choosing their victims and planning this out well in advance to leave nothing behind. They know precisely what they're up against when covering their tracks and are accounting for that."

"It wouldn't be the first time someone's tried to do so," Victor said. "But I would say they've been the most successful."

"We'll have to figure out how they're doing it," Morris said, "if we want Vivian or anyone else to have any chance of tracking them down."

"If we think of or come across anything that will help us make that determination, we'll let you know, Detective." Victor gave a curt nod in his direction with his next sentence. "Brant, a pleasure, although I'm sure these are not the circumstances we would have preferred to meet again over."

"Indeed not," Brant said, although his gaze was not on Victor but me. "Perhaps we can arrange another time to get together and discuss my reasoning for being in town."

"Certainly," Victor said, sounding wryly amused. "Just send a note to the Company, and it will manage to find its way to my desk. Viv?"

I rose and stepped back over the body to follow Victor out the door to where our guide waited, hovering in the hallway. He led us back to the entrance, and we exited without another word spoken, the ride away from the asylum filled with silence.

CHAPTER FOURTEEN

Case 1895-11-HO-003258
Autopsy revealed no unnatural cause of death.
Coroner has ruled it accidental of unknown ori-
gin.

Victor left me at home, which seemed dark and unwelcoming, even in the white glow of the afternoon sunlight bouncing off the mounds of snow still sitting atop people's roofs. It had been swept almost completely from the roads and sidewalks; the only drifts that remained were mud-spattered pieces shoved up against the curbs and the walls of buildings.

I stood on my front stoop, staring at the door and the knocker, the bulk of it which was in the vague shape of a peony.

It was the knocker that had convinced me to purchase the house in the first place, and stepping inside was what convinced me I had found a home. All the colors had been warm, with the blush of spring and the heat of summer, golden glows and pretty pastels.

It did not feel that way to me today.

Instead, it felt as if a presence had taken up residence, slowly creeping out from the center in dark tendrils and clinging roots that crawled their way up the walls and along the ceiling. It had me standing on the stairs, a hand on the doorknob, reluctant to open it and step inside.

I shook the feeling off.

There was no physical difference in my foyer, but the air inside felt thick, something palpable. I hovered at the threshold and glanced at the parlor, which was filled with wan light filtering its way in through the windows. A look up the stairs told me I didn't want to enter my second floor, where the shadows waited, gathering and looming above me. I stayed still, uncertain and wondering if I left and returned, would the feeling that someone else was in my house remain?

I tried to count the days. Had it been long enough that I had the excuse of picking my clothing up from the laundress so that I would have a reason to leave? Would a short trip down the sidewalk be enough for this staleness, this oddity to leave my house? I could go, retrieve my items, and pick up a pie from the pub. The wait should mean I would be out close to an hour or more to get dinner.

I checked the buttons on my jacket and fussed for a moment with my scarf, the knitted yarn sticking to the leather of my gloves. Then I went right back out my front door, locked it securely behind me, and practically skipped down the stairs in haste. I headed to the right, winding my way among the people, my stride much the same as theirs—huddled down, shoulders up by my ears, that slight bend at the waist into the bitter cold, hands shoved into my pockets.

I did not feel lighter the farther away from my house I moved. Instead, I felt heavier, each step like moving through mud, thick and sucking at my soles and heels. Had I not been quite so stubborn, having now made up my mind to see Kate, I may have given in to that feeling and turned back around to sleep in the parlor. I sped up my pace, which at least had the benefit of warming up my limbs, and set my heart to racing as I ran the last two blocks down to Kate's place of business.

I reached her door just as someone else was coming out, the two of us managing that awkward dance back and forth before we slipped past each other, him to the street, and me into her foyer. Kate was inside, examining the shirts the previous patron had left behind. She looked up as I moved into her line of sight and then set the fabric down, brushing her hands off on the front of her apron.

"Vivian," she said with a smile. "I wasn't expecting to see you until tomorrow."

"I seem to have miscounted my days," I said, trying to match her cheer, but it felt false, stiff, and pasted on.

Kate didn't seem to notice anything amiss. "Stand here just a minute. I've got your items ready, so it's a good thing you came by." She disappeared down the hallway.

I shifted, passing my weight from one foot to another as I waited, trying and failing not to fidget. It was not only one minute, judging by the incessant ticking of a clock she had somewhere just off her foyer.

I started counting the clicks of the hands when she returned, carrying my bag of clothing.

She set it down on top of the shirts with a thump. "Alright there, everything freshly pressed and folded. Do try to get them home and hang them up quickly so no wrinkles set in."

I snagged the bag up, settling it securely in my arms. "I'll probably be back sometime tomorrow or next week with more."

She nodded and picked up the sleeve she had been looking over. "I'll be here."

I hesitated, but with nothing to say and no conversation to carry, I turned and headed back onto the sidewalk. I took a minute to orient myself, mapping out in my head where the nearest pub was before picking a direction.

It wasn't long before I joined a crowd of people. I ducked my way through the pub door on one of its swings as someone else exited and found myself surrounded by the heat not only of a roaring fire and numerous lit lanterns but the warmth of too many bodies pressed closely together in too small of a space.

I was going to have to find a way to shove through the press to get up to the bar near the kitchen, where an entirely separate line from the ale-seeking patrons waited.

A hand landed on my shoulder, and I twisted, dipping to the side. The fingers slid free, and I was face to face with Lucien, who looked just as surprised as I felt. There was a flush to his normally pale cheeks as he stared down at me.

"Lord LeVerre," I said stiffly.

"Lucien," he corrected.

"I don't feel comfortable enough to address you by your given name," I said, turning back toward the line. I raised myself up on my toes so I could try to see over the number of heads. I grimaced: if anything, it seemed to have grown in those few brief moments.

"Are you here to meet someone?" Lucien asked. I could barely hear him over the din, and I was obliged to set my heels back on the ground and turn toward him again, leaning in so he could repeat the words closer to my ear. "Are you here to meet someone?" His breath brushed against my neck, and while I heard him more clearly, I could have sworn he lowered the volume of his voice to force me to shift nearer.

"No," I said and immediately regretted the word. His eyes lit up, golden tones in the way the flames in the lanterns and on the hearth danced.

"I've a table," he said. "And an impatient waiter guarding it for me so I could speak to you. Why don't you join me before he decides he has better things to do with his time than ensure a solitary man saves his dinner while he flirts with a peer?"

I took as much of a step back as I could. "I think said man will still be dining alone."

"And what if he merely wants time to converse?"

"About?" I asked warily.

"Your flower shop."

"What about it?"

"Come sit down. It will be easier to explain when you have the space for it." He started forward into the crowd, with half a glance back at me as if he knew I would follow.

I did, my intentions to retrieve a meal and immediately retreat back home disregarded for curiosity's sake.

"When I have the space for it?"

He motioned to the table we had arrived at, a booth currently guarded by a harried waiter who gave Lucien a curt nod and the barest of smiles. "An order for the lady?" they asked.

"Cold, sweetened tea in a glass, please," I said before Lucien could order for me.

"Alright." They disappeared into the crowd.

I eyed the table. There was a full pint of beer on one side of its surface, so I slid onto the cushions across from it. I set my bag of laundry on the bench next to me to guarantee Lucien couldn't decide to trade seats, and unsure what else to do with them, I laid my hands in my lap. Lucien followed me into the booth, sitting in front of his drink and leaning forward, elbows up on the table.

"Well, I'm here," I said. "What questions do you have for me?"

"How much of a business plan have you put together? Vendors? A space?"

I rubbed at the seam of my glove. I was sure the hole was gradually, steadily, becoming larger, and I needed to repair it before I made it any worse. "I have a potential storefront," I said slowly. "And some contacts for the inventory. I know I would need at least one other employee to begin with, although the shop would be small to start."

"How would you let people know your flower shop is open?"

I gave him a sidelong glance. "An open sign."

He chuckled, and I outright glared at him. "I meant no offense," he said. "But how will you get the word out to potential customers? Are you planning on just showing up one day and hoping they'll walk in your door?"

"I assumed that was how it works," I said. The words sounded weak, unsure, and disgruntled that I had missed a step in what it took to open a new business.

He shook his head. "What you need is marketing."

"Marketing," I said dubiously.

"Word of mouth." He scooted forward as if by pressing his chest up against the edge of the table, he could somehow make his point more tangible. He lifted his cup out of the way of his arms and shifted it to the side. "Someone who, before you're even open, lets potential clientele know about your flower shop."

"And how would I do that?" I asked. "If I have no shop yet?"

He waved a hand, a dismissive sweep of his fingers. "You do that while you're preparing the space, so you have the shop; you're just not open to the public yet. You want to whet their appetites, get them hungry for the arrangements you create."

It was my turn to laugh. "Lucien, they're only flowers."

"Not," he said—and there was a gleam in his eyes I didn't like, the spark that traveled through them and the curved smile on his face—"to the *bourgeoisie*."

"I doubt that those of high society will be coming down to my modest shop," I said.

"They will if you convince them that these are *the* mark of the wealthy. Anyone who is someone will have an arrangement, a corsage, even a single bloom from Miss *Tailor's* store."

"And who exactly will be convincing them that my flowers are meant only for those in the know?"

"Well, I suppose I would be doing that," he said, and he sounded quite serious.

"And how will you be doing that?" I asked. "I thought you no longer had friends among them."

He shrugged. "They won't prevent my reentrance into their elevated company. And certainly, it would take some convincing that I'm not merely a downer, flinging myself onto their couches to mourn and languish like an unwanted poet."

"What—" I said, paused when the waiter returned and set my glass on the table.

"Any food?" they asked.

"Do you have any soup?" I asked. I wanted something warm.

"Caramelized onion."

"I'll take a bowl of that, please."

"Sir?"

"I'll have the same," Lucien said. "Something hot would be welcome."

The waiter nodded and disappeared.

I waited another beat before picking back up the sentence I had started. "What exactly do you get, or expect, out of this?"

"Expect out of what?" Lucien asked. He picked up his beer, took a sip, and a grimace flickered across his lips—there and gone as he set the glass down.

"Something wrong?" I asked.

"Hmm?"

I motioned at his pint. "Is there something wrong with your drink? You made a face."

He looked at the glass still clutched in his hands, seemingly confused by its placement there. "No, it's just more—bitter than I would prefer." He slid it just off to the side. "Expect out of what?"

"Out of all this work, you would be doing to convince strangers to frequent my flower shop."

"The flower shop I intend to fund?" he asked. "It would hardly be a good use of my investment if I allowed it to fail because I did nothing, now would it?"

"Hardly," I admitted. "Why would you fund it to begin with?"

He tapped a single finger on the table, his brow furrowed and a thoughtful frown on his face. "Beyond my hopes that maybe it will result in a cordial, somewhat warm relationship between us?"

"Only cordial?" I asked warily.

"You've made your current stance on anything more than that quite clear," he said mildly. "So yes, only cordial."

"So then what beyond that?"

"I have been—lingering in that house, and it finally feels like I've awakened." He leaned forward, elbows back on the table, as he caught my gaze and held it fast, and I wasn't sure I would be able to look away. The noise of the pub, the din of the patrons, that ever-present roar was melting away, receding into silence. "I need an outside project."

"And I am that project?"

"I would like for you to be." There was an under-current to what he said, a push and pull, as if what I should have heard was *you already are*, but the words slipped past my ears unnoticed.

"What about your mother?" I asked.

He blinked, and whatever spell I had found myself under, struck still by his eyes, seemed to shatter, and I jumped. It was as if someone had found a way to turn up the volume in the room, an out-of-tune orchestra that had gone from the first, single, lonely note into a battle march.

"What about her?" he asked, an unexpected chill in his voice.

"If you're still searching for her—" I hesitated, unsure if the hardness in his gaze was due to the shifting lights and shadows from the gathered bodies passing between our table and the lanterns. I vacillated, attempting an explanation for the question as if I needed to have one prepared. "If your case remains with my involvement, your planned funding—"

"Would have a negative effect on your current employment?" he asked. Whatever frostiness that had been in his tone vanished, melting snow under a warm spring sun. "Understandable that the subject may then cause you some concern."

He pulled his pint back toward himself and gave it a turn, examining the glass. "I am," he paused. I could see the tip of his tongue pushing just against the front of his teeth before he pressed his lips together in a thin line. "I am beginning to lose hope, if I'm being entirely honest."

"Has the Company sent you a decision?"

"No. But the further it stretches, the longer I have to wait, the more discouraged I become."

"It may very well be a good thing," I said, "that they're moving so slowly. It certainly means they haven't outright rejected your case."

He sighed and sat back. "I do suppose I have that." He tapped his finger on the table again. "You remind me a bit of her," he said. There must have been something in my expression as he hurried to clarify. "Her movements. You both carry the same kind of tranquil, unconscious grace."

"I would not be one to consider myself graceful," I said.

"She didn't either," he said, and his eyes were unfocused, seemingly fixed on a point somewhere beyond me without really seeing. "But it was there. You're much the same in that regard."

"I suppose I should take that as a compliment."

"It was meant to be. Less about your similarities and more in the way you hold yourself." He paused, rubbing at the wet ring of condensation his glass had left on the wood. "But I suppose that may not be the kind of comparison a woman wants to hear."

"Perhaps not," I acknowledged. "I suppose it would depend on the woman."

The smile he gave me had an air of timidity about it, but it was off, like an emotion he meant to portray but had very little practice in showing. "I suppose so."

The rest of our meal had been spent in conversation over flowers, in particular, whether a hothouse would be needed to ensure the business had blooms out of season. And while I had said certainly, but there was nowhere in the city that had the space for one, Lucien seemed convinced he could find such a building.

I refused his offer of a ride home, insisting that I preferred to walk, even with my bag of laundry. I maneuvered my way down the sidewalk, past shuttered businesses and equally closed-up houses in the dark, with only the streetlamps to guide me, and I wondered just how it was he happened to be in this neighborhood. Not that it was far from the Company itself, which he would have reason to frequent for now, but it was an out-of-the-way area for him to end up in.

As such, I spent time checking over my shoulder and along the road for any sign that he had followed me. I couldn't quite put my finger on what it was about him that made me so wary. A couple of seemingly unintentional moments notwithstanding, he had appeared relatively harmless.

But maybe that was how all dangerous men were.

In spite of my mounting trepidation, I entertained the idea of signing whatever paperwork it took for him to fund my shop. I turned the corner onto my street, casting another glance back, but everything was as empty as before, and I hurried forward. Once I reached my house, I raced up the steps to get in through the door and lock it behind me. I hoisted the laundry bag back off the floor from where I had dropped it in my haste to get the door fastened shut and turned to head up the stairs.

I paused on the first step, staring into the darkness above, but the looming sense of something lying in wait had receded, almost as if it had left the house when I did. I shook my head. I was jumping at shadows again, and it was getting to the point where it was becoming childish.

The lantern in my bedroom was lit, and I didn't pause to consider whether I had left it on. I must have, as there was no one else in my house. The shawl still covered the mirror at the dresser, but a part of it was pulled to the side as if a hand had snagged the edge to tug it out of the way of their view.

I ignored it as well, humming the first notes of a song I couldn't place as I emptied my clothes from the bag, giving the garments gentle shakes to ensure they were free of wrinkles before hanging them up in the wardrobe.

Vivian.

My hands stuttered to a stop, my fingers clutching at the fabric as I took a cautious peek over my shoulder. I was alone in my room still, and I stood there silently as the minutes ticked past, trying to decide if I had, in fact, heard a voice behind me, with a timbre I couldn't identify with the way it slid among the octaves. If I turned back around, would I hear it again?

I studied the room—eyes roving over the furniture, following the lines of the window, searching. There was nothing there. I turned my attention to the skirt still in my hands, brushing at the fabric where I had gripped it, fluffing the cloth, then smoothing it once

I had it hung up. That finished, I turned to face the room again, trying to discern if anything had changed in those few minutes.

The shawl was pulled back over the mirror, the whole of the glass obscured, only the side of the frame exposed. It made me think of a recently shut door. Curiosity tugged at me. As certain as I was that I had to have been imagining it or mistaken as to the placement of the shawl, now I wanted to know what exactly was behind it.

I stepped over to it, hand hovering at the fabric, and I paused, staring at my own fingers encased still in the leather glove. I tugged both gloves off and lifted the shawl out of the way, the fabric slipping along my palm as I moved it. I took one long breath in and looked into the mirror.

I was staring at myself.

I let out the breath I had been holding, half laughing. I wasn't entirely sure what it was I had been expecting. Those reflections from my childhood?

There was a thump from outside the room, and I turned my head, staring past the door where the light spilled into the hallway, and saw nothing there. After a moment of no further noise, I decided it must have been the house settling. I glanced at the glass, intending to place the shawl back where it had been hanging, and found a woman I didn't know staring at me. I was frozen in place, eyes locked on hers.

She slammed the flat of her palm against the glass with a thud.

I shrieked and jumped backward, dragging the fabric with me. It slithered off the frame. The back of my knees hit the end of the bed, and I teetered, eyes fastened on the figure in the mirror. She watched me, seemingly nonplussed by my reaction, her russet-colored gaze boring holes.

I knew those eyes.

"Lady LeVerre?" I whispered the words in that moment before I lost my fight with gravity; forced to let my knees fold beneath me, I collapsed onto the bed.

When I looked back at the mirror, I found only myself.

I left the shawl on the bed, moved back to the dresser, and touched the glass, palm to palm, with my own reflection, pressing on it as though one or both of us could push past the solid barrier. I leaned in toward it so that my breath fogged the surface, leaving a trailing mist across it.

But it was empty.

"You look like shit, Viv."

"Good morning to you too, Victor," I said sourly.

He settled in the chair on the other side of my desk, the same one Lucien had sat in when he had come and waited for me. "Are the nightmares back?" he asked.

"No," I said, rubbing at my wrist—surreptitiously, I hoped. It itched like a healing wound, yet every touch seemed to drive shards of glass deeper in.

"Then what's the reason for the poor sleep this time?"

"Lady LeVerre," I said, opting for half the truth. To tell Victor I was seeing things in the mirror when I was wide awake felt like something I wasn't yet ready to reveal.

"Ah," he said. "A worry about the fact that it may forever remain an unsolved case or a worry about the fact that someone will have to inform her son of that fact?"

"The unsolved case bit," I said. "Since I doubt we will be the ones who have to inform Lord LeVerre of any such thing once they've decided what they're willing to do in regard to his warrants."

Victor sighed and leaned back in his chair. "And in all honesty, the Company has at least two people whose abilities are relegated to lie detection, so it's unlikely our services would be needed at that point." He rubbed at his jaw and set his hand back on his thigh, that muffled *tap, tap, tap* as he drummed them against the fabric of his pants. "So we can truly wash our hands of him."

Victor would consider the matter settled, and I bit my tongue on telling him that Lucien had displayed an overt—had outright stated—an interest in helping me procure the space needed to begin my flower shop.

"No cases today?" I asked.

"Not that we've been assigned to yet," he said. "The paperwork on my desk is caught up, and they've had no movement on the other three that they would need to call us in for."

"Not even to go examine the homes for the most recent two?" I asked.

He shrugged. "Not that they've told me, although we could certainly submit a request ourselves. Might help move the two of them forward so they stop sitting on whatever form Morris turned in."

"They may want to hurry, for once," I said. "I get the distinct feeling there will be a lot more bodies on the floor before whoever this is is done."

Victor got up and sidled his way between my and Margaret's desks and pulled open a drawer. He examined its interior for a moment, snagged a set of papers, and set them on my desk even as he resumed his seat. He plucked up the topmost one and pulled it toward him as he picked up my pen. "We have two missing women whose homes we can go examine and one whose home we've already been to."

"And there was nothing there," I murmured.

"But maybe there's something at—" he paused, set his pen down to retrieve his notebook from his pocket, and thumbed through the pages. "Judith Harper's that will tell us if she met someone new recently."

"And Flannegan's fiancée? You think she also may have met someone new?"

He shrugged. "It doesn't have to be a romantic *tête-à-tête*. It could be a new friend, a new neighbor, someone she wouldn't find threatening."

"And will you be turning in two forms or one?"

Victor sighed, twiddling the pen between his fingers. "If I tell them the cases may be connected, it should encourage them to move Morris's request along a bit faster, so the one form, for two birds."

I waved a hand at the stack. "Well then, be my guest."

"Hmph," was all he said at first as he bent over the paper and began meticulously filling out the first line.

I began rifling through the others, looking among the forms for any pages he may have missed that would need to be submitted along with his current sheet.

"Have you heard anything from Lord LeVerre lately?" He asked it so casually that I paused in my movements.

"Why?" I asked after a long moment of silence.

"Last I knew, he had shown an interest in your flower shop." He shot me a look, a quick flick of his eyes up from the page to meet mine before he looked back down again. "And he does not seem the type to let go of something he has latched onto easily."

"Are you going to warn me against financially tying myself to him again?" I asked. "Because I've heard you each time you've done so."

Victor set down his pen and looked me directly in the eye. "But have you listened?"

"I have not signed or agreed to anything he has suggested," I said stubbornly.

"So you have spoken to him about it, though."

"Yes," I admitted. "I came across him at a pub not far from Kate's when I stopped in for dinner—or he came across me, and he asked me to join him."

Victor said nothing.

I continued on, the urge to fill the silence bubbling up in my throat. "It was only for a meal and in a public space. I don't think there was any harm in that."

"Normally, I would agree with you," Victor said and picked his pen back up.

"Does his house really bother you that much?" I asked.

"It's not just the house, it's the man," he said. "And I can't put my finger on the *why,* or I would tell you."

I tried to pick at the seam on my glove, running my thumb both along and across it, wearing away at the threads myself.

Victor finished scrawling out one last sentence and got up from his seat. "I'm going to go turn this in, and if we're lucky, we'll be sent out before the afternoon."

"And if we're not lucky?" I asked.

"Well, we'll have nothing to do but sit around and fill out more paperwork for the next week or so."

I sighed as he left, muttering while staring at my desk and the stack of forms. "It almost makes you hope for a murder just to have something to do."

CHAPTER FIFTEEN

My dearest Eleanor, why do you not answer me? I know you're there, listening to me in the dark. It's as if you're just around the corner, and every time I round it, you slip away again. If I leave the lights low, will it tempt you out of wherever you've been hiding?

It was fortunate that, for once, the cogs in the machine that was the Company ran quickly, and Victor and I found ourselves interrupted during our respective lunches. We climbed into the carriage with sandwiches still in hand and sent a note to Morris via courier instructing her to meet us perhaps two steps ahead.

"You need to get the cushions in this thing replaced," I grumbled, seated once again on that self-same spring. If anything was going to drive me mad, it was that, and not the woman in my mirror or the nightmares.

"Where will I find the time to take it in?" Victor asked mildly.

"Once this whole thing is resolved, I'll go in for half to fix it."

"Deal," Victor said.

We spent the rest of the ride in silence, swallowing down our sandwiches as quickly as we could without choking, and were both finished by the time we pulled up to Miss Harper's townhouse.

It was in a row of them quite similar to mine, two stories high—three if you counted the attic as a space—arranged in groups of five side-by-side before a gap between the buildings created an alley to get around to the back.

Miss Harper's home was on the end of one of these rows, and the sun reflecting off the pairs of front windows gave it a blank-faced look in the dull red brick. She had painted the wooden shutters and the front door to match—an off-white tone that gave the whole thing the appearance of needing to be washed, like the house itself was streaked with grime.

We had beaten Morris here, and so now we were at odds ends, with the option of either sitting in the carriage or standing on the front stoop while we waited.

Victor and I piled out of the carriage and headed for the stairs—it wouldn't make much of a difference in the cold when the interior of the carriage was the same as the air outside. We huddled together at the bottom of the stairs rather than up by the door, and neither one of us spoke, content to watch the passersby.

"Morris's taking an awfully long time," Victor said.

"Hmm," I agreed, jiggling in place, attempting to keep some heat flowing to the limbs, particularly my toes which were beginning to go numb.

He shifted and rose up on the balls of his feet as if he wasn't already tall enough to see over the scant few heads of anyone else coming down the sidewalk.

"Ah, there she is." He settled back on his heels with a resigned sigh. "She's brought Brant with her."

"Is that an issue?" I asked, glancing over my shoulder in the direction he had been looking.

"It's a curiosity," he said.

"That doesn't explain why you sound so bothered by it."

"More of an explanation as to why he's in town would be appreciated," Victor grumbled. "We've never had a case follow us home like this before."

"We've never had a case quite so odd before," I said.

"Detective Morris, Detective Brant," Victor said cheerfully as they drew nearer, without any bite to his tone to indicate his earlier irritation.

"Victor," Morris said, sounding amused, as if she could tell that his joviality was a mask. "Vivian."

"Detective Morris," I said, and inclined my head. "Detective Brant." I added his name onto my greeting almost as an afterthought.

"Miss Tailor," he said. "I would say it's a pleasure, but the circumstances don't seem to warrant those words."

Morris waved a hand at the door. "Well, shall we?"

"We already would have if we had a key," Victor said.

"That would, perhaps, be a helpful thing," Morris said agreeably as she fished around in her coat pocket and pulled out a key with an evidence tag. She unlocked the door, pushed it open, and for a moment we stared into the sunlit foyer before she stepped inside.

"Miss Tailor?" Brant said. "After you."

I huffed, went up the steps, and followed Morris into the building.

The interior was chilly—not quite as cold as the air outside—but the chill in a home where the occupant has left and not bothered to leave any sort of heat source on.

Victor and Brant crowded in behind me, and I was forced to take another step deeper in to make room. Morris snapped the door shut behind them, and the space immediately darkened.

"Well, where do you want to start?" Morris asked.

I looked around. To my right was a parlor—a double-wide door that led into a room with couches and chairs crowded around a low slung table, their backs to the large bay windows and instead facing a fireplace at the rear. A gold gilt mirror hung over the mantel, and the grate below it was empty.

In front of me, a hall led deeper into the house and a set of stairs led up, and to my left was nothing but an empty wall.

"Might as well start here," I said, and headed into the parlor. "If she had any recent guests, I assume she would've invited them into this room."

"Depends on the kind of guest," Brant said.

I shot him a glance over my shoulder, but he wasn't looking at me. Instead, he appeared to be studying the wood that framed the doorway and the carvings along the top. I turned back toward the room, hesitating as I studied the furniture.

It didn't look as though it got much use. Almost as pristine in appearance as it probably was the day the occupant had brought it home.

I tugged one of my gloves off and set my hand against the back of the couch, along the top of its frame, and found it flooded with laughter, the edges of conversation, the rattle of teacups on their saucers, and the clinking of spoons against the porcelain. The thump of a book as it was set down on the table.

There was cheer and delight, the sense that these meetings occurred as often as the people in these memories could find the time to get together—weekly if they could, monthly at a minimum. But there was no new presence among them, the grooves between them worn down and smooth, fitting together as neatly as pieces in a puzzle. There was nothing there that felt out of sync, out of place with the camaraderie they had grown into.

I drifted along the back of the couch, let my hand slide down the length of its wood, toward its arm, and made the leap from there to the armchair to follow its shape as well.

There was no change there. I stepped away from the furniture toward the wall, touched my fingers to its plaster, and found only more of these echoes.

It was a bright room, a happy room, and I walked its edges until I reached the mantel and set my palm against its carved wood.

His regret was sour on my tongue, thick and cloying, and if I let my hand stay still for long enough, I could choke on it until I was drowning.

I yanked my hand away, and looked up to find myself staring directly into the mirror, the couch, chairs and tables reflected behind me.

There was a ripple in the glass, and I couldn't be sure if it was a defect in the mirror itself or movement.

"Viv," Victor said. "Have you found anything?"

Hesitantly I reached out, brushed the tips of my fingers against the mantel, but it was still there: Lucien's sorrow, as strong as if he had only just left the room. I wavered, standing on this precipice, split between these choices.

"Viv?" Victor repeated, and still I felt stuck, the words sitting on my tongue, and all I needed to do was spit them out, but the muscle was frozen.

Would I tie myself to a man who may have had a hand in murder for a flower shop?

"Lucien LeVerre," I said.

"What?" Victor said.

"Who?" Morris asked.

"Lord LeVerre was here?" Brant asked.

"Yes," I said.

"When?" Victor asked sharply. "How long ago? For how long?"

I sighed and set my hand on the mantel yet again, that melancholy crowding up against all my senses until I could no longer breathe, and the reflection of the room behind me swam, my own image distorting. I could have sworn another presence was pressed against my back, their whispering voice in my ear before I finally pulled my fingers away. "Within the last week," I said. "It does not feel...long enough to have been a social visit, but his emotions were strong."

There was the scratch of pencil on paper to my left and I could only assume all three of them had pulled out identical notepads and were scribbling madly away to take down the information I had just imparted.

"What kind of emotion?" Morris asked.

"Regret," I said.

"For what he was going to do?"

I shook my head—I could still taste it. It lingered there at the back of my throat, creating a knot that was hard to swallow past. "No...and yes."

"Yes and no?" Brant asked. "How is it both?"

"Humans are complex creatures, are we not?" I said, instead of directly answering his question. "How can we be both joyful and sad in the same moment? It is like that." I took a breath, closed my eyes, and opened them to find myself staring directly at my reflection and found there was a shadow in her gaze, a gleam there that I didn't like.

I turned away from the mirror.

"He has regrets for what he has done and what he has not done, tied up in the sorrow over what he must do. It is knotted and tangled together, and I can tell you what he felt and who it was, but I cannot tell you his motivation. That is for you to discover."

I walked out of the room, slipping past the spot where all three of them were huddled together in the doorframe, then through the front door shutting it behind me.

Victor found me in the carriage, shoved as far as I could get into one corner to try to move away from that thrice-damned spring so I at least wasn't sitting directly on the thing. I was sure the flesh where it pressed up against me on these rides was nothing but pulp at this point, one massive bruise that would burst like rotten fruit if any more pressure was put upon it.

"Morris and Brant have headed back to her station," he said from the door.

"Hmm," I said, more an acknowledgement that he had spoken than that I had truly heard his words.

"They only want to speak to Lord LeVerre—have him sit down and answer some questions," he said.

I snorted.

Victor sighed, climbed into the carriage, and sat across from me. "They did ask that we inform the Company so that if he comes by, they're aware that the police wish to have him in for an interview."

He tapped on the side of the carriage wall and muttered to it. The wheels creaked, and the whole thing shuddered as it began rolling forward.

The silence between us only lengthened the farther from Miss Harper's townhouse we went.

He jiggled his leg, drummed his fingers upon his thigh, and cleared his throat. "Morris wants you to go to the home of Flannegan's fiancée and check there as well, to see if he just happened to visit both locations."

"And what," I said acidly, "are the odds that he hasn't?"

"It may yet turn out to be innocent," Victor said, although he did not sound as though he believed it.

There was no reason for a man of Lucien's stature to have been in Miss Harper's neighborhood to begin with. Not when he was a man of no little means. He had already proven a penchant for showing up in odd places—places where you would not find a member of the peerage unless they were, in their words, "slumming it."

"Back to the office for you to write up the report?" I asked.

"It's where we usually go first," Victor said. "And we'll have to wait to hear from Flannegan as to when and where to meet him."

"And if we even have approval for it," I sighed, slumping back against my seat.

"That as well," Victor acknowledged.

We went silent again, the only noises the rumble of the wheels against the road and the creak of the carriage's frame as it shuddered whenever it hit a bump. I fiddled with the seam in my glove, once again wearing away at the threads that clung to the leather.

Victor cleared his throat. My eyes stayed fastened on my hands.

He cleared his throat again, and when I still didn't look up, he spoke. "Viv."

I raised my head, and he caught my gaze with his. "If you run into him outside the Company walls, I don't want you to be the one who informs him that the police would like to speak with him," he said.

I hesitated before I answered, trying to weigh what I knew of Lucien in my mind against his actions, his words, and how they didn't line up with the way fear skittered along my spine whenever he was near. "You sincerely think he's a danger to me?"

"I can't say if he is, but I don't want to find out," he said. "What kind of interest do you think he took in

Harper to convince her to open her door to him in the first place?"

I opened my mouth and shut it, taking the time to actually consider the question that Victor had asked and not throw back a flippant answer. "He's only been in town for the past week, so where did they meet?"

Victor leaned back, both hands set on his thighs, and jiggled his knee. The man couldn't sit still any more than I could. "Her home is on the other side of the city from the Company, so there would've been little to no reason for him to be over that way."

"Are there any hotels in that district?" I asked. "We don't know where he's been staying."

Victor pursed his lips. "None I'm aware of, and if there are, then they're not the reputable kind."

"And you only frequent reputable hotels I'm sure," I teased solemnly.

He snorted. "I don't frequent hotels to begin with. Too many people passing through, and they're some of the few places I can almost guarantee a vision, but I can't place who or what it belongs to with so many echoes around."

I straightened in my seat. "Hotels."

"Yes, we were just discussing hotels."

"Not that. I mean, yes, that, but if we could find out which hotel Luci—Lord LeVerre has been staying at, maybe you could trigger a vision, and we could get evidence one way or another of his involvement."

"It may be worth the attempt," Victor mused. "And provided we stick to the public areas of the hotel, no warrants or police presence needed for that." He shifted again, tugging his notepad free from his pocket.

"I'll want to send a note to Morris and have her ferret out where he's been staying." He jotted something down, and then tapped the tip of his pencil against the pad, brow furrowed. "Has he asked you anything about the cases you're working?"

"Not specifically, no," I said. "He had asked if we had any new ones, but has let that matter lie since."

"So not a sensation seeker," Victor muttered. He fiddled with the pencil, sliding it back and forth between his fingers. "What could be the motivation here?"

I shrugged. "I believe that's Morris's problem to discover."

He snorted. "Does it not bother you?"

I opened my mouth and closed it, snapping my teeth shut around the irritated words I wanted to hurl at him.

He had done nothing to deserve them. And I could not blame him for Lucien having a facet I had been trying to ignore.

"It does," I admitted. "But I am not sure I wish to know."

We didn't speak again for the remainder of the ride.

When we finally arrived back at the Company's doorstep, the cold had deepened. As sharp as broken glass, it cut right through the layers of fabric I was wrapped in and left me chilled to the bone in the short walk from the sidewalk and through the front door.

Inside, the heat was akin to stepping into a sauna. The Company was apparently in the mood to spare no expense, and I could feel my fingers and toes thaw almost immediately.

"My office or yours?" Victor asked as we made our way past the front desk.

"Yours," I said.

It was only a matter of minutes before we were getting ourselves settled, and Victor was pulling out the old familiar forms and a pen. I sat and watched as he filled out the page, ink blossoming on the paper as it took on the shape of his flowing script.

"Here we are again," I said.

"Quite," he said. He pulled out his pocket watch, checked the time, and grimaced. "Do you want to take a trip to the café to pick us up some sandwiches, or would you rather I get one of the office mice to handle it?"

"I believe the correct term is *administrative assistants*," I said.

"No one uses that title," he said absently, filling out another line.

"I use it."

"When you want to tweak my nose." He rubbed his forehead, along the edge of his brow. "I'll have to send notes to both Morris and Flannegan, and I suppose I should send one to Brant as well so we can discuss what brought him into town to begin with."

"In essence, the boring work."

"Yes. Which is why I asked if you wanted to be the one to run an errand or if you would prefer to sit and watch me, unless you have paperwork to fill out yourself?"

I wasn't hungry, and I also did not wish to go walk into the air outside, but it seemed far worse to send someone else out into the cold for me. I got up, snagged my coat off the rack, and began pulling it on, followed swiftly by my scarf and hat.

"I take it that means you've got it?" Victor asked, raising one eyebrow at me.

"Yes," I said, fussing with the buttons on my coat and the placement of my scarf.

"Viv," Victor said, and I paused to look up from my hands and meet his eyes. "If you happen to run into Lord LeVerre, please be careful."

"If you are so concerned," I said, "perhaps you should instead come with me?"

He set down his pen and shoved his chair back as he stood. "You're right." He came around the desk and grabbed his own coat, scarf, and hat and then motioned at the door. "After you."

The two of us traipsed down the hall, the stairs, past reception, and then out the front to the sidewalk and the piercing chill. It didn't just nip at my cheeks and my nose—it bit them, as if it had become a living thing with a mouthful of slavering teeth.

It was not the most pleasant of walks, considering not only the cold but the manner in which Victor and I hustled as quickly as we could without breaking into a run to reach the warmth of the café. We slipped through its doors, both of us gasping in the heat, as desperate for it as we would have been had we been deprived of air.

We had managed to hit a particularly slow period. The tables were nearly empty, with maybe half a dozen people dotted throughout the space.

"Perhaps we should sit instead?" Victor asked. "After that walk, I think I would prefer something much hotter than a sandwich before heading back."

"I find myself in much the same position," I said. I took the time to look around again, even though I had already counted the heads of the people already seated and knew that none of them were Lucien.

I didn't know what either of us would say to him were we to see him in public. Go about our day? Pretend that we had discovered nothing, circumstantial as it could be considered, and wait for Morris and her cohorts to "invite" him to the station to answer questions?

If we mentioned anything to him, forewarned would be forearmed, and Morris would not appreciate us giving him time to get his story straight.

"Viv, come on," Victor said, and I started. He and the host were both looking at me, and I realized he had been handling the securing of a table for us while I was busy ruminating.

"Sorry," I said. "I was puzzling."

Victor shook his head as I fell into step with him. "Yes, you are."

The host seated us and left us with paper menus before I responded to Victor's not-quite-a-dig. "I meant, I was puzzling over what, if anything, we should say to Lord LeVerre if we were to run into him in a public space."

"We say nothing," Victor said, picking up his menu. "We exchange the usual social pleasantries, avoid any discussion of our current cases, or if he asks, deflect."

"I understand that," I said. "I—just..." I sighed. "Nevermind."

Victor set his menu down. "Nevermind what?"

I waved a hand somewhat helplessly at the café, which wasn't at all the thing I wanted to encompass. "I've never had a case where it was someone I at least had a passing familiarity with. Certainly not someone I had a risk of running into."

"And not someone who had openly expressed an interest in you in some capacity?"

This time I motioned at Victor. "That, exactly."

Victor rubbed his fingers on the table. "It's why I am worried about you running into him in the first place."

I looked down at my own menu, but the words were blurs, my eyes unable to focus on their shapes and orders. "If he is the one murdering those men and taking those women, where is he keeping them?"

"I don't know," Victor said. "And hopefully that means Morris is digging into whether he owns any property in the city. Because he would not be able to sneak three women, in particular if it was against their will, up to a hotel room."

I pushed the menu away from me. "We'll need Morris to obtain a warrant to check his rooms if we find evidence of him in the fiancée's home."

"Yet another bridge to cross when we come to it," Victor said, picking his own menu back up.

I did not return to the Company's building once we had eaten; instead, I insisted on going home, and Victor had taken the time to escort me.

Now I was standing still, my hand resting against the lock as if I intended to step back outside once Victor had disappeared from sight. But what good would wandering the streets expecting to run into Lucien do me, or anyone else for that matter?

I would, in fact, only be hurting Victor, to ignore his advice and the care he had taken to keep me safe.

As early as we had eaten, the shadows in my little home were already beginning to lengthen, the light draining away as the sun began its slow descent to sink beneath the horizon.

I did not want to sleep in my room, but the couch in the parlor was beginning to wear on me. It was not meant for sleeping, and at this point I wasn't even entirely sure it was meant for lounging despite its shape.

I turned to glance up the stairs and to the landing there, but they still held a modicum of slanting sunlight streaming in from the front bedroom windows. I could sleep in there. If I shut and locked the door behind me, I should feel safe enough.

Once our current case was resolved, I would hire someone to come to the house and drag my mirror off to the dump or a secondhand shop.

I shook off my nerves. They would do me no good dawdling in the foyer instead of taking advantage of what light was left to retrieve anything from my room

I wanted for the night, so I headed upstairs. I paused at the door itself, my hand hovering over the knob, trying to recall whether I had shut the door behind me that morning.

I couldn't remember. My habits felt as though they had all been thrown askew. Scattered and tossed about by the current events.

I shoved the door open. The lamp was off, the room itself dim, darkened in the corners, and the only part that seemed to stand out was the bed itself, positioned so the light from the windows would pool on the blankets.

I crossed hurriedly over to the lamp and switched it on so its blue-tinted glow flooded the room, as bright as I could make it. It made the room feel colder—sterile in a way—but I would take that discomfort while I collected my belongings and moved them to the other bedroom.

I grabbed an armload of assorted clothing, bundling them into my arms without a single care as to whether I was wrinkling the fabrics, and left my room to dump the armful onto the bed in the other.

The room itself felt far warmer, and I did not think I could attribute it all to the sunlight that was left.

I went back, fetched my shoes, and then again to fetch my nightgowns.

That done, I stopped in the doorway, letting my eyes skip over the room while I considered whether there was anything else I needed to get or could do without for the night.

Vivian.

My name floated in the air, softly whispered—a kind of caress—and yet the hairs on the back of my neck stood, gooseflesh prickling along in its wake.

Vivian.

It called again, whatever revenant it was this voice was attached to, and against my better judgment, I stepped into the room and turned toward the mirror there.

My shawl had fallen free of the glass, a heap of fabric sitting on the vanity, and all I could see reflected back at me was the vague shape of a woman.

Vivian?

The voice sounded plaintive now—a plea—but there was an undertone, a current I was not sure I wanted to be wading into lest I be swept away by something far more powerful than I had estimated. I moved closer to the mirror, my feet not my own, my limbs driven by the call of that voice, that timbre that captured my mind. All other sounds had fallen away: there was only my breath, the beating of my heart, and their gentle, entreating tone.

The figure in the mirror began taking on a more solid shape, the blurred edges sharpening the closer I came to it, until she seemed to bloom out of its depths—the Lady LeVerre.

She was attired much as I was, although I was sure the fabrics of her clothing were far richer than the ones that had slid through my fingers. She wore a simple white and blousy shirt, with long cuffed sleeves that were surprisingly loose along the arms in spite of how closely trimmed it was to her waist. A dark skirt disappeared below the edge of the glass the closer I moved to it as she stepped forward along with me.

It would appear that the popular styles of hair had remained much the same in the past seven years, for hers was an artfully disheveled bun, strands left loose to frame her face, which was similar to my own, delicate and pointed.

It was her eyes that truly caught me though. A golden russet in one moment, the color shifting and darkening until I could have sworn they were far closer to red.

She set her hand on the glass, palm and fingers pressed to its surface and I was staring at the lines in the skin, picking out the shapes as if I were a fortune-teller who could read what they would tell me. *Come to me, Vivian*, her voice crooned. *Help me.*

I reached out, my own fingers trembling, and I paused to stare at the back of my hand and the leather glove it was still encased in.

When I looked back at the mirror, it was to see only me, my hand halfway to the glass.

CHAPTER SIXTEEN

December 2, 1888

Lord LeVerre stopped at the station today to request we leave Lady LeVerre's case open for a little longer. He seemed certain she would return, and that it was only a matter of time. Something was missing from my office when he left, but I couldn't place my finger on what it was.

C old winter light shone directly in my face when I woke the next morning, and I was starkly reminded of why I had chosen not to make the front room my bedroom to begin with.

I rose, used the necessities, splashed water on my face, and regretted it instantly as it was like bathing my skin with ice. I dressed for the day, all the while trying to keep from straying toward my locked bedroom door.

It was nagging at me, sitting in the back of my mind, this need to go inside and touch my fingers to the glass, to try saying her name to see if she would return.

I had slept with my gloves on, and now that I was ready for the day, I retrieved them from the nightstand where I had set them when I got up. I hesitated, rubbing at the leather, picking over the worn seam.

I needed to repair it.

I pulled them on and headed downstairs to the kitchen where I busied myself with the daily routine of breakfast and coffee, but I kept glancing at the ceiling above me.

I wanted to go back up the stairs and unlock the door.

I did not like this insistence, the way it whispered and cajoled, crooned and begged in turns, an undercurrent to it that told me if I didn't listen it would shortly turn to anger. It reminded me of Lucien—the way it twisted in my guts, crawled its way up my spine, and sat at my shoulder. That knife's edge walk.

The poker was in the parlor. Perhaps I should take the heavy metal to it, shatter the glass until the mirror was shards and dust and grit scattered across my vanity and the floor.

I ate mechanically and drank my coffee, but couldn't taste the liquid on my tongue. I washed the dishes and set them aside to dry.

I had nothing else I could do in my house but listen to that voice repeat my name. It was there—in the air—slipping its way down the stairs. I was sure that it would drive me mad if I stayed.

I retrieved my coat, scarf, and hat from the rack by the front door, stepped outside, and locked it behind me.

I hesitated with my hand still on the knob, the key still in the lock. There was nothing that said I had to go into the office. I could go back inside, up to my room and stand in front of my mirror all day if I wanted to.

It was as if there were strings attached to my limbs: someone had tied them to my wrists and ankles, and now they were trying to figure out the combination needed to make me dance to their tune.

I turned away from my door, hurried down the steps and up the sidewalk to the only building I was sure would be a safe haven in this city. I had a stitch forming in my side by the time I reached it, but I didn't pause until I had gotten through the door and into the lobby.

The receptionist looked up long enough to ascertain who had just come in, and looked back down at whatever paperwork it was she had on her desk. I bustled past her into the hall and then the stairwell. My steps didn't slow until I reached the second floor and had to decide if I wanted to see if Victor was already in, or continue on to my office.

He would ask me what was wrong, and how could I tell him that Lady LeVerre was haunting my mirror?

I moved past the second floor, and sought the sanctuary of my own space and desk.

The room was empty, my erstwhile office companion somewhere else per her preferences. There were times when I wasn't entirely sure she existed, and then she would pop up, either exiting as I was entering, or I would find her sitting at her desk, reading a book or filling out forms before one or both of us would be summoned for another case to resolve.

I took the pause I needed to catch my breath and ease the burning muscle before I set my hat, scarf, and coat on the rack and took a seat behind my desk.

It took me a long minute to finally relax, but when I did, I sagged back against the chair, my limbs as loose as I could make them. I finally felt as if I had the space to breathe. I had been drowning and hadn't realized it, inundated with a need I couldn't understand even as I fought against it.

I wanted to laugh at myself, to shake my head and repeat that it was only a mirror—only a reflection—an overactive imagination wrought by fever dreams and lingering nightmares.

I wasn't sure that I could.

I pressed my hands to my face, palms over my eyes, the tips of my fingers in my hair, as any laugh that tried to bubble its way to the surface felt too close to hysterics and would shortly dissolve into tears.

There was a knock on the wood of the doorframe, and I started, jerking upright in my chair, my heart beating frantically in my chest, to find Victor standing there.

"Fuck, Viv," he said. "You look awful."

"I couldn't sleep," I said.

He sat on the chair across from my desk. "Nightmares again?"

"Yes," I said. It wasn't quite a lie—at least, I didn't think it was. Surely the experiences I was having with my own mirror were nothing more than that. I was dreaming and didn't know it when I was walking those nightmarish landscapes—real enough that I was mixing them up with the world at large instead of having a clear and consistent line between the two.

"Do you want to try staying at my apartment for a night or two to see if that clears them up?" he asked.

I shook my head and rubbed a hand on my face. "No, I think we just need this case resolved and then they should go away. It's the oddness of the whole thing that's affecting me."

He still looked concerned, with worry in his eyes that lightened the gray, making them less storm clouds and more a hint of rain.

"Truly," I said. "It's just the way their emotions linger with no answers."

He was quiet, watching me before he nodded. "Alright. Well then, you'll be happy to know we've an appointment with Flannegan at ten o'clock for you to try reading his fiancée's house to see if Lord LeVerre has been inside it."

"And if I find evidence he has been?" I asked.

"I assume Morris and Flannegan will track him down, because at that point it looks less circumstantial and far more suspicious." He pulled out his pocket watch, glanced at the face, and tucked it away again. "And not to rush you, but it's already half past. If we don't want to be late we need to be heading out the door now." He got up from his chair and I followed, snagging my coat, scarf, and hat free of the rack as we headed out my door. I somehow managed to pull them on as we walked along the hall and down the stairs.

Victor's carriage was, as usual, parked outside, and the two of us climbed in and were off shortly after.

It did take us close to the whole of that half hour for the carriage to navigate the streets, and when it finally pulled up in front of our destination, one peek out the window determined that Flannegan was already waiting on the front steps. Yet another townhouse in a row of homes, empty flower boxes at the front, trimmed in white.

"Only him?" I asked.

"Only him," Victor confirmed as he pushed the door open and got out. "Good morning, Detective."

"Morris says you may have a suspect," Flannegan said by way of greeting, and I paused in my own exit, half-out of the carriage.

"We may," Victor said. "But it's a bit early to be sure."

"He was at one of the victim's houses, was he not?"

"Yes." Victor's tone was clipped.

"Well then," Flannegan said as if that decided the matter.

"We do need to determine if the same person had access to—I'm sorry, we weren't provided her name."

"Mary O'Brian."

"Miss O'Brian," Victor finished. "If my sister could read the interior of the house and its contents, please."

"Right," Flannegan said, he turned and opened the door. He stepped inside, and Victor and I followed from the cold winter sun to a chilly and dimly lit foyer. It was a similar layout to my own—the parlor to the left, a hallway that led deeper into the building, and stairs in front that were wreathed in shadows.

I wasn't sure I wanted to find out what waited there for us in the dark.

I headed for the parlor, where it was brightly lit comparatively, with weak sunlight spilling out over the wood floor, its cheerfully colored rugs, and worn but deep couch and armchairs. There were tables with various knickknacks scattered throughout, and old-fashioned lanterns rather than spelled lamps. The fireplace was empty, cleared of even ashes.

A mirror hung above its mantel, framed in flaking gold although the glass appeared relatively free of tarnish. I could see the three of us reflected in it where we stood—me hovering at the parlor door and the two men behind me.

"Well?" Flannegan asked.

"If you could please exercise some patience, Detective," Victor said, but I could barely hear him. The sounds of their voices had become muted, as if I was swimming underwater.

The woman in the mirror wasn't me—I was sure of it, despite our similar features. The smile on her face was off—too sharp—and the gleam in her eyes reflected a hunger I had never felt.

"Viv," Victor's voice broke through, and I started, turned to face him. "Are you ready?" he asked.

"Yes," I said, hastily pulling off my glove, and trying to ignore the steady not-quite-a-glare that Flannegan was giving me. I kept my glove clutched in one hand, and then set my free palm against the back of the couch.

The fabric was incredibly soft beneath the tips of my fingers, and the emotions drifting up to me were of contentment and joy.

He had proposed to her while they sat on this couch together—a small, sweet gesture and moment between them, no grand sweeping declarations of love—but it made my heart ache all the more with it. It was a quiet, daily kind of love, one that put down roots so deep there was no pulling them free from the soil, and what was planted there would remain with him for the rest of his life.

And he was looking at living it without her.

This remnant of her was beginning to fade, that slow sinking into darkness, and soon all that would be left was that sense of her feelings being wrapped in cotton. Any time I touched any of her items, it would be like an unboxing before I stowed them away in storage again.

"Anything?" Flannegan asked.

"Not yet," I said. "At least, not of anyone she did not know or had only just met." I slid my hand along the couch as I walked. "You proposed to her on this couch."

"I did," he said tightly. "What else can you read there?"

"Just that," I said. "Those small moments between you two."

I stepped away from the couch and set my hand on the frame of one of the armchairs, but there I found only chatter, the excited gossip of what I assumed was her closest neighbor, the clatter of tea cups, and the snap of gingerbread being broken in half.

I glanced at the mirror, caught in the space between the mantel and the chair, unsure that I wanted to make that leap and come within touching distance of the glass.

But there was only me reflected in it, gray eyes and a pale face with shadowed, hollow cheeks. No wonder Victor had said I looked awful.

I touched the tips of my fingers to the mantel.

He had been here. The wood was absolutely flood-ed with his regret, and I wondered if he wore it wrapped around himself like a cloak, his own constant companion. He had run his hand along the mantel much the same as I was doing now, following the line of its edge as he walked. There was a moment where he paused, considering something about the house—such a fleeting thought that the emotion was there and gone before I could delve into it.

I lifted my hand, set it back down, palm against the wood, warm where the sun sat in the same spot, swamped by his regret, but this time I knew what I was watching for.

The house was too small. He felt squeezed in by it, the walls too close despite the brightness of the rooms. And then it was gone again, swallowed by his melancholy.

I brought my hand up to my chest, turned to face Flannegan and Victor. "Was she planning on selling the house?"

"Yes," Flannegan said. "Our wedding was supposed to be next week, so she listed it with a solicitor in the hopes that we could get it sold quickly." He waited, eyes on me, his lip trembling while he hesitated. "Is there any news you can give me about her? About what happened?"

Now it was my turn to pause, while the words stuck in my throat and coated my tongue—dust and ash.

"Miss Tailor," he said quietly. "Will we find her alive?"

I swallowed back against the knot, the building nausea working its way upwards. "I'm sorry," I whispered. "But we won't."

He blinked, nodded, and took in a shuddering breath, his eyes glazed and shiny. "Right," he said gruffly, his voice thick. "If you—anything you did find, please report it to Morris—I want...I want..." He was casting about, turning his head as if he was trying to find a spot to sit in a crowded room before he gave up and sank to the floor, his back against the doorframe. "I would like a moment to be alone," he whispered.

"Viv," Victor said, but I was already navigating my way back to the foyer, slipping carefully past Flannegan and around Victor to go stand by the front door while Victor knelt next to the man, his words mere murmurs. He patted him gently on the shoulder, got to his feet, and we went out the door while Flannegan began to weep.

We were down the steps and already at the carriage before I said anything. "Should we be leaving him alone like that?"

Victor cast a glance back at the house and its windows. "No," he said. "But it's what he said he wanted."

The ride back to the Company was subdued, the mood much the same once we had reached Victor's office.

He was the first to break the silence. "Did you find any evidence that the nurse was dead when you read her house?"

"No," I said. "But she was more recently taken, wasn't she?"

He pulled open a drawer, yet more forms that he set on the surface of the desk, shuffled through them before picking one. "Was it Lord LeVerre in the house again?"

"Yes," I said.

He began writing hastily, his normally neat, flowing script gone beneath scribbled words.

I doubted we would find Judith Harper or the nameless woman from our first case alive.

"The first woman, you suspect she's deceased as well?" he asked, echoing my thoughts.

"It would seem likely," I said. "I could read the houses again for both of them, to be certain."

"We'll need to ask Morris if Harper had recently listed her home with a solicitor; that would explain the connection there, but the first..."

"Pure coincidence?" I suggested. "We had only been in town for a night."

Victor frowned. "How did he get here so quickly?"

"Who?"

"Lord LeVerre. If we had only been in town for a night, he had to have left right after we did to get here in time to murder that man and take his daughter." He drummed his fingers on the desk; his pen had gone still. "He wouldn't have had time to discuss the warrants with Brant otherwise."

"If he's lying about not being a murderer," I said quietly, "he could very well have lied about attempting to secure them."

Victor made a face, a furrowing of his brow and a thinning of his lips as he stared down at the paper. "It's possible he went to town to see Brant, was told no, and then immediately followed us here to speak to the Company."

I sat quietly. "He doesn't seem the type to take hearing that word well, whether his mother is involved or not."

"No," Victor said wryly. "He does not." He went back to filling out the form on his desk, reached back into the pile to pull out blank papers, penned a quick note across them, and folded them up, making the paper into its own envelope. He shoved away from the desk. "I'll be right back," he said. "Don't go anywhere." He disappeared out the door. His footsteps clicked down the hall.

I certainly had no intention of getting up and leaving the room, so his warning, or request, was entirely unnecessary. Where would I go anyway? Up to my own lonely office in the hopes that I might find Margaret, a woman I barely knew or spoke to?

Or was he worried I would leave the building to seek out Lucien? Nosy I might be when it came to someone as a client—poking around where I perhaps should not—but actively seeking out a man who may have kidnapped and murdered three separate women seemed like a bad decision even I would not make.

Victor's chair creaked when he came in and sat back down. It creaked again as he shifted, settling against its back. "I think the best thing while we wait may be for me to take you home so you can rest."

I opened my mouth to protest, but what could I say without sounding like a child, scared of the dark with nothing there but shadows to be frightened of? And if I did say anything about the nightmares, Victor would offer to let me rest at his apartment, but what if what I was seeing was real? Would it follow me there and infect his home as well?

"Alright," I said.

He got back up from his chair, and I hesitated a minute longer before I followed him out his office door.

CHAPTER SEVENTEEN

File N-1647

Item I: Small novel—cover and title are faded and flaking off. Remnants of petals pressed between its pages are embedded in the paper. No notations as to who the item belonged to have been made.

My house was quiet, sitting silently in the afternoon sun. I would have wavered, standing uncertainly on my own front step for far longer than I did with Victor watching me from the carriage. Instead, I had hurried inside, eager to at least get out of the cold and into the warmth. It was half past one at this point, which meant I had quite the length of time to while away.

I spared a glance at the stairs, my gaze following their length to the upper landing, but from where I stood, I could see nothing amiss—no looming or gathering of the dark above me. In fact, everything seemed ordinary.

I headed for the kitchen. I paused in its doorway once I reached it, waiting to see if I could hear footsteps, or the moan of wood that would indicate someone was waiting upstairs in my room for me, but there was nothing. After another moment of hesitation I stepped into the room itself. There was nothing to clean or straighten, and I had a while before dinner.

I made my way to ice box. If nothing else, I could take stock of what I had, and go to the grocer's for anything I was running low on. I opened its door, half-bent at the waist as I looked over the items inside: eggs, butter, cheese, a glass pint of milk, but no meat wrapped in its familiar paper and twine packaging. I had used up any of the sausage that Victor had brought me, and it would appear he had procured nothing else from the butcher.

Above me the ceiling groaned, a heavy kind of scraping that sounded as if someone was shoving the furniture about. I froze where I was, my heartbeat in my ears, its thrumming hammering against my ribs. Slowly—so very slowly—I straightened and closed the door to the icebox, my head cocked to the side as I waited for another sound. Although how I was supposed to hear it above my frantic pulse, I wasn't sure.

The rapid *tap, tap, tap* of someone light on their feet as they moved about the room sounded as if they were circling or pacing—a quick, scurrying back and forth.

I followed their movements, creeping out of the kitchen and up the hall, their footsteps echoing. The closer I came to the stairs, the quieter their movements became, almost as if they themselves were waiting with bated breath to see just what it was I would do.

I went for the poker in the parlor. I pulled it free of its stand before I headed for the stairs and then up to the second floor—my own movements deliberate, my free hand trailing along the banister. I would not warn them of what I intended to do if I could help it.

Perhaps it was a good thing I had left my gloves on—the leather between my sweating, clammy palms and the rough metal. My grip was so tight my fingers ached, my whole arm trembling.

My bedroom door was cracked open, and I was certain I had locked it the night before, and left it locked this morning before I had exited my house.

I crept up to the door, the poker raised as high as I could manage to swing it, and I shoved the door open. It swung freely—no objects in the way to block its path—and when I peered into the room, nothing was changed. My bed, my wardrobe, my vanity—all the pieces were exactly where they had been the night before.

Even the mirror remained in its same spot, the shawl still drawn over the glass to block its view of the room.

I lowered the poker, hesitating in the doorframe. I had heard footsteps; I was sure of it. I spared another glance at the mirror, took a breath, hefted the poker back up, walked over to the vanity, and yanked the shawl free, the fabric slithering off the glass in one swooping waterfall.

There was only my reflection staring back at me.

I was tempted to reach out and touch my palm to the glass to see what would happen, or to smash the mirror, crack the glass into millions of shattered pieces.

Instead I turned around and left the room, slammed the door shut behind me, and locked it. I took the poker back to the parlor and left it in its place with the other tools. I snagged my coat, hat, and scarf up off their rack and pulled them on before I went out the front door, locked that behind me too, hurried down the steps, and took a right to head up the sidewalk.

I had no destination in mind.

After a bit, my racing heart began to calm, whatever anger or fear it was I was carrying draining away, and I paused in my steps to take in just where I had ended up.

My feet had taken me in the direction of the shops and the grocer's, and since I had been planning a trip to the butcher to begin with, I headed there first.

The shop itself was a cheerful little building, painted white on the outside with two large bay windows through which one could easily peer into the store. The floors were tiled, and the walls at the back behind the counter the same.

"Miss Tailor," said the man standing behind its polished wood surface, "I'm glad to see you up and about." He paused, brow furrowed while he studied me. "Your brother said you were sick, but if I were him, I would say you still are."

"Sickness followed by poor sleep," I said. "I haven't had much of a chance to recover from it."

"Aye, that would certainly do it," he said, but he sounded uncertain. "What can I get for you today?"

"Just sausages, the small ones for breakfast," I said. "I don't know that I'm up to cooking anything more complex."

He nodded and began pulling the requested items from the chilled, glass-fronted display case. I waited impatiently, as whatever energy I had managed to gather together seemed to be going the same way as my irritation, dribbling away until I was sure I would sag like a puppet whose strings had been cut, collapsing into a pile of limbs on the butcher shop floor.

He wrapped the sausages up into a neat paper package tied with twine. I paid him, took my purchase, and left. Now that I had procured a single item, I was left at odds ends, not quite ready to head back to my house, even if it was only for long enough to put the meat into the ice box.

Instead I wandered a bit farther up the road, both through and with the streams of people who were also frequenting the area, until I came upon an empty storefront.

It also had a pair of bay windows—tall and narrow ones, the frames holding the panes painted a dark pine green. The rest of the front was the same color, with peeling gold letters above the door. The interior of it was dark, but I knew when I walked up and pressed my face to the glass to peer inside, I would see a dust-covered counter toward the back, with a cash register resting on its surface, and beyond that, a door that led into the storage space, and lightly stained, wide-planked wood floors. There were two round tables for merchandise that had been left by the previous occupant—whatever their offerings had been, I didn't know. It had lamps on the wall, but having never been inside, I didn't know if they were oil or magic.

"Is this the storefront you spoke of?"

I jerked, and nearly dropped my package. When I turned, I was face to face with Lucien. My mouth went dry, my tongue stuck to its roof, and for a long, flustered moment I could say nothing at all. But we were standing in the middle of a crowded sidewalk, so what could he possibly do to me here?

"Yes," I finally said.

He shifted, turning to study the building. With his eyes off me I could let out a breath, feel the stiffening muscles along my back and shoulders relax. "It's quite small."

I tilted my chin up. "It's the perfect size."

"Oh, no doubt about that," he said, and gave me a sidelong glance that made me want to skip a step backwards. "It has an air of *intimacy* about it."

I didn't like the way the word lingered in the air between us. If anything, I was certainly full of regrets that I had discussed my plans with this man in the first place. I had given him knowledge without knowing what he truly was.

"Are you staying nearby?" I asked. "I didn't know there were any hotels in the area."

"No," he said. "I'm afraid that I'm currently located across town. It's farther from the Company than I would have preferred, and doesn't make looking for a more permanent location any easier."

"You're moving here?"

"It would be hard to keep an eye on my investment if I'm having to traipse back and forth between here and the country." He stepped forward and ran a finger down the wood framing the panes of glass. He bent at the waist, knocked on the sill and then beneath it. "Seems solid enough. I don't see any signs of rot." He reached into his pocket, pulled out a key, unlocked the front door, and swung it open.

I stared into the opening, past the afternoon sun filtering through the dust motes in the air. The floor inside was dull, and it would need a good cleaning, perhaps even a refinishing to protect the surface from scuffs and marks.

My brain and tongue finally caught up with each other. "You bought it?"

"I did."

"But..." I peered back into the interior. "We don't even have an agreement laid out yet."

He waved it aside. "It's a good investment regardless of who the proprietor is. You'd have to lease the space from me until you've made enough profit to buy it outright, same as you would have had to do with the previous owner. I can do the exact same thing with someone else if you've had a change of heart and no longer want your flower shop." He looked directly back at me. There was a smile on his lips that seemed to shift from shy to sly and back again, and I wasn't sure which one was the mask and which one was the true him. "Would you like to tour it?"

"I..." I took a glance at the streets, a quick one out of the corners of my eyes. It was broad daylight, the sidewalk filled with people, and there was no way they had missed the two of us as they walked around me where I stood, nearly blocking the way.

I was quite possibly one of the few people in a position where I could ask Lucien questions without raising his suspicions.

"Yes," I said, and then moved past him, my skirts brushing against his legs as I stepped over the threshold and into the dim space beyond.

He followed me in and shut the door behind us. Despite the fact that its entire face was more panes of glass, the room felt darker when the latch clicked. I ignored the uncertain chill that crept its way up my spine, spread out along my shoulders and up my neck, leaving prickles in my skin in its wake. I moved deeper into the shop, and trailed my gloved fingers down the surface of one of the tables, leaving pathways in the gathered dust.

"I was thinking," Lucien said as he walked along the edges of the room, pointing out spaces on the walls to me, "that we would want to hang mirrors, full height ones on either side to help keep the room bright but also make it appear larger than it is."

I paused, still standing by the table, so its bulk was between us, whereas he was by the wall, his fingers pressed to the plaster although he had twisted to face me. "Floor to ceiling?" I asked hesitantly.

"Not quite," he said. "That would be unsightly. More about starting at the ankles and then just above your head, nearly big enough to be a door." He motioned at the wall sketching out where the mirror would hang. "About this wide, and framed. So if you look at it, you could almost mistake it for an additional room, or maybe even a painting, a reflection caught in time."

I eyed the amount of space he was indicating. "Those would not come cheap."

"We would purchase them out of the startup funds."

"And these startup funds would come from where?"

"Well, that depends on how much of a personal stake you want in your own shop," he said. "I could fund you one hundred percent of the way."

"For how much of the ownership?" I asked warily. "And what would my responsibilities towards paying back those funds be if the shop were to fail?"

"If the shop fails, it fails, and that would be the end of it. Investments like these are always a gamble," he said. He stepped away from the wall and came towards my table, so now we stood directly across from one another.

"That does not tell me how much of my shop you expect to own in exchange for those funds."

"All of it," he said baldly.

"All of it." I couldn't help the way my voice faltered.

"Whatever agreement we come to would include a clause allowing you the opportunity to buy me out, in whatever fashion you wish, whether that's over time or all at once."

I laughed, and it sounded bitter to my ears. "You honestly expect my shop to make enough money that I could afford to buy you out in one fell swoop?"

He edged around the table, coming in closer toward me, and I stood my ground, waiting to hear just what honeyed promises he intended to pour into my ears. "I absolutely expect it to, with my help."

"And if you control one hundred percent of my store, how exactly am I to make enough profit myself to buy you out with the money I receive? I wouldn't be anything more than an employee in my own store. Without any possession, where are my dividends?"

"I suppose," he said seriously, now that he was looming above me, his russet eyes locked on mine, "that they would all be going into my pocket."

"And that would make it impossible for me to buy you out."

He grinned, a quick flash of a smile that exposed his teeth. "I suppose it would, yes."

"And which method of ownership are you trying to encourage here?" I asked. "The one where I have some skin in the game, or the one where I can never remove you from my life unless I give up my flowers entirely?"

"Do you want honesty, or do you want pretty lies?" he asked. He eased back a step, tapping his fingers on the table beside us. "If I have full control, and the shop goes under, you suffer none of the losses, as whole as you were before this venture. But it would mean you are stuck with my company for as long as the business exists—until either one of us dies, or retires, I suppose."

I hesitated, letting the silence between us grow, before I finally asked the question that had been sitting on the tip of my tongue. "How did you know which building to buy?"

He smiled at me again, and if there was any one thing he did that set me on edge, made me want to back away and flee, it was whenever he would bare his teeth. "A calculated gamble. I could have chosen the wrong storefront all together. But there are only so many empty stores so close to the area in which you stated you lived, so the odds that I would get lucky and strike gold looked to be in my favor."

"So when you weren't haunting the Company's hallowed halls, or conveniently wandering the streets nearby, you had a solicitor showing you about?"

"I did," he admitted.

"To houses too?"

"Yes."

"Have you found any that interested you?" I was skirting as close as I dared to the subject.

He left his hand resting on the table and watched me long enough that I could feel sweat gathering on my brow and along my hairline, ready to drip down the back of my neck. I was ever grateful for the leather of my gloves, which hid my palms from view, and no one else would ever know that they had gone cold and clammy. "Sadly, no," he said, and turned away, heading over to the counter and began examining the cash register. He poked his fingers over its metal curlicues, the decorative embossing on its surface. "You would think the previous tenant would have taken something as valuable as this."

"It may have been more trouble to remove it than it was worth," I said, lingering by the table, as much as I was tempted to join him in looking the item over.

He gave it a shove, grunting when it didn't move. "It's bolted down."

I couldn't help the laugh that rose in my throat. "They generally are."

"For what reason?" he asked. "I would think its very substance would make it too hard to simply lift and run off with."

This time I did cross the space between us, slipping past him so I was behind the counter with the wood between us, pointing at the keys. "The drawer locks, and remains locked except for between sales when you add up the prices and hit the total. The only way to get at the money it holds is to either take the time to get behind the counter and hold off the employees while you key items in, and hope the store owner didn't get it spelled. *Or* you can attempt to snatch it off the counter and pray you move quickly enough that you can try to break it open in a secondary location."

He looked up from where my fingers were dancing over the buttons of the till to meet my gaze again, and my hand stilled, locked in place while I was caught by the red gleam in those russet eyes.

"You seem to have thought this through quite a bit," he said.

"You think through how a criminal would act in certain circumstances when you're someone in my position quite often," I said.

"And how would he act now?" he asked.

If I hadn't already been frozen, stuck to the floor with my hand resting on the register, I would have been at his words. I hesitated. "In a case where he discovers he can neither open nor take the till with him?" I asked.

There was a flash of amusement in his eyes, something akin to a cat toying with a mouse. "Yes, what then?"

"I suppose he would run."

He was watching me again, a slight tilt to his head as he regarded me. He lifted his hand, it stalled halfway up. "I often wonder..." he began.

"You often wonder?" I prodded, when he said nothing else.

"If I were to touch you skin to skin, what secrets of mine would you find?"

I opened my mouth, shut it, and there was a flush gathering across my cheeks and up the back of my neck, the heat of it pooling in my chest.

"Palm to palm," he hastily clarified. "Nothing more."

"I've never read the living, only the dead," I said shortly.

"Ah," he said. "I forgot; we've been over this before. What do you think you would get from a living person, if anything at all?"

"Surface emotions, most likely," I said. "How they're feeling in the moment."

"So potentially, you could tell how I'm feeling, right now, here?"

"Possibly," I said warily. "But I do not know that I would want to be reading the emotions of someone who is either a potential employer or business partner."

"Because of the interest I've shown in you previously?"

"That certainly is a part of it." I moved away from the till, down the counter so that I could open space between us, but he followed after me, the wood the only barrier. "And I do not know that I want to venture down a path that would give me information I do not want to have."

He met me at the end of the counter, blocking my way out from behind its surface. "And what if it is information I wish to impart?" He set one hand on top of the wood, leaned in toward me, and the only way I had to go was to step back, deeper into the space and farther from the windows and the street. "When I am with you, I feel as though I have awakened from a fever dream. The air around me was stale—the colors and light gone from the world. You bring it back in with you, and I cannot bear the thought of losing it all again."

I was blushing madly, unable to speak and interrupt this apparent confession of love, unsure of which direction I dared even take.

"I am in thrall," he murmured, his eyes fastened on my throat, and I could have sworn locked directly on the pulse that frantically fluttered there, "and I have nowhere to turn to."

"Have you heard any news about your mother's case?" I squeaked.

He blinked—his eyes flicked up to my face, back down again—then thankfully he straightened, easing away enough at least that I could catch my breath, but not enough that I could slip around him to head for the door. He left his hand on the wood, the long fingers spread, and I glanced down at them.

He was wearing gloves.

"No," he said. "I've written to the Company, asking for some kind of update on whether they'll assist me with obtaining those warrants, but from what I understand," and here his voice hardened, the tone chipped stone, "Brant has also come to town and I believe is blocking that progress."

"Oh," I said quietly. "But—why would he do that?"

"I don't know," he said, and his voice was growing colder with every word, the bitter bite of winter borne from his tongue. "But I will not—cannot rest until I know what happened. I owe her that much at least, as she made me what I am."

"She had such a heavy hand in influencing the man you are today?"

"She *was* my mother," he said, but the words had a cadence to them, the rote of information repeated until it would trip off the tongue and sound like fact.

"I'm just—surprised," I ventured, "that a family with your standing chose not to hire a nanny or a governess."

His eyes were searching mine, and there was something in the way they flickered as if he was working through what he *should* say rather than *how* to say it. "My—mother—was insistent that she be the one to school me until I was old enough to be sent away to one that could teach me the things she had no knowledge of."

"Oh." I was hesitating again, wondering if I told Lucien I was seeing a woman I was certain was his mother in my mirror, if he would think me mad. Or maybe he would think I was on his side, as feverishly obsessed with finding her as he was, my own failures at reading her items aside. Or perhaps part and parcel of why she haunted me now.

Maybe the only way for me to know would be to return to his manor. With a man I suspected of at minimum murdering three men and kidnapping and killing three women—Flannegan's fiancée at least—and I stood there a moment longer with the realization that I hadn't even bothered to remember the woman's name.

"What is that you have there?" Lucien asked. He sounded honestly curious, and it interrupted my tumbling thoughts and half-formed plans of fetching Victor and confessing all to both of them at once. Mad I might be, but I would go nowhere else alone with the man standing in front of me.

I looked down at the package I still held in one hand. "Sausages."

"Sausages?"

"Yes. You know, ground meat in casings meant for frying and eating." I was babbling at the moment, but I was trying to think of a way that would get Lucien to back up farther, a movement that would let me get by him without having to shove him out of the way and run. He would know something was off if I pushed him out of my way to dart out the door. "I need to get home and get them into the icebox before they go off."

He took a step back, then another, which allowed me to move past him and toward the front of the store, although he kept pace with me as we headed to the door. "We certainly wouldn't want you to get sick from eating meat that's gone bad."

I paused, turning toward him with one hand on the knob. I was trying not to meet his eyes, focusing my gaze instead on the space between them—his fore-head, his nose—but I could not get my own to settle onto a single spot. Instead I looked down, my eyes on the floor and the tips of his shoes. "I would like to speak to Victor about your case, to see if maybe..." I lost the thread of what I was trying to say, unwilling to promise anything when I was already on uncertain ground.

"Can either of you make your employers move with any more speed?" he asked. "Because the plodding from them is all I've seen."

"Unfortunately, no," I said wryly. "They are of the opinion that they will get to everything in due time and not a moment sooner."

"So then, just what will you and your brother be able to do to assist me any further than you already have?"

I licked my lips, and then decided to let the words lie, to not give him any details more than I had at this point.

I could only bring myself to so much haste. "I would like a chance to speak to Victor first, to see if he agrees that my idea has any merit."

"Then I suppose we should part ways until we have reason to speak again."

"I suppose," I said. I could not bring myself to turn the knob and step out the door, this reluctance chafing at my nerves. "I don't know which hotel you're staying at, so how will I send a note?"

"The Hotel Morning Glory," he said, amusement threaded into his tone again. "It seemed fitting, considering I came here to seek out you and your would-be flower shop."

My fingers had tightened on the knob, and now they loosened. "I thought you came because Brant would not assist you in obtaining warrants."

"Can it not be both?"

"I believe I have actively discouraged you in pursuing the second."

"I think you have the order of them backwards," he said, edging in closer to me, enough that his shoes were brushing up against my hem.

"Then I will continue to discourage you in your pursuit of the first," I said shortly. "Even if there were no other reasons, I will not mix business and pleasure."

"There are plenty of husband and wife businesses out there who appear to be operating smoothly and doing quite well for themselves."

I snorted. "You barely know me, and *we* barely know each other. Even if marriage was on the table, it's too soon to even come under consideration." I finally looked up and caught his gaze with mine. My voice was as firm as I could make it, although it and my conviction seemed to want to waver. The noise of the outside streets was fading, the colors of the sunlight and dancing dust motes smearing together, and the only thing in my field of view were his eyes.

"Then, maybe over time, we can come to know each other better."

I shook my head, trying to clear the way his words seemed to weave their way through my thoughts, wisps of fog in my mind. He reached down, set his hand over the top of mine on the knob, turned it so we opened the door together, and the sounds of chatter and clicking footsteps flooded their way into the space. He released his grip on my hand and motioned at the streets outside. "After you," he said.

I blinked, tore my gaze from his, and slipped out the door and onto the sidewalk, moving as speedily away from him as I could without breaking into a run.

CHAPTER EIGHTEEN

File N-1647
Interview with witnesses suggests the victim may have gone to visit her mother.
Further investigation led only to Highgate.

I did not go home. Instead, I went back to the Company's office building, past the receptionist, and straight for Victor's office.

It was empty.

Rather than try to figure out where he had gone, I sat in the chair across from his desk, my package of sausages clutched in my hands. I stared down at them, unseeing, trying to recall where I had gotten them.

I perhaps should have been more disturbed by the fact that the most recent events of the day were made of mist, and all I could focus on was the image of Lucien's eyes on my throat. I did not like it, or the way fear pooled at the base of my spine, thick and dark like the shadows at the top of the stairs and at the door of my bedroom.

"Viv," Victor's voice came from behind me, and I looked up even as I twisted in my chair to face him.

"I sent you home to rest, so how is it you came back looking worse than when you left?"

I set my package on his desk. "I went to pick up sausages and ran into Lucien on my way home."

"Lord LeVerre?" he asked, a correction in his tone.

"Yes, him," I said waspishly. "I ran into *Lord LeVerre* on the way home."

He didn't acknowledge my snappishness. "Are you alright?"

"I'm here in one piece, aren't I?"

"That doesn't mean that you're well," he said, moving around both me and the desk to sit in his own seat. "What happened?"

"He has managed to purchase my storefront," I said.

Victor's brow furrowed, his lips thinned. "How did he know which building to buy?"

"I don't know," I said peevishly. "I never told him which one I was considering, and he claims it was a matter of luck and deduction."

Victor snorted. "Quite some reasoning in that case." He drummed his fingers on the surface of the desk as he leaned forward. "Did his powers of deduction happen to lead to a conversation between you two?"

"Yes."

He sighed. Rubbed his forehead, along the ridge of his brow and between his eyes. "I wish you had taken the first opportunity to walk away rather than engage with him."

"We were on a public street surrounded by people."

"Were you?" he asked. "Or did you go into the shop with him?"

I flushed, skipped past his question. "I know which hotel he's at."

Victor shot me a sharp look. "You did, didn't you?"

"Did you not hear me? I know where he's been staying."

"I heard you," he said shortly. "You went alone, into an empty building, with a man who has potentially murdered up to six people in the space of a week."

"When you say it like that, it sounds worse than it was."

"It's only not worse because he let you walk back out!"

If anything, my flush was deepening, the heat of shame spreading through my chest and into my neck and cheeks. "It was a bad decision, I'll admit."

"Thank fuck for that acknowledgement," he muttered.

I wanted to snap at him, and the only thing that stayed my tongue was the knowledge that he was right. "We at least now have the excuse to be at his hotel and to examine the space without him being any the wiser."

He sighed and sat back, his shoes scuffing against the wood of the floor. "And what are we supposed to be accomplishing that would make visiting him at his hotel part of it?"

"Seeing if we can get any movement on his case with regards to the warrants." I said. "He seems to be under the impression that Brant is putting pressure on the Company to delay in giving him a decision."

"Is that all?"

"It's all I've promised him." I hesitated, and then plowed forward with the half-formed plan that had bloomed into my mind while I was standing in that shop. "I think perhaps we should go back to his manor and see what else we can find."

Victor's eyes narrowed until they were almost slits, a frown on his lips. "In regards to what?"

"I would say under the guise of finding out what happened to his mother," I said. "But in truth, to touch everything I can possibly read about him and why he really followed us to the city." Victor waited, staring at me silently, and I kept going. "If he's gone after six people here, how many do you think may have gone missing out in the country over the years?" I hesitated, and then went for my one, last possibility. "Maybe he's the one behind his mother's disappearance."

"Then why bring us into it at all?" Victor asked.

"He could in fact be sensation seeking," I suggested. "No one knows what happened to her, and in truth, no one other than him seems particularly concerned."

"He *wants* people to know that he got away with it?"

I shrugged. "Or he merely wants the attention that comes with being the son of a victim. That kind of sensation and all of that emotion has leaked away and he wants to recapture it."

"So he risks being exposed to get back his sympathy." Victor rubbed his chin. "It has merit; we've seen those kinds of cases before." He leaned forward again. "What was it you wanted to do?"

"We take Morris and Brant with us to his manor, and begin investigating with this new theory in mind."

"And what do we tell Lord LeVerre it is we're doing?"

"Finding his mother."

He tapped his desk. "Do you think he'll want Brant there to begin with?"

"Probably not."

"Let me send a note to Morris, and see how she would want to approach this. I think if we come in too strongly we'll spook him and get stuck at a dead end to both cases." He gave me one last glance. "And you should go home and actually *rest*."

To say I approached my own house with trepidation was to put it lightly.

I did so with empty hands, my sausages left in the trash of Victor's office with the warning that he would want to make sure it got taken out before the room began to smell.

After hesitating on my front steps—something I seemed to be doing more and more—I unlocked the door and went inside. The interior was dim and quiet, with no movement looming on the stairs above me, the parlor to my left empty.

I wasn't sure I should have expected anything else.

Hunger drove me from the foyer, down the hall, and into my kitchen. I glanced up at the ceiling and back at the stairs the entire way. Once there, I continued to look up, eyes tracing along the plaster above me.

When nothing occurred, I settled in for a meal that was a repeat of what I had eaten our first night back from Lucien's manor: cheese, an apple, some bread. I sat still after I finished, half poised to leap from my chair, but the space above me was quiet.

I rose from my seat and made my way to the parlor where I picked up the poker before I headed up the stairs.

The second floor hall was also silent, the only light filtering in the wan glow of the late afternoon sun. The door to my bedroom was shut tight, and when I tested the knob, it was locked—exactly as I had left it this morning.

When I moved back from it, I tread over a lump on the floor—something hard between the sole of my boot and the wood—and when I shifted my foot and skirts out of the way to find what I had stepped on, my own shadow blocked my view.

I knelt and reached out, searching blindly in this dark space, fingers brushing, scrabbling across the floor until they hit upon what I had stumbled over. I picked it up, lifting it so I could see its shape in what light was left.

It was the little hand mirror that had been sitting on my vanity for the past week or so. I stared into its glass, at the familiar shape of the face that stared back.

The palm of a hand hit its surface.

I shrieked and dropped the thing before I could fully register if I had truly seen what I thought I saw.

It tumbled to the floor with a clatter, a lucky landing that didn't immediately shatter it upon impact.

I scrambled back, away from it and my bedroom door, until I was seated across the hall, back pressed to the wall, poker clutched across my knees, legs tangled in my skirts. I stayed there, watching both the mirror and the door, until the rapid pace of my heart began to slow and I felt as though I was drawing in full breaths instead of desperate gasps of air.

The laugh that wrenched itself free of my chest was more sob than giggle. It took some convincing of my limbs to get them to move. I crawled back toward the mirror, near enough that I could use the end of the poker to shove it under my bedroom door, through the crack between its bottom edge and the floor.

I pushed it in as far as I dared let the poker go, then swung it so the mirror was shoved off to the side before I yanked the poker back, as if I thought if I let the item linger long enough, something on the other side would grab hold of my only weapon.

I didn't bother trying to check my handiwork. I climbed to my feet and backed away, feeling about behind myself until I managed to cross over the threshold of the front bedroom and could safely close and lock that door—left alone in the one room that still held some of the dying sunlight.

I collapsed down onto the mattress, and stared blankly at the painted wood surface, the only barrier between me and the rest of the house.

I must have managed to sweep the mirror up on one of my trips to and from the room, and that I had dropped it on the floor without noticing its presence.

I could not even begin to fathom how to explain seeing a hand come from within the mirror to hit the other side of the glass, fingers and nails scratching at the surface like a scuttling crab.

I was trying to remember details—how long the nails were, whether I had seen the flash of gems or metal that would mean it had been wearing rings, or the lacy edge of a cuff that would indicate sleeves. But all I could see was the pale, bloodless skin of the palm where it pressed against the glass.

I shook my head, leaned forward with my own palms pressed to my eyes, elbows on my knees while I tried to banish the image from my memory. I did not need to be adding more fodder to the nightmares I had already been having, and surely the only logical explanation was hallucinations brought on by exhaustion.

I was not seeing ghosts in my house, or revenants in my mirrors. They were tricks my own mind was playing on me, and I was letting my imagination get out of hand.

I was not entirely convinced of the truth of it by the time I unfolded from my position, the room nearly swathed in complete darkness. I took the time to position the poker beneath my pillows before I undressed and changed into my nightgown.

The poker might be useless against haunts, but I would hold it in reserve in case the wraith that seemed to be infesting my house turned out to be someone or something far more solid. If Lucien had, by luck or design, managed to find the very shop I had mentioned in such an offhand way to him, I would not trust that he had not found his way to my house as well.

I settled into bed, the blankets pulled up to my chin, one hand under my pillow, fingers wrapped around the rough metal of the poker's handle.

I was standing in an otherwise empty field, directly in front of a mirror. It was framed in heavily carved and gilded wood, the glass at least as tall as I was, if not taller. I was staring at the edges, down at my feet, and the poking foliage around me. Anywhere that my reflection was not.

The grassy stretch I stood in was all shades of gray, the other colors leached out of it until it was a pale reflection of a cold and endless moor.

His chest was pressed to my back, his voice a purr in my ear, edged, it seemed, with delight at finding me here. "*Vivian*," he said, and gently he touched his ungloved fingers to the loose strands of my hair, brushed them away from my face, his bare skin sliding against my cheeks then following down the line of my throat, his palm pressed to my fluttering pulse.

His hand was as empty as glass, entirely devoid of emotions or swarming memories, and I found myself reveling in it, something as simple as another person's touch, the tactile sensation that left goosebumps and nothing else in its wake. I closed my eyes, ready to lean back into it and give myself over to this craving when the feel of his hand drifted away like smoke.

Vivian.

I finally looked up straight at my own image in the mirror, caught her eye, and for a moment it was just us.

A hand slammed its palm against the glass, and I jumped. The limb ended at the elbow, mist and fog in the shadows. It was followed by a second, a third, until the whole of the mirror was filled with hands, fingers scrabbling at the surface, pushing against the glass until it groaned, and spider web cracks began to form.

Light streamed directly into my face, and I lay there, staring up at the ceiling, trying to gauge if I felt any more rested than I had the day before, but if I was being honest, I merely felt drained. I rolled onto my side enough that I could check the door, but it was shut tight so I doubted I could blame any nocturnal visitors for my current exhaustion.

I had nowhere I had to be—at least not until a message from Victor was delivered detailing what our next steps were—so I could simply go back to sleep.

I was letting my eyes drift closed when I heard the echo of a door slamming shut. I froze where I was, ears straining to listen, trying to determine which door it was I had heard.

There were footsteps coming up the stairs.

They were followed by a knock on my bedroom door, then Victor's voice, muffled by the wood and the distance between the two rooms. "Viv?"

"In here!" I called, shoving the blankets back and hastening to get my feet on the floor. "Give me a moment to unlock the door."

It was only a minute at most before I pulled the door open to find Victor standing on the other side of it, looking somewhat confused, but it wasn't long before his face cleared. "You changed rooms."

"Yes," I said, although the answer seemed facetious.

He held up a paper wrapped package. "I brought you sausages to replace the others."

"Thank you."

"I'll go get them cooking, and you come down when you're ready."

"We have an assignment?"

The noise he made was somewhere between a snort and a sigh. "In a manner of speaking, but it would be the same assignment as before."

"Ah. I'll only be another minute."

He turned and headed down the stairs while I shut my door and took the time to get dressed. I hesitated when it came to removing the poker from under my pillow, as I was sure I would want it when I came back for the night. But I also didn't want to explain to Victor why I had it in my bed to begin with.

I left it where it was and went down to the kitchen.

Victor was in the midst of cooking the sausages and some of my eggs, with a steaming cup of coffee already sitting on the table for me. I claimed a chair and the mug, and waited for him to finish his task. When he was done, he set two plates on the table and sat across from me. He took a sip from his own cup before he said anything.

"Morris and Brant," he grimaced at the second name, "only want to go to Lord LeVerre's hotel to see if we can find any evidence of the missing women in his rooms."

"What about his mother?" I asked.

"They are unconcerned about a cold case."

I opened my mouth and shut it, my brow wrinkled, lips pinched. "That seems unusual for Brant. Didn't he say this was a case that stuck with him?"

"He and Morris agree—and I cannot blame them—that we should stick to the current case because the odds that we can help any of these women are far higher."

"One of them is already dead," I said quietly. "What are the odds the others are not?"

"Did you find anything to indicate Miss Harper's death while we were in her house?"

"No," I said. "But she was the last one taken."

"So maybe we can still help her."

I stared down at my plate of food—the fried eggs and the links of sausage—and swallowed. "And after we have finished with this case? What then? His mother is merely forgotten?"

"We may have to let the case go, yes," Victor said cautiously. "If the client is incapable of—"

"Incapable," I sneered. "A pretty way to phrase it."

"We've never had the client who hired us arrested for murder before, so I'm not quite sure what you expect me to refer to it as here."

I deflated, slumping back against my chair. "I don't know myself." I took a sip of my coffee, mulling it over in my mind. Maybe what was needed was time and space, and eventually Lady LeVerre's wraith would stop haunting me, her case buried beneath the myriad of things that made up daily life. I could let it lie until it became fallow, like the empty field in my dreams. Or I could confess all to Victor, that for some reason, I could not let this case go. It followed me.

I set my cup down. "Are we supposed to meet them at the hotel?"

"Yes," Victor said, and pulled out his pocket watch. "At half past eleven."

"That's a little late in the morning."

"They wanted time to pull a team of officers together, just in case."

"Will the coroner be on standby as well?"

"I believe they're hoping they'll be able to instead use a doctor."

"And what do you think?" I asked. "Do you think that they'll have need for a doctor?"

"I would say I am hopeful as well, yes."

I sat there quietly, mulling it over, trying to think of an argument that would allow us to return to Lucien's manor regardless of today's outcome. "What about John and the cook? Someone will need to go check on them at a minimum, won't they?"

"I assume so, but that doesn't come under our purview."

I rubbed at a whorl of wood on the surface of the table, tracing its shape with the tip of one gloved finger.

"You haven't eaten," Victor said. "You need to eat."

"I would not say that I'm hungry."

My mind kept straying upstairs. I could almost see my bedroom door as strongly as if I was standing directly in front of it. If I couldn't get to Lucien's house, perhaps I could try talking to Lady LeVerre through my mirror. To see if saying her name back to her got her attention when she was calling mine.

"Viv," Victor said, and I focused in on him, his gray eyes trained on mine. "You need to eat something even if you're not hungry; you don't look well."

I grimaced. I speared a sausage with my fork and bit into it.

Victor sighed. "Thank you. Mother will have my hide if I let you waste away to nothing." He glanced at his pocket watch. "Once you've finished, we'll head over to the hotel."

CHAPTER NINETEEN

I wish I could hate you, Eleanor. I seem incapable of such strong emotion after all this time. I am faded, haunted by the echoes of your voice, the image of your face. Our home is decaying, and I along with it.

The front of the hotel looked as though the whole of the building needed a good wash, streaks of grime and dirt smeared on the walls, and more of it on the windows.

Next to me, Victor made a face, as we both peered out of the carriage at it, shoulder to shoulder. "This is where he's been staying?"

"It could very well be nicer on the inside," I said, although I couldn't help the doubt that crept into my tone. "Maybe the mess is from the recent snow and anything in the street that was kicked up when the pavement got cleared."

"I suppose it wouldn't make much sense to try to clean it in this cold," Victor muttered.

I pressed my face to the glass. "Where are Morris and Brant and whatever team they've put together?"

"Inside, I wager."

"Well then we're not much help out here, are we?" I asked before shoving the carriage door open hard enough that Victor nearly toppled out of the newly gaping hole in its side. He shot me a glare as he recovered and then climbed from our conveyance onto the sidewalk. "Sorry," I said.

He stepped back enough that I could make my way onto the pavement beside him. "Next time, could you check to make sure I'm not leaning against the door before you open it?"

"Yes," I said meekly.

"Thank you." He paused long enough to give the hotel one last considering look. "Might as well check inside." He headed for the door, and I followed.

There was no doorman at the front, so we stepped through into the lobby—a space that while brightly lit, matched the exterior in terms of overall wear. The seating—couches and chairs gathered around a roaring fireplace—looked to have flattened cushions, and scuff marks covered the surfaces of the nearby tables. The walls were dingy, in need of being wiped down and painted over with a fresh coat. Any wood framing was dull.

Victor paused, a few feet past the entrance, one hand pressed to his chest.

"Is it the dust?" I asked.

"Yes," he said. "Ash and iron. I can feel it gathering in my lungs, the way it squeezes out the air."

I hovered next to him, peering about the space. "Then perhaps we should be moving quickly, before it gets worse." I found who I was looking for, and gave

Victor's arm a tug so he followed after me, albeit with a quick stumble.

Morris and Brant, as he now appeared to be her constant companion, were standing at the counter, speaking to either an employee or a hotel manager, in low voices. They both looked up as we approached them, while the man behind the counter appeared flustered, uncertainty dancing across his face in his furrowed brow and pinched lips.

"Miss Tailor, a pleasure," Brant said.

Morris was less circumspect. "Shit, Vivian, have you been sleeping at all?"

"Not really, and when I do, not well," I said.

"Cases getting to you?" she asked.

"This one is, yes."

She nodded. "You should take some time off after this, a couple weeks, maybe a month. Go out to the seaside or something."

"Traveling isn't—easy, for Viv," Victor said quietly. He hadn't yet seemed to regain his equilibrium, rubbing a hand first along the ridge of his brow, down his face, and then back to his chest just over his heart.

"Ah," she said. "Take a day trip. There's some gardens to the east side of the city."

"In this cold?" I asked.

She waved hand. "They've got winter-happy plants."

"You mean evergreens."

"There's a few that only bloom in the cold. Might be a good place for some research." She tilted her head toward the man behind the counter. "Hotel manager here was just about to show us to Lord LeVerre's room."

"I will do no—"

She rolled her eyes. "Relax, sir. We're only here as visitors; no need to get uppity. If you don't want to show us, please *inform* us as to which room he's in."

The man huffed, pulled a book out from beneath the counter, and thumped it down onto the surface with only as much gusto as he could and still maintain some air of dignity. He opened it and began flipping through the pages.

"I thought you were bringing additional company," I said, eyeing the glaringly empty space behind us.

"My request for...assistance...was denied. The manager," Morris said, "was just telling us that he's only ever seen Lord LeVerre come in and leave alone. And is insistent that the staff would say the same."

"Does his room have any windows?" I asked.

"Of course it has windows," the manager snapped. "All the rooms have windows."

"Do they unlock?"

"Why wouldn't they?" he asked irritably. "This isn't a prison; this is a hotel." He ran a finger down the paper, mouthing words and numbers until he reached somewhere just past the page's midpoint. "Room 357."

"Third floor?" Brant asked.

"That is generally how the numbering in hotels works, yes," the manager said stiffly. "Now, if you will *please* go about your business *discreetly*."

"Come on then: stairs," Morris said, and headed for a hallway located on the right-hand side of the lobby, directly across from the counter.

"Is Lord LeVerre—aware we're coming?" Victor asked. He was beginning to sound if as if he was having difficulty breathing, and I was unsure if it was a symptom of his visions.

"Not as far as I know," Morris said. "So we'd best hope he's in his room and not out and about wandering the streets."

The remainder of the hotel that we saw was not in any better condition than the front or the lobby. The carpet on the floor was bare, worn down to the point of being almost entirely useless in terms of muffling footsteps. There were marks in the plaster, chipped, white flecks in the otherwise painted walls. It appeared that there was only any shine to the wood at all because people did in fact make use of the banister on the stairs, the surface gleaming and polished where hundreds of hands had gripped or slid along it.

"This is not where I would have expected a man of his means to stay," Brant puffed as we climbed upwards.

"Maybe he's pinching his pennies," Victor said, leaning back to peer up the stairwell. He wavered on his feet, but caught his balance before I could reach out to steady him.

"Or maybe he's not as wealthy as he makes himself out to be," Morris said. "My money is on that."

I kept my thoughts to myself—the words that had tumbled from Lucien's mouth about the hotel name being fitting as his reason for choosing it clutched to my chest like a particularly good hand of cards. I could inform Morris of his motives if we found any evidence of the missing women in his rooms or the rest of the hotel.

The hallway we found ourselves in was quite dim compared to the lobby—only a single window down at one end to let in any sunlight, and the rest of the space threadbare carpet and closed doors. All three of us hesitated, studying the space while we determined which way to turn.

"Left or right?" Morris asked.

"Right," Victor said.

"You get a vision?" Morris asked.

Victor pointed at the door across from where we stood. "That's 333, and they go up from there—339, 345..."

Morris headed in the direction Victor had pointed, the rest of us following after her, while she counted the doors. "Room 351..." She stopped in front of the next one. "Room 357." She squared her shoulders and glanced back at Brant. "You ready?"

He nodded, and Morris knocked on the door, a hard rap of her knuckles against the wood, brusque with a certain kind of urgency.

She said nothing, and I felt a prickling kind of unease, that she wouldn't alert Lucien as to who was at his door. Who the sense of discomfort was for, I wasn't sure.

The door opened, and Lucien peered out at us, his eyes skipping over Morris and Brant, first to Victor then to me. "Mr. and Miss Tailor, to what do I owe the honor?"

"Lord LeVerre, I'm Detective Morris," Morris said, "I believe you're familiar with Detective Brant?"

Lucien's eyes narrowed. "In passing."

"May we come in?" Morris asked, blandly.

Lucien didn't move, his eyes focused past Morris and on me. "I assume this isn't a social call?"

"I'm afraid not," Morris said. "Perhaps it would be best if we came inside and all sat down?"

Lucien stepped back, pulled the door as wide as it would go, and motioned at the interior room. "Be my guest."

Morris, Brant, and Victor filed past him, and when I went to step over the threshold, I paused, hovering there beside Lucien, halfway through the frame as I studied the room. He had mirrors hung on all four walls, including the one situated above the fireplace. And to the right side of the room I could see a second door with mirrors placed on either side of it.

"Something wrong, Miss Tailor?" Lucien asked quietly.

"I didn't realize you were quite so fond of your reflection, Lucien," I said.

I almost missed the satisfied smile that flickered across his face before it settled into a more genial expression. "I would say it keeps me company most nights. Unless it goes wandering about."

I twisted, staring up at him. He blinked, the amused look on his face fading, and he opened his mouth as if he had something else to say.

"Lord LeVerre, if you could join us?" Morris said.

"Yes, my apologies," he said, and moved away from me toward the couches and armchairs gathered together in the middle of the room. He had left his hotel room door open, and perhaps that was for the best.

"Miss Tailor?" Morris said. "If you could please also join the rest of the group?"

I followed after Lucien, and sat down in one of the armchairs, as far from him as I could get with the seating arrangements. Morris and Brant had already claimed the couch, sitting side by side and Victor remained standing, just off to the left of its arm. I glanced around the room, at the mirrors and our reflections, the space at least bright enough from the morning sun streaming in the windows that the images in the glass were nothing more than pale imitations of the people in the room.

"So," Lucien said, lounging in his chair. "To what do I owe the pleasure of having not one, but two detectives call on me?"

Morris cleared her throat. "Currently, our investigation has three dead men and three missing women. Evidence that you were at the houses of two of these women has been found."

"The addresses?" Lucien asked.

"This is not an interview, Lord LeVerre," Morris said. "We've brought Miss Tailor with us to read your rooms and tell us if any of the three women have been here."

Lucien's gaze wandered over to me, and I did not like the way his eyes settled on my throat, or the tilt to his head as he studied me. "Really." I looked at my hands, the way my fingers were twisted together in my lap. Lucien shifted in his chair. "Has Miss Tailor informed you that we were in discussions regarding the funding of a business she intended to start?"

"I was aware," Victor said. "And I made sure that Morris knew."

"And you are not worried that she is perhaps compromised?"

"No," Victor said shortly. "Because if she was, she wouldn't have told us you were at those houses to begin with." He appeared to be growing paler the longer we were here, and it made me nervous that whatever vision that seemed to be attempting to push its way to the surface would affect him so.

"Fair point," Lucien said silkily. "Do you have a warrant?"

"Yes," Morris said, pulling the aforementioned document from within her jacket pocket. She unfolded it and held it out toward Lucien. "Feel free to read through it; there's a copy with the Company and another copy with the court so you could keep this one if you like."

There was no smile on Lucien's face now as he took the paper from Morris's hand and unfolded it, eyes narrowing as he read through the lines of text. When he finished he set it on the table next to himself. "I am also suspected of murdering those three men?"

"Those are the current theories, yes."

"I suppose that if I were to tell you I didn't do it, you won't believe me?"

"We follow the evidence, sir. And currently, the only evidence we have of someone being in contact with at least two of those women, is tied to you."

Lucien turned back toward me. "Am I truly the only other voice in those rooms, Miss Tailor?" He scooted forward on his chair, leaning so his elbows were resting on his knees. "Or was I the only familiar one you could bear to expose?"

I snapped my head up. "Victor would never—"

"I don't mean your brother."

I stopped, my mouth still hanging open like a gasping fish, before I shut it, trying and failing to keep my confusion from flickering across my face.

Lucien's eyes flicked toward Brant, then skipped along the walls and back again. He leaned back in his chair before I could register the meaning of his glances. "As I was saying—"

"There is no one seated in this room that I would cover up a murder—let alone three—for," I said tightly.

"Not even yourself?" Lucien asked.

I hesitated before I answered, because in truth, who could say what they would or would not do faced with such a situation, if they had never before encountered it. "No."

The smile on his face this time was knowing, sly. "As honest and true as an arrow?"

"For this, yes."

"If we could proceed?" Morris interrupted. "I'm sure whatever *tête-à-tête* it is you would like to have can wait until we establish innocence or guilt." The look she leveled at Lucien was hard—the protective glare of a mother hen shielding her flock—whereas the one she turned in my direction softened, concern in her face and in her tone. "Miss Tailor, if you could?"

I nodded, rose to my feet, and tugged off my right hand glove, pausing as I considered just where to start. I had very little to go on, because while shabby, the room itself was clean, so I moved around to set my hand on the back of the chair I had just been sitting in.

There were dozens of voices to shift and sink into, all of them babbling at once, barking laughter and titters, followed by wave after wave of increasing grief. I was swamped in it, the way it sucked me down, clinging to my legs and knees, desperately trying to worm its way upward toward my heart, even after I pulled my hand away. But there was no sign of Lucien, his regret, or of any of the women.

"Something wrong with this chair?" I asked.

"Doubtful," Lucien said. "I merely have my preferences and that one was not it." He motioned toward Morris and Brant. "I've never sat on the couch either."

I drifted over toward it and ran my palm along the dull wood of its back. Both Morris and Brant leaned forward and twisted to face me as I passed and slipped through their layered emotions, one spiky and irritated, their calm surface akin to a duck on the pond, and the other a patience that stretched as far as the eye could see—someone willing to wait, biding their time until their prey made a mistake.

Beyond them, gasps and moans, panting breaths that had me snatching my hand away, a flush in my cheeks.

"Encounter something?" Lucien asked.

"No," I said, relieved that my voice came out steadily instead of squeaking, thin like a reed. I focused on the chair he was in. "If you would?"

"I'm quite comfortable where I am," he said mildly.

I narrowed my eyes at him, but he stared back at me innocently, eyes wide and unblinking, as if he couldn't fathom any reason as to why I might ask him to move. I stepped away from the couch, set the tips of my fingers against the frame of his chair while he twisted to smile up at me, something hard in those russet eyes of his, flecks of garnet in the gold.

There was only Lucien, his regret a dragging need—a stone around his neck—dust and dirt thick in his throat. There was longing there, buried deep beneath it, and a whispering voice that skittered at the back of my mind.

Vivian.

I pulled my hand away, my eyes still locked on his. "You—"

"Have you found any evidence of those women yet, Miss Tailor?" he asked. "Perhaps you should try the walls?" He tilted his head, an inclining motion toward the second room. "Or the bedroom?"

They were only dreams, nightmares, I was sure of it. I had checked every nook and cranny, under the bed, in the wardrobe behind my own clothing, each door and window, including their locks, and had found no evidence of a living person inside my house.

The only image in the looking glass beside my own had been that of his mother.

I could hide the trembling of my hand by lowering it against my skirts, and I took the time to wipe my palm on the fabric and remove the clammy feel of sweat gathering across the skin as I turned and moved toward the walls. I had not recovered by the time I brushed my fingers against the plaster, following the line of the chair rail as I made my way around the room. I paused in front of one of the mirrors.

All I saw was my reflection, and the backwards image of the room behind me. I pulled my fingers across the glass, but there was nothing there. It was as blank as it always was.

I moved from the mirror to the fireplace, but the only thing there was the brusque quickness of a maid removing old ashes and building up the next fire. The rest of the room held no other answers for me either.

I paused on the threshold of the bedroom door, hesitating as I stared into the darkened space. The curtains had been drawn across the windows, and whatever light that managed to leak past them didn't go far, leaving the rest of the room in shadow. What I could make out wasn't much—the hulking shape of an unmade bed, the blankets and sheets still kicked back toward its foot, the pillows dented.

Considering what I already encountered on the couch, I wasn't sure I wanted to know what other similar activities would have occurred in a hotel bed.

I turned toward Lucien. "Are there lamps in this room?"

"On the nightstands," he said.

I looked back at the space. I would have to step into the dark and cross the room to reach the lights.

I moved away from the door, stepping just off to one side of it and motioned at the frame. "If you would go turn them on?"

"Surely you're not scared of the dark, are you, Miss Tailor?"

I pursed my lips, pressing them tightly together while I attempted not to grit my teeth and grind out an answer. "No."

"Then no," he said. "The floor is clear, and there's nothing in there for you to trip over, if that's your concern."

"How considerate of you," I said dryly.

"Far be it from me to make it any easier on my accusers," he said. "Were you here for a social visit, I would certainly turn on the lights for you rather than expect you to stumble about."

"Were I here for a social visit, I wouldn't be entering your bedroom at all."

"How...disappointing."

"Sir," Victor snapped. He stepped around the couch, slipped past me into the dark bedroom, and had become a shadow himself within mere moments of crossing the threshold. I hovered there by the door, waiting, until I heard the familiar click, and the blue glow of a spelled lamp filled the space, throwing a pallor over the furniture and walls.

I wasn't entirely sure the room was any more inviting with the lights on than it had been when it was dark.

Victor came out of the room and moved to one side. "All clear."

I stepped through the door.

The first thing I noticed should perhaps have been the bed and its tousled blankets with the way it dominated the space, but instead I was studying the walls, my eyes drifting over the mirrors lined up one by one on the side across from the windows, and the many mes all staring back from their various angles of view.

I turned toward the sitting room, Lucien the only person framed by the wood lining the door, a picture perfect positioning. "Why all the mirrors?" I asked.

He shifted in his seat so that he could look directly at me without having to turn his head. "Would you believe me if I said it was pure vanity?"

I glanced at the mirrors and my reflections, sure that I had caught a flicker of movement that meant they had in fact been looking off elsewhere, or turned in a different direction before I brought my eyes back to the glass. "Not entirely."

He smiled at me, a baring of his teeth. "And if I instead told you it was to make the space feel larger?"

"That I might believe," I admitted. "Although why you would want to add to the looming shadows, I don't know."

"Are you sure you're not frightened by the dark, Miss Tailor?" he asked. "Perhaps have a tendency to jump at shadows and reflections?"

"Quite sure," I said, although he took my measure and I wasn't sure how, beyond my initial recalcitrance to enter his bedroom, which could have been chalked up to any number of things.

"And yet you still hesitate, even with the lights on." He rose from his seat, brushing at his waistcoat and pants as he did so. "If we could perhaps get on with it, and then you and your detectives can take your leave."

I turned on my heel, marched over to the bed, bent, and set my palm directly on the mattress.

I was drowning, struggling to find which way was up and break through to the surface, but there was nothing within reach of me but black waters—so dark, so deep was this need, this obsession, that to say it had drenched the bed was to put it lightly. It was a yawning pit, a void with no way out, a screaming black hole that poured into me until I was suffocating, crushed beneath its pressure.

It swept me away—flashes of memories rushing by, an avalanche, a tidal wave of them. I could not catch my breath, and I was lost in it with no way to wrest myself free. There was Lucien, fully grown but that awkward stage of being when one has only just become an adult. He was dancing a waltz with a woman, the sparkling, dazzling beauty of the ballroom pale in comparison to her light. And while she appeared just as young as he, there was a knowing look on her face, a sly smile on her lips and in the coy glance of her russet eyes.

I was dragged along, or away—I could hardly tell which—flashes of a white dress, two hands and a pair of rings, among which Lucien's face stood out clearly, delight in his gaze and in his boyish grin, his mouth forming the words to vows I could not hear over the din of anguished, raging howls that filled my ears and blocked all other sound.

I landed in Lady LeVerre's bedroom—the walls closing in on me, the shadows looming at the ceilings, gathered and waiting—while she stood beside the couch with a body splayed out across its surface. She and Lucien were arguing in hushed voices—him motioning frantically at the woman on the chaise, Lady LeVerre pleading with him, her turns of phrase sweet, promising, alluring—until his shoulders slumped, the bitter taste of fear that he would lose her otherwise flooding my senses. It rotted away piece by piece, until what love there had been was replaced with an unending need.

And it only repeated one word.

I yanked my hand back and staggered, and I couldn't catch my breath with the way my heart squeezed itself shut in my chest.

"You look like her, you know," Lucien said from the doorway.

"Like your mother?" I asked, though I was barely aware of the words. I wasn't even sure I had actually spoken until he replied.

"My mother," he scoffed. "No, my *wife*."

I turned, and caught a glimpse of something crumpled on the floor behind him. I blinked, a roaring in my ears because surely I was imagining what I saw. Morris and Brant were here too, and they wouldn't have allowed Lucien the chance to go after Victor. They certainly wouldn't be allowing him to wander freely about if he had.

Lucien stepped into the room, and I moved, intending to slide past him and examine the shape—the broad back of someone's jacket.

He grabbed my arm, brought me to a halt, and I was left with only that image, the distance still between us while I tried to comprehend what had happened.

"Victor?" I called his name, and there was a quaver in my tone. This wasn't happening, this wasn't real, and I would wake back in my own house, in my own bed. This was just another nightmare that had crept up on me unexpectedly. "Morris? Brant?" The pitch of my voice climbed higher. They wouldn't have left us alone in this hotel with Lucien, not when they were so convinced he was guilty, evidence in his room or not.

He had been in the victims' houses.

"Vivian," he said. I turned, and made the mistake of looking directly into his eyes. He smiled at me, giving my arm a tug until the two of us were positioned in front of one of the looking glasses. He reached up, grasped my chin, and twisted my head so I was looking directly at the mirror and our reflections with their matching russet colored gazes, their palms pressed to the creaking, crackling, splintering glass. "Did you honestly think the only monsters that existed were human?"

About the Author

Jamie lives in Charlotte, NC with her husband who is a SAHD to their three feral children, three badly behaved dogs, and two rescue fish. She has a love for all things pop culture, watches too many documentaries, is obsessed with behind the scenes on movies and TV shows, and has been fascinated by mythology and monsters, and how they reflect our own darker humanity, for the majority of her life. (Her favorite college course was a Gothic Fiction Course and the pride and joy of her possessions were her copies of *The Complete Idiots Guide to Vampires* until someone stole it and *The Complete Idiots Guide to Ghosts & Hauntings* which she still has to this day). You can find her on Threads, Insta, TikTok and BlueSky under the handle @VillainLeaning.

Acknowledgements

Jenn, you had one job (not really, you had three and wrangling me and my bouncing ideas around is, sadly, one of them) and I hope you continue to hold down the fort of my dramatics as my friend for years to come. Have you read yet?

For the friends who are tireless in their support and championship, thank you all so much. I am so grateful to have met you. Y'all know who you are.

For the friends I've lost along the way, I hope you're happy.

OTHER WORKS BY JAMIE JACKSON

Adventures of a Villain Leaning Humanoid Series:
Fear and Fury
Torment and Tarnish
Scorn and Sorrow
Deception and Damage
Ache and Anguish
Compulsion and Control
Vengeance and Violence
Obstinance and Obsession

Standalones:
The Sparrow and the Oak Tree
Bound to the Fate of Kings

www.ingramcontent.com/pod-product-compliance
Lightning Source LLC
Chambersburg PA
CBHW021134260626
47169CB00005B/1605